The Lizzy & Darcy Letters

Lizzy & Darcy in Lockdown

and

Lizzy & Darcy Unleashed

By Joanna O'Connor

Inspired by Jane Austen's
esteemed characters

Jeannette
With love
Joanna O'Connor

Lizzy & Darcy
in
Lockdown

For my beloved, beautiful,
fun-loving Mama

Dear Reader,

It's spring 1812 and Miss Elizabeth Bennet finds herself in quarantine lockdown at Hunsford Parsonage with the Collinses, resorting at last to the company, by letter, of Mr Fitzwilliam Darcy, who is likewise inadvertently incarcerated at Rosings Park with his Aunt, Lady Catherine de Bourgh, his cousin Anne, and his other cousin, Colonel Fitzwilliam.

Whilst my intention is a light and humorous glimpse into a challenging situation, I assure you that weightier matters will be addressed and respected as the letters progress.

I appreciate your presence, wish you well, and offer my felicitations.

Yours etc.

Joanna

P.S. A Glossary is to be found at the end of the book.

<u>Key</u>

(Bracketed and written in Italics) = thoughts that are not sent.

*Referring to Mr Wickham

** Referring to Miss Caroline Bingley

***Referring to Mr Collins's offer of marriage to Lizzy

**** Lizzy is enquiring as to Darcy's involvement in Bingley's removal from Meryton; Colonel Fitzwilliam has hinted at this in his previous letter

_____ Indicates a pause in the letter, while the writer collects themselves

_____ A pause while Darcy answers a knock at his door and speaks with Colonel Fitzwilliam.

Letter One

Tuesday 5th May, Hunsford Parsonage

Dear Mr Darcy,

I confess myself at something of a loss to explain the impropriety of my writing to you in this manner; but finding myself in lockdown after only three weeks in Hunsford with the Collinses, and having exhausted friends and relatives with repeated requests for diversion over the proceeding almost six, I must reach out to my extended acquaintance in the hopes of finding one - besides Jane - who is not already out of humour with this epidemic. Now, I give my full assurance of that being the one and only time you will hear me directly mention what is our present national - or even international - dilemma, for it does not amuse me, and - as you may remember - I dearly love a laugh.

There seems plenty, however, that surrounds the Unmentionable that *is* diverting, and - as one who is often a keen observer of the follies of others - I hope you may not object to joining me as witness to the microcosm in which we now find ourselves fixed *(or perhaps you will, in which case I really shall be none the worse)*.

My father has often referred to each of us existing within our 'own small worlds,' and in this case, he has become quite literally and figuratively correct, for my world currently consists only of Mr Collins *(whom I recently refused in marriage)*, my dear friend Charlotte *(who accepted him instead)*, Charlotte's sister Maria *(a dear girl of whom I know rather little, despite a lengthy acquaintance)*, and what missives we receive from Meryton and Rosings.

Since the National Household Isolation Edict, Mr Collins has given orders that we are all to remain separate from one another and in our rooms, with brief exceptions. Charlotte is permitted to leave hers three times a day to prepare the repast - the cook and housemaid having been hastily returned to their families - whereupon Mr Collins, wrapped in muslin, will - at a safe distance - usher her from the kitchen and deliver our food upstairs on trays. He has devised a system of miniature bell ringing, so that each may open their door to their own specific ding, thus avoiding any chance of cross-contamination. I am, naturally, infinitely tempted to open my door to Maria's tune, but have managed to resist the impulse for now. Prior to lockdown, Charlotte, it seems, had already adopted the attitude of letting her lord and master have his own way in everything, for the sake of peace - a decision, I believe, which may well fire back loudly upon her in the future (*if not already*).

Mr Collins himself walks freely about the house (*hopefully fully clothed, although I seek no proof*). Once a day, he dons his beekeeping attire and braves the arduous journey to Rosings, where he signals his deference to your Aunt *(Lady Catherine de Bourgh)*, and delivers written greetings to a small table you have no doubt noticed, that he carried over for just that purpose. Suffice to say he delivers far more than he receives. He would go more often but, as you know, we are only to go out for daily exercise, to gather food, or to visit a vulnerable elderly person. By the by, if this letter seems lightly singed to you, it is because Mr Collins waves any letters - received or delivered - over a lit candle, for 'we cannot be too careful, Cousin Elizabeth.' Mr Collins, of course, keeps himself constantly informed and is even purchasing his own newspapers (also promptly singed). Consequently, he is more afraid than any other of my acquaintance. I've often reflected that we are seldom as cautious as we might be when allowing our heads to be filled with the opinions of others. A risky old business, in truth, which should be undertaken with the same prudence one might give to imbibing one of Mr Collins's home cures.

For my part, my only real fear at present is that - should we run out of provisions - we will be forced to resort to Mr Collins's potatoe patch. Such a display of unnerving forms as you have ever seen! Charlotte says it occurred owing to his planting in November during an early frost and not knowing how to chit them.

Yours etc.

P.S. Mr Collins has even tethered the village cat outside, for fear that she might be carrier. He has fashioned her a wooden collar and chain, and there she sits in a disconsolate heap, her green eyes looking up at my casement window in pleading submission.

Letter Two

Wednesday 6th May, Rosings Park

Dear Miss Bennet,

I admit myself surprised to receive your letter. But also... *(gratified...? Satisfied? No, that's worse. Flattered? Good Lord, no. Stunned...?! Gratified... Gra-ti-fi-ca-tion...)* Pleased.

(It will have to be pleased)

———

At present, there is little to report that may amuse from Rosings. We mostly keep to our rooms. My Aunt has *(exerted her influence)* managed to persuade three servants to remain *(at a reduced salary)*, and the Housekeeper, Mrs Norris (who I think had nowhere else to go), so at present we must make do.

It is a strange kind of independence. But not unwelcome.

(Like your letter)

———

The weather is unseasonably warm. Which is also...
not unwelcome.

_____

Mr Collins has skills I knew not of. I believe he has
sent several homemade tonics to my Aunt. May I
ask what effect they are like to have?

I trust your family is, thus far, well.

Yours etc.

P.S. With respect, potato is spelled without an e,
unless you intend a plural, in which case 'es.' A
common error.

P.P.S. I fear for Mr Collins, once the cat goes free.

Letter Three

Thursday 7th May, Hunsford Parsonage

Dear Sir,

Thank you for your letter, and for your kind enquiry after my family. They are all quite well. My mother has placed my father under lock and key, in order to preserve his health as far as ever she may. My younger sisters *(with the exception of Lydia)* are to leave provisions for him outside his library, where a day bed has been moved. He does not consider this a hardship, and writes that he finds himself at last supremely grateful for the estate's entailment, as it allows him to read and reflect in almost uninterrupted bliss.

Mama's progress through the last few weeks has been somewhat unsteady. Her first reaction was to give a good venting to everyone, during which she rid the house of every circulating library book; something for which she now admits some remorse, for all the books in the house are now out of bounds with my merry father. My mother herself is not a great reader, but Mary considers her intellectual advancement most seriously impeded by the new restrictions.

Next, Mama set about stock piling as much food as she could, siting the Bible as reason. One of our meadows was flooded in January, then in February Kitty set fire to the hearth rug in the drawing room, so it seemed likely - with impending pestilence in March - that famine was also on the way. Jane tried at length to reason with her by letter, siting Joseph as Vizier of Egypt (Genesis 41) and paralleling his good economic sense with that of our government, but to no avail. She was not to be persuaded. Having filled the pantry with as much lardy cake and ginger wine as could be made, she is now to be found - most days - weeping in her bedroom, often joined by Mary or Kitty. Thank heavens for Jane, whose communications are all calmness and optimism; perhaps aided by the fact that she remains in London with my Aunt and Uncle Gardiner.

Aunt Phillips is the shining missive of bad news. Every family has one. She comes in state to Longbourn at least twice a week to deliver some scripted epistle of doom that floors my mother, but by which she herself is somehow completely unaffected; perhaps because she knows how much has been embellished on the way. Her good humour and dire portents make for a most confusing combination. One of her early triumphs was a note held up to the window to say that the whole neighbourhood was to be completely overwhelmed within a week by the army, home from abroad, who would dismiss the ever-popular militia to remoter climes, and then assume a power that would keep us locked inside our homes, without outdoor exercise, by any necessary force. Strict rations would be distributed door to door at an allotted time. This was later proved to be a falsehood, concocted by members of the militia themselves who it transpired had spelled official with a u. But my mother was quite beside herself.

One wonders how the government might organise the distribution of food to every household anyway, especially as most of the population was - before the Unmentionable - already mostly without it. But I am not supposed to consider these things, being a foolish female.

Ah yes, regarding your Aunt and the tonics. Mr Collins's most recent home cures have been devised upon the four elements. Thus hot, cold, dry and moist - which handily sums up the immediate reaction of the victim when consumed. His concoction of pond water, pumiced dandelion petals and pulverised mushroom wiped Charlotte out with the gripe for four days straight. Spousal duty, I imagine, for mine went instantly into a basin.

When this is at an end, I will ask Mr Collins to enlighten you on all of which he is capable.

Please remember me to Colonel Fitzwilliam, if you should see him. I imagine one might pass days in Rosings without fear of bumping into one another.

I hope her ladyship and Miss de Bourgh do tolerably well and are enjoying their prodigious fireplace and sixty-four windows.

Yours etc.

P.S. Your reply was extremely brief. But - in spite of corrections to both spelling *and* grammar - I am, as you can see, undeterred *(indeed, I am quite grateful for a source of near companionship)*. If you are willing then I will deliver further letters myself in the morning at seven, when the household is not yet up. Mr Collins deems my writing to you inappropriate, therefore this will be the path of least resistance. I shall be punctual; thus you may collect from said table at five past seven without fear of either damp or impropriety. I would welcome the freedom of an early walk and will be breaking no rules as it is exercise and solitary.

P.P.S. When you speak of independence, what exactly do you mean?

Letter Four

Friday 8th May, Rosings Park

Dear Madam,

Thank you for your lengthy communication. I am most gratified to hear that your family is much as ever. I shall endeavour to fulfil your wishes and supply you with a more detailed description of my current environment; although I must first mention that, regarding Mr Collins, I would rather you did not.

I caught sight of Colonel Fitzwilliam in the breakfast room this morning, he at one end of the table and I at the other. We might have played Shuttlecock from that distance. We exchanged hasty greetings and I conveyed your good wishes to which he rejoined with his own. He seems well and as amiable as ever, though he has run out of military equipment to polish.

My Aunt and cousin take the carriage out each day for exercise and are in reasonable spirits. At least, I perceive no great difference in either. Anne fashions a new talisman for her collection every day; but again, this is nothing novel.

How-ever did you know of the sixty-four windows? I have been twice around the building this afternoon to disprove the truth of that statement, but must regretfully assent to your superior knowledge.

Do you ride, Miss Bennet? I am sure you are most welcome to take a suitable mare from the stables at Rosings should you wish. For my part, my daily rides are becoming more and more extensive and - if I do not apply due care - I will find myself back in Derbyshire before I know it, whereupon I shall no doubt receive a hefty fine and be returned by carriage to Rosings. A circumstance which might be just as well, for Pemberley is currently completely unoccupied, my sister being still confined in town and all the servants temporarily dismissed; and if left there I would no doubt find myself soon a Timon, hunting for scraps and decrying others for the crime of being man.

You ask of my new found independence? I suspect you imply that I am at last learning to pull on my own breeches, or pull off my own boots. Is that so? I know enough of your disposition to suspect some mockery at my expense.

I have a letter this morning from one who would claim an acquaintance with you: Miss Bingley. She urges me to grow a beard, something that is now the fashion in London since we none of us may tend to our own locks. Since my independence does not yet include the easy use of a razor, I may have to regretfully comply. Mr Brummel would not be impressed. Shall I remember you to the lady, when I make my reply?

Although I appreciate that we are yet young in this occurring, I cannot help but pause to reflect upon the encouraging aspects of what is about us. The newspaper gives dire prognostications, which may be expected; but around us we may see many acts of kindness and compassion, letters filled with loving wishes, and a pause in factories, and war, while we unite in battle of another kind. What will this world be grown to, I wonder, when we emerge from this? A better one, I hope.

Yours etc.

P.S. I am willing, but cannot be so unchivalrous as to expect you to walk to Rosings in order to collect a letter by my hand. I shall therefore deliver mine at the same time, to the hollow in the old elm on the green by the Parsonage. I offer my assurance that I shall turn a blind eye to any further spelling or grammatical misdemeanours, except to respectfully mention that the 'siting' to which you refer is spelled with a c, and not an s. A common misconception. Now I am done.

P.P.S. What do you do for entertainment of an evening, when not writing *inappropriate* letters?

Letter Five

Saturday 9th May, Hunsford Parsonage

Dear Sir,

Thank you for your slightly longer epistle. I shall answer your questions briefly and in order: -

a) Mr Collins is responsible for all I know of Rosings, despite my best efforts, I was bound to absorb something; b) Thank you, but I am no horsewoman; c) Yes. Both breeches *and* boots; d) Regarding Miss Bingley, no, thank you; e) Regarding the world, I hope so too. You must remember to pay your taxes...

Mr Collins has contracted the Unmentionable. Indeed, it seems impossible that he might ever have avoided it, having thought of nothing else since its original announcement. His symptoms are thankfully only slight, but enough to take him to his bed, thus allowing the three women in his keeping to roam free. I confess, the light hurt my eyes at first and I was unsure as to what day it was, or even what month. But now I am taking the stairs two at a time, and wandering the garden openly - at a safe distance from Maria and Charlotte, of course - and the trees are all a-leaf and in blossom, and the garden at the very least in bud, if not in bloom, and I am feeling all at once the hope of spring.

Mr Collins had plans to give an Ascension missive from the top of the church tower, but for now we must postpone that pleasure, and his parishioners will be left in peace a few more weeks. I admit I admired his confidence at believing his voice might reach so far and wide, but from the plans in his study it seems he was constructing a sort of papier-mâché trumpet, which would have aided his acoustics. This, he has fondly dubbed 'the Lady Catherine,' a compliment of which your Aunt will no doubt be most sensible.

I did not know of Miss de Bourgh's collection. My sister Mary is quite vigorously superstitious too. In February, she became afraid of the colour red. Just the mention of it would send her into spasms of anxiety. Naturally, everywhere she went red was mentioned or displayed. Now she writes that she can barely move through a doorway without performing some extensive ritual. It is no exaggeration to say that, despite these precautions, she is quite the unluckiest of people in general. In fact, I sometimes wonder whether the very rituals she employs for preservation somehow attract disaster - her focal point being unfailingly upon what she fears. Jane, on the other hand, whose focus is so very amiable and her observations always upon what is lovely and good, has few experiences that are not equally so *(with the exception of your friend Mr Bingley fleeing the county).*

Did I mention that when the quarantine Edict was first issued, Mr Collins - in a heartbeat - jumped the hedge and hightailed it over two fields before he realized he had nowhere to go? For this I really cannot blame him, for it took everything in my power to resist the same impulse. Shakespeare and Goldsmith both agree - the better part of valour is discretion, or desertion - for he did not once glance back for Charlotte. *(He who fights and runs away lives to be tedious another day...)* They say when unusual times arise, we find out what we are made of... and what those around us are made of also.

Ah yes, my evening entertainment. Prior to his confinement, Mr Collins supplied each of us with a copy of the Reverend Fordyce's 'Sermons to Young Women,' two volumes, which I now enclose as loan that you may come to know him better. I must confess, it *has* amused me greatly. It is exactly the sort of book I would expect Mr Collins to have numerous copies of. Otherwise, I brought with me only three novels - none of which you might approve - and have read each several times.

But now, of course, I am a free woman. Thus, this evening I lay outside upon the front bench, with the Free Cat upon my chest, and we watched the world go by in the sky above our heads. I saw the clouds tinted with sunlight move so gently across the sky, and little birds flap, flap, flap and glide. I saw Venus appear when the sky was yet quite blue, before the trees turned to silhouette and a pinkish-mauve tint brushed in pastel shades across the heavens. I saw bees and a dragonfly. The sound of bees intoxicates me.

Yours etc.

P.S. No comment.

P.P.S. I wonder, is this not a perfect opportunity for Lady Catherine to learn the pianoforte?

Letter Six

Monday 11th May, Rosings Park

Dear Madam,

I have no doubt my Aunt will indeed be delighted by Mr Collins's kind Eponym, but shall defer the pleasure of telling her till you may personally be present. Please convey my sympathies to Mr Collins, and my best wishes for his speedy recovery. If we lived in a world where all good things were possible at once, I might convey the opposite wishes to yourself and your female companions. But, alas, it is not so.

On Wednesday Lady Catherine sneezed four times in a row and is now likewise indisposed. She has - at the greatest expense - secured the resident services of an esteemed physician, who brings her meals which she refuses to *eat (and whom she alternately barks at and pleads with not to abandon her)*. I should like to tell you of her courage in the face of what is, almost certainly, a mild cold. My cousin is perhaps for the first time in her life separated from her mother, and removed to the furthest part of the house on account of her congenital delicacy.

I admit myself presently fascinated - in the face of little alternate diversion - to witness how the Unmentionable affects the people nearest to me. I observe that what was already predominantly present or inherent is merely exacerbated; thus, Anne is afeard for her health and given to emotions, yet Bingley's letters are all light-hearted affability and hopefulness, Georgiana is cautiously willing to believe in a bright future, while Miss Bingley refers mostly to the inappropriate behaviour of others and gives lengthy descriptions of quarantine vogues. Thus, with my Aunt being much as she ever was, I await her renaissance without unease. We must, however, defer her piano instruction till then.

What of Mrs Collins and Miss Lucas? You seldom mention either.

I wonder if you are not rather too hard on the regrettable Mr Collins? I am sure he must mean well, and some of his interventions have been, surely, rather inspired. Freedom aside, how do you all manage without his foraging efforts? Have you enough? A serious question.

What of your elder sister? Will she remain indefinitely in London, or are there efforts being made to bring her home?

Do you hear from any others of our acquaintance[*]?

Thank you for Fordyce. It shall relieve me of my current revisiting of 'The History of Little Goody Two-Shoes.' In return, please find 'A Vindication of the Rights of Woman' by Mary Wollstonecraft, which I have recently completed, and admired.

May I send you anything else from my collection? You might find the 'Meditations' of Marcus Aurelius - although also not a fiction - edifying.

Yours etc.

P.S. Breeches, boots and beard! Partially. I have now wielded a razor successfully in the direction of my lower face, although am not yet confident enough of my abilities to shave about my mouth. Thus, I look - if I do say so myself - rather Shakespearean.

P.P.S. I hope all at Hunsford will accept an additional gift of what I am told is a 'pottle' of 'forced strawberries' appropriated from the Rosings Greenhouses. Mrs Norris, the Rosings Housekeeper, is a formidable lady who guards the kitchens and hot houses with the same verve with which she guards the tea, so the pottle is all I could procure for now; but I have my eye upon a ripening pineapple.

Letter Seven

Tuesday 12th May, Hunsford Parsonage: from the Wilderness Within

Dear Mr Darcy,

Thank you for the Wollstonecraft; I have read it many times, but shall be delighted to revisit. I am familiar with Aurelius's 'Meditations,' and found them impressive, for an Emperor. I particularly enjoyed his remark 'put an end once for all to this discussion of what a good man should be, and be one.' I do like my philosophers to the point.

I doubt you will find any relief in Fordyce, but, if you should, do be sure and mark the page.

Please convey my regrets to Lady Catherine and, indeed, to Miss de Bourgh, and my good wishes for a speedy end to suffering.

I am sure you are right with regard to Mr Collins. Within our family he has seldom been thought of with any particular warmth, even before his actual person was known to us. Entailed estates do not encourage affection, you know. This might not have been insurmountable, upon meeting, had he been a less *(conceited, pompous, narrow-minded)* silly man. I do of course appreciate that he is not without his merits - for instance, I am grateful for the origin of his postal system, and even for the singing of letters. But as to the enslaving of felines - well there, I fear, he has lost my good opinion for all time. You know how that feels*.

It therefore behoves me to tell you that Mr Collins is a most demanding patient. Charlotte is up and downstairs at all hours, warming water and making up poultices. Thankfully, she is infinitely serene. She has quite the most beautiful singing voice, the kind you might pay to hear. When she is happy, she goes to the farthest end of the garden and sings up to the sky. She might have been another Angelica Catalani. But then, who knows what may become of Charlotte yet? People have run into the night and changed their lives - why not she? Do we not all have friends we wish this for? But there are some doors which may be only opened from within.

Prior to his trial by sneezing, Mr Collins insisted that Charlotte learn a sesquipedalian a day, to improve her vocabulary *(and impress your Aunt)*. Now that he is bed ridden and 'like to die,' he has increased it to three. As he has little more than a slight temperature and a sniffle, it seems unnecessary. But ensuring that Charlotte is not left with idle hands or poor word power seems to give him peace.

Speaking of which, Mr Collins, it transpires, is a Seasonal Snooper. Charlotte has found all manner of spy glasses, telescopes and even a polemoscope in a study drawer where she had initially been seeking accounts. I am not sure the Reverend Fordyce would approve. Certainly not publicly, at least.

I am becoming something of an experimental cook. This afternoon, I made 'Honey Clouds' for which I whipped egg-whites into peaks with honey, then burnt them in a pan. They were pleasant enough 'passable, Eliza, for a gentleman's daughter' said Charlotte. She and Maria are both excellent cooks, and I begin to realise the value and independence which comes from possessing the ability to prepare a meal from scratch. I am fascinated by the sugar nips.

At present, we have plenty of milk from the three Collins goats: Evan, Tilly and Beryl. Ever practical Charlotte also makes goat's butter and goat's milk soap. We have a plentiful supply of eggs from chickens quite recklessly oblivious to lockdown.

Your strawberries were most welcome, thank you. We made Strawberry fritters and they were a decadent change from pears and apples. I would enclose the recipe, but I doubt your new found independence would yet accommodate such things. Charlotte is an excellent housekeeper, quite in her element, and has a larder filled with pickles and preserves. The only thing we might shortly lack is flour, but I hear this is a common cry at present; and, of course, the harvest was so sparse last year.

By the by, I am not at all surprised to learn that Lady Catherine's Housekeeper is a formidable woman. It seems fitting. Our Housekeeper at Longbourn is disposed to nervous fits and vapours, and my father would be rid of her, if he could.

I am often most mindful of my good fortune to be out in the wilderness at this time, away from the city, with provisions enough; and every day amazed at what was once done for me without my notice. I am not afraid of it continuing much beyond this Edict, but nevertheless, I am sensible at last.

Jane's account of London is cheerful enough. She remarks upon the Unmentionable only to say how much she now appreciates the shops and coffee houses and tradesmen and our freedoms prior, and looks forward to their return. If our lives are restricted in the country, theirs are much more so in town. Jane writes that they keep strictly within the house and make do. In the early stages, my Aunt and Uncle attempted to arrange for Jane's safe carriage home - indeed, Mama was clear that all were welcome at Longbourn - but it was simply not to be. The Edict was written, read, and London and all of us sealed off before anyone could make a move. Cheapside is not, however, as it may sound to you, and they will all do well there, I hope. How does your sister?

I am unused yet to this night-time quiet, coming from a house of bustle; but it is a friendly kind of silence (Mr Collins's grumbles not withstanding). I spend as much of the day as I can out-of-doors and have even taken to lying in the grass - although if you ever say so, I shall deny it. There's something that happens to one, when frequently in nature. I would describe it as a feeling of harmony or unity. Something challenging to put into words, but I feel the better for it.

The free cat now follows me almost everywhere I go, although she adamantly refuses ever to come inside the house. I have fashioned her a shelter out of wood and straw and she seems happy enough. She purrs almost constantly and licks my hand with her little rough tongue. I wonder how I shall ever leave her behind, when all this is over.

Yours etc.

P.S. I've never had a sense that I would contract the Unmentionable, even with Mr Collins in close proximity. I don't know why. That being said, I stay put. I stay put because others are afraid and they need me to stay put. I wanted you to know this *(for I cannot imagine what you will think, should you hear of Lydia's antics)*.

Letter Eight

Wednesday 13th May, Rosings Sanitorium

Dear Madam,

Thank you for your letter - a most welcome diversion to the routine of isolation.

I trust you are truly as hopeful as you seem with regard to Miss Bennet and the Gardiners? I have every confidence that they will all remain safe and sound till this has passed.

Georgiana was in excellent health, when last I heard. I thank you for your enquiry. Our residence in London is removed enough and the grounds are plentiful for exercise. I hope for the best, and would do infinitely more were it within my power.

Whatever, may I ask, is a 'Seasonal Snooper'?

Bingley once told me that both his sisters possess a wide selection of spying fans. Mrs Hurst, in fact, owns a quizzing glass through which she likes to peer. You may remember this from the Netherfield Ball last year *(how very long ago that seems).*

Do you find you lose track of time and that days fly by?

You are likely quite right and I am beyond them yet, but Colonel Fitzwilliam has boldly declared that he is well acquainted with fritters and will cook us up a batch tomorrow night when Mrs Norris has gone to bed.

Speaking of the proverbial, Cousin Anne's isolation has taken an interesting turn. She was found out by said Housekeeper to be hoarding large amounts of food from the dry larder within her chamber. We are under strict rationing on Lady Catherine's orders who, like Mr Collins, is perhaps afraid we are none of us suffering enough. When confronted by the lady, my cousin bellowed 'I don't want to play the ------ pianoforte!' until Mrs Norris quailed. Anne then took four macarons and crammed them all at once into her mouth. Not a sight I thought I'd ever see, on either count. She has grown quite wild with dark imaginings, it seems, and although, naturally, I cannot entirely condone her behaviour, I may still sympathise. Mrs Norris was heard to mutter that Miss de Bourgh was 'most unladylike' and 'would have no gown left to fit her if she continued in that manner.' It may be noted, that while my cousin could do well by the gaining of weight, Mrs Norris could not. But that is most improper of me. For now, though, our Housekeeper is quite chastened and takes to her room rather early in the evening. I shall ask my cousin what she might do about the tea allocation, for Colonel Fitzwilliam grows quite fretful on just one cup a day.

I have never lain upon the grass. At least, not since early childhood: I may have to try. Is there a knack to it, or does one just lie straight down?

How is the Free Cat? Have you given her a name?

I sympathise with your sister. With the shopkeepers, tradesmen, warehouses and coffee houses all closed down, we may realise at last how much we owe to them. Wood Street, Milk Street, Bread Street, Honey Lane, Friday Street; I have a broader view of Cheapside, indeed of many matters, than you might realise. But perhaps you confuse me with Miss Bingley?

I never had a moment's doubt at your willingness to comply with that which gives the greatest good to all. I wonder, though, why you might believe I should?

Yours etc.

———

P.S. Evan?

Letter Nine

Saturday 16th May, Hunsford Feline Reformatory

Dear Sir,

Thank you for your letter and the ten sacks of flour. We now have nothing left to want.

Why, clearly a Seasonal Snooper is a person who has nurtured a tendency to peep through windows that are not their own *(all sixty-four of them)*; but rather than it being a daily habit, it is more of a weekly or monthly occurrence.

I am most thankful to hear of Miss Darcy's well-being and happy location. If one must be in London at present, those are surely quite the best surroundings in which to find oneself. I am sure she will do well there and keep in the best of health.

I have named the Once-Free Cat 'Felicity,' and she is currently cantankerous. Mr Collins had a gruelling night the one before last *(or rather we did)*, but is now, it seems, over the worst. At least, he is expressing boredom and calling for amusement. He who never reads novels... Thus, he left his chamber for the first time today, and the free cat made her way up there at once and did something unmentionable, but not unpardonable, upon his pillow. As Mr Collins has no sense of natural justice *(or humour)*, she is now disgraced in chains once more. I will set her loose as soon as I may, and Charlotte has asked me to take her away with me once this is done; she is quite out of humour still about the spy glasses.

I am learning all sorts of things I thought I never should. Such as scything - beware your ankles and those of others. And the washing of clothes. What a lengthy process! We begin early and are barely done by four. Mama was always adamant that we should neither cook nor wash clothing for ourselves and, while fully comprehending her motives, I begin to wonder how I could ever have believed such dependency to be of value. It occurs to me that Charlotte wants so little, because she can do much for herself. Mind you, there are some tasks which she performs without a thought that I am sure I *never* could.

Incidentally, Charlotte has politely asked me to refrain from any further creative cooking; she says we have not the provisions for my many mistakes. I am to follow her instructions and not to deviate. Mr Collins has attempted to reassert his authority and return us to our rooms, but to no avail. We have tasted too much liberty to let it go again without a fight.

Question: if you buy security, do you lose freedom?

With surprise, I must confess some sympathy for Miss Bingley, Mrs Hurst and their spying fans. How else may a woman ascertain the character of a new acquaintance, when she is so very limited in what she might say or do publicly?

I accept the society in which I find myself, because I must; but do not admire it much. Nor would I admire a man who attempts to raise himself not by personal evolution, but rather at the expense of woman, reducing her to a simpering ninny that he might educate her better. Our inferiority is imposed and not inherent, thus while society insists upon this quite ludicrous patriarchal hierarchy, we must resign ourselves to the alchemy of observation that we might better know the characters of those with whom we associate, to make the most rational decisions that we may. I look forward to a time when we all are wiser in our treatment of one another, where women are no longer 'out' upon display, paraded about with a looming expiration date of which we are all too sensible. I apologise in advance for this outburst. I do wish Mr Collins would return to bed.

I sympathise also with your cousin. With the life she has thus far led, an eruption seemed inevitable. People fear anger, their own most of all, for it is not counted as a virtue. But if you cannot admit your own frustrations, albeit briefly, privately, how may you possibly progress beyond them? Personally, I find retreating to my room, closing the door and jumping up and down repeating 'I'm right, I'm right, I'm right,' of the greatest assistance.

My cousins are fond of cricket, and I have discovered, too, that the whacking of a ball hard across a lawn is a great relief to any feelings of frustration. Might you and the Colonel contrive a game with Miss de Bourgh?

Yours etc.

P.S. Yes, Evan. She is a very robust goat. I thought of Fitzwilliam, but, indeed, there do seem rather many of that name already.

P.P.S. As a gentleman keenly attuned to the misconduct of others, I am half afeard of news you may have heard from home. If you know aught of any of our near acquaintance in Meryton, regarding quarantine restrictions, I would ask you to be frank with me at once. If not, accept my apologies and my silence upon the matter.

Letter Ten

Monday 18th May, Rosings Asclepion

Dear Madam,

I confess that news of your youngest sister's conduct has reached my ears. The source I will not divulge**, but as it is one to whom I would not fully give my trust, I would ask you to acquaint me with whatsoever you may wish, should you wish it.

Regarding the question of security, I am not convinced that one may purchase it at all. I am certain that freedom, as with all points of import, must be found first and foremost within oneself. Attaching one to other out of need and scarcity, rather than for a mutual, ardent and abiding love, an equal desire for participation, seems fraught with possibility for disappointment - on either side. Why do you ask?

I appreciate your 'outburst,' although I do not see it as such. Indeed, I fully comprehend your feelings and shall, if you would hear them, add my own. I believe that many of my sex are also bound, indeed, *frustrated* by the conventions of which you speak. While they may serve some, they most emphatically do not serve all. I might also add that while we men may experience sentiments similar, if not equal, to women, we are required to be stalwart in face of sorrow, composed in face of danger, and unflinching in each unpleasant duty. Just as you bear feelings of inequality, which I fully concede, there is much expected of my sex. Fathers, knowing this, are more rigorous with their sons than daughters, for reasons that we, as children, might not fully comprehend. I was fortunate. My father was kind.

Regarding marriage, I am fully expected to make a match which meets my own feelings last, and those of my peers first. Whilst I might truly seek an equal companion in life, the equality of rank is felt - by many - to be of far more import than equality of character. A woman of great spirit might have the most unfortunate of families, which would make the match insupportable. One with each seeming credential of good breeding may be an utter bore, having focused every effort upon superficiality and none at all on character. When engaging another for a dance, one takes a great risk. Our dances are long, and if one has made a foolish or a desperate choice, there will be an half hour to fill with idle chit chat. A skill I have no wish to acquire. I write as I think - forgive me.

If not an impertinence, may I ask what brings you happiness? I have had cause of late to consider this at length. The answer is not what once I thought.

Now, I must tell you of The Rise of Lady Catherine. I am sure it will come as no surprise to you to hear that my Aunt - formidable woman that she is - has overcome the Unmentionable, if indeed she ever had it. Twice, we were called upon to say our goodbyes. The first time, Lady Catherine lay in state, looking - I must say - alarmingly frail, having taken no repast for many days. She suffered each one of us to say what we might, then told Anne she was 'quite busting from the seams' (she is not); the Colonel that he was 'quite shockingly unkempt' (he is); and myself she affected not to recognise, but avowed that 'whoever I was' she was 'most seriously displeased with me.'

Last night, we were once more summoned, but my Aunt would neither look at nor acknowledge any one of us. Anne was quite beside herself with fearful remorse and at once set about ridding her room of any remaining provisions, asking the Colonel and I to assist her in the building of a bonfire where she might dispose of all evidence of a recent foray into archery. We agreed, reluctantly. It has been most gratifying - if a little unsettling - to see her so recently invigorated. The Colonel, especially, has been quite captivated.

This morning, quite convinced of the worst, we made our way to the breakfast room, only to find Lady Catherine ready stationed, expostulating and rapping out enough commands to right a year of wrongs. Our exclamations upon her miraculous renaissance were met with bemusement and derision. It transpires she had dismissed her physician late last night for 'gross incompetence' and 'intolerable breath,' an action with which I have much sympathy, for the man seemed far more attentive to her passing than her healing.

I confess I was greatly tempted to give my Aunt a very sound rebuke for alarming us all like that. Twice. But before I could open my mouth she said 'Nephew, if you for two moments together believed _I_ could be felled by a paltry little bug like that, you are not the Fitzwilliam I thought you were.' She's right, of course, I never did believe it entirely. 'Sometimes, I like to rest and recuperate, without the fuss and bother of all of you,' she continued. 'So, I simply… withdraw.'

We all have our ways. I have great affection for my Aunt - she and my mother were deeply fond of one another - and I am most relieved at her revival. I would add that, knowing she, both illness and recovery might quite justly be attributed to boredom and wilfulness in equal measure. She has ever been one to make the most of her position.

Ah yes, you speak of gardening. The gardens at Rosings are now quite overgrown, the ground staff having been dismissed long before. The Colonel and I began their maintenance recently, enlisting our cousin, who had still energy to spare. By the by, both the Colonel and I attempted to persuade Anne to join us for cricket, as you suggested, but she declined. She had developed a preference for archery, aforementioned, citing that she saw an actual use for it - whatever that means - and was quickly an accurate shot. It may please the soon-to-be-free-again cat to note, that Anne's chosen targets were a large pile of written civilities from Mr Collins to my Aunt.

Yours etc.

P.S. Another question; if you might go anywhere today, where might you go?

Letter Eleven

Wednesday 20th May, Hunsford Salon

Dear Sir,

I am most gratified to hear of your Aunt's miraculous recovery. I never doubted it would be so. I do find it in my heart, though, to hope your cousin's retreat may be short-lived. To have gained so much ground in so short a time is something of a value not to be decried.

Charlotte has at last put a stop to the newspaper, after finding Maria pouring over one in floods of tears. Thomas Gray was right, ignorance *is* bliss

Mr Collins, in his recuperating solitude, has taken up a paint brush and is endeavouring to paint each of us. He has some skill. Naturally his chief subject is your Aunt, something which may well offend his wife - although of that he will never be sensible. He has endeavoured to 'beautify' Lady Catherine, by lengthening her nose and neck, enhancing the colour of her eyes, and filling out her lips. I leave it to you to determine whether this is truly a kindness, or an affront. Although I cannot be sure whether your Aunt will notice the changes, for they are subtly done, I am quite certain that - given the right circumstances and at the earliest opportunity - Mr Collins will draw her attention to each, that she might recognise and applaud his skill. In which case, may Heaven help him.

Regarding happiness: my sister Jane, my Father, when I see him, Charlotte, long walks outdoors (no turning about rooms for me), having a purpose, dancing *(even if one must suffer partners who are simply 'tolerable')*, Felicity, a good book, stimulating conversation, a curiosity satisfied, *(your letters... for the most part)* and you?

If I were free to go out, I would either take a carriage to my Aunt and Uncle and Jane in Gracechurch Street and we would go to the theatre, or I would go home to Longbourn and sit outside with my father at dusk while he smokes his pipe, and we would admire the serenity together and pour out amusements.

I am grateful to you for your description of what it is to be man. My chief experience of such is Papa, who seldom communicates such matters. I confess, though, to having had a strong inclining that we might not be *quite* as different as supposed.

You speak of a lady's family being potentially 'insupportable.' I could not marry a man who might allow himself to think so meanly of mine. *That* would be insupportable to me.

Regarding all of us, I would simply say - we have inherited this world, and only we may improve it with comprehension of what does not serve us more, and notions of what may better do. I would rather an equal partner of an unconscionable or insipid family, than an insipid partner of whom my family approves. But to each his own *(do I contradict myself?!)*.

A further wondering - what might make one lose the good opinion of a person whom one had known since childhood*? To whom, one might say, one owed one's allegiance? Or is it that, once grown, one now perceives a difference in rank and fortune not apparent before? That the very views that might dis-incline one from a woman of good character, on account of her 'insupportable' family, might also dim your view of friend and equal, now proven lesser by birth (though not by nature) and thus considered no longer friend?

Question: Is it possible ever to rediscover something you believe may permanently be lost?

Yours etc.

P.S. I confess, I was tempted to speak of Lydia's transgressions, but I realize now how wrong of me that is. Lydia is but fifteen. She is flighty and ebullient and trying. But she is still my sister. Your family is your family. Our loyalty to one another is of great value; not just to blood family, but to those of long acquaintance. We are alarmed that the behaviour of our nearest and dearest is a reflection upon us, and thus we are ashamed of them. But there is no love in that. I am learning that when you speak of love, you speak, truly, of appreciation. Therefore, you must attend to what you may appreciate most in one another and give all your consideration to that; their 'flaws,' and 'imperfections,' you do not see. That is much the politer way to be, do not you think? But we are afraid to show love, for fear of disappointment or rejection, and we look for flaws, that we might early save ourselves.

———

Perhaps you might tell me what you have heard, that I might tell you of its falsehood?

P.P.S. Regarding freedom, I could not agree with you more. It is seldom that one may have the opportunity to see, at such close quarters, the price one might have paid***.

Letter Twelve

Thursday 21st May, Rosings Park

Dear Madam,

I believe you speak once more of the differing accounts that puzzled you exceedingly[*]. You ask a pertinent question. Without hesitation, I answer - one who has harmed one whom I love. I recall having once declared before you that my good opinion, once lost, was lost forever. Or something to that effect. Thus, we find our words of a moment return to haunt us; for I have often thought of what I said, and whether there was fully truth in it. But we must not quote ourselves or one another over time, for it implies an expectation that growth has not occurred.

In the case to which I suspect you specifically refer however; my feelings are unaltered. Indeed, unalterable.

Very well, I will relate in brief what I have heard of your youngest sister; but I do so most unwillingly, knowing it will cause you pain.

_____

There are reports that she is 'not one to remain at home.' That she, by some - and I quote - 'self-ordained edict, in direct opposition to the one by which the rest must currently abide' - deems herself one of the few able to wander at liberty and is regularly to be seen about the town with young Mr Denny, where they endeavour to encourage friends and neighbours out of quarantine to join them at Lottery Tickets or Whist. In fact, so eager is the youngest Miss Bennet to be out and social, it is purported that she has attempted to organise a masked ball. Howsoever, I gather there have been few sponsors.

There is one other, of my knowledge, whose conduct is pronounced equally inappropriate[*]. A recent - and favourite - acquaintance of yours, who has - it seems - been stockpiling flour and buying up salted meat, then selling these on at vast profit. As this information comes from the source aforementioned[**], not *wholly* to be relied upon, I must withhold my judgement *(somewhat)*; though it seems well within the character revealed to me over lengthy acquaintance, with no recent amendment to which I might cling.

Our loyalty is of great value, I agree. But we must take the foremost care where we bestow it. Also, our hearts.

Lady Catherine spent much of yesterday in the organisation of a recovery celebration. It was a sight to behold. Mainly because the attending guests - all three of us - were a sight to behold. Under usual circumstances, Lady Catherine experiences a biannual 'cheeriness' which usually results in a large gathering of friends, who are welcomed with open arms, treated with warmth and generosity, and then dismissed in high dudgeon a day or so later. It is an interesting ritual, but most amusing when one knows what to expect. On this occasion, my Aunt had ordered the preparation of an extravagant meal, which I regret included the pineapple I had hoped to send to you. She had prepared guest cards for each of us, upon which she had written - in her own hand - what she considered to be our most pressing faults. After supper, we were each commanded to offer a form of improvised entertainment. Out of what must surely have been utter desperation, the Colonel opted to dance, Anne to sing, and I to recite excerpts from 'The Faerie Queen.' It did not go well.

Ah, regarding Mr Collins's foray into the world of art; you need not fear. My Aunt has many paintings completed in similar fashion. Indeed, she invites such skill. Rest-assured, he would do far worse to present her otherwise.

Regarding happiness: my grounds at Pemberley, sincere friendship *(even with one who laughs at me, knowing that I might not always bear it well)*, a sense of freedom (intangible as that may seem), my sister Georgiana, the conviction that I am of value, intellectual stimulation.

(You: in spite of your unfortunate heritage. You)

Yours etc.

P.S. Answer: I doubt it. If you whole-heartedly believe something to be true, then life will prove it so. Thus, a belief in loss may result only in further absence.

P.P.S. I enclose an epistle from Colonel Fitzwilliam, who wishes to assure himself that you are well.

Letter Thirteen

Friday 22nd May, Hunsford Parsnip

Dear Sir,

Unfortunately, what you relate accords with what I too have heard *(thoughtless, thoughtless Lydia!)*. I am disappointed by Mr Denny. I thought he was of sounder character; and I think both my sister and he may grossly have misunderstood the purpose of masks.

I have always been able to find a place of allowing in my heart for Lydia. Foolish as she may be, I never previously considered her quite so devoid of the kindness and compassion that binds us each to other. She speaks a great deal about not caring, and now I must believe her. She brings dishonour upon my family and heaven knows what repercussions await when all this Unmentionableness is at an end. She who has broken quarantine again and again without thought or concern for others. I do not fear for my family. They are made of sterner stuff than one might think. But where so many who have so little abide resolutely by the Edict, she, who has so much, does not. Perhaps you will say that she is 'but fifteen'; but I can promise you that she will be just the same when she is 'but sixty'!

But then, we all have our foibles, do we not? We are all foolish at times, or careless. But there is - ultimately - growth in it. The on-going pulse of personality. There must be growth. Otherwise, there are only ever-increasing loops *(my mind is going in loops)*.

How-ever shall I forgive her?

As a matter of fact, I *have* heard of others who do not abide by the Edict. Meryton's rather lately disgraced Master of Ceremonies is one, I hear, often to be spotted keeping assignations with his most recent mistress. But the less said of him, or his rather singular vessel, the better.

I doubt the acquaintance[*] in question has done any such thing. Or if he has, then indeed it is simply an action taken to assist others; to distribute produce fairly. If the source of which you speak is one whom I suspect[**], she will no doubt have little to say in favour of a person who acts in trade. We understand one another only as far as our prejudices allow, do we not? I will not ask you to relent in your aversion, but simply to consider if it serves you still?

I feel I have been most frivolous regarding the Unmentionable. From a distance, it is easy to imagine it a fiction. Something that all abide by out of duty, but not for any true necessity. In our isolation, within the country, it can be easy to...look away. Charlotte and Maria's Grandmama has... departed this world. She was ill only a week. Their mother is left in the greatest remorse, having been unable to attend. All are devastated. I met her many times at home. She was a dear woman - kind and generous. I am a foolish, flighty person.

Now to Mr Collins.

(Oh how I do hide behind Mr Collins...)

Mr Collins, it seems, has little knowledge of the local flora and fauna, in spite of possessing many books describing such. Thus, I found him out early this morning, waving a large axe towards a gentle row of Hawthorne and Hazelnut trees near the border of the Hunsford grounds. Upon rushing towards him and voicing seven-foot-distant protests, I discovered he considered his near-victims not trees, but 'weeds.' I undeceived him immediately. 'Are the trees in the field human, that they should be besieged by you?' I cried. Truly, I have been too much alone. He was most taken aback, responding that he had no intention of besieging anyone, least of all 'you, dear cousin Elizabeth. For family, and the accord within, is everything.' Which would have been plenty, indeed pleasantry, enough had he not felt obliged to add that 'within family, one must prepare oneself for all forms of irrationality, and un-reasonability, and irascibility, especially among the women-folk; and tolerance and forgiveness one must practice and have readily to hand, to soothe those fevered, feeble brows commanded to one's charge.' With this he dropt the axe and made his way in haste towards the house, where he no doubt went at once to Charlotte with complaint. Once I had hidden the axe away forever and for good, I reflected upon our system of education, that teaches the young so little of the plants and trees and creatures within our trust. Mr Collins might - and does - furnish one with the quasi-accurate date of any battle, whether requested or no; but is this truly a useful, transferable intelligence, I wonder, comparatively speaking?

I have yet two letters from Kitty, another from my father and a small package from Jane to read and respond to. Thus, we are told that the post will soon cease for the time being, so our knowledge of friends and family becomes utterly restricted.

Please know that my daily thoughts and prayers include your sister.

I am very glad of this correspondence. Thank you.

Yours etc.

P.S. Please do not reproach yourself for the pineapple. I am sure we would not have had the first idea how to eat it. I only wish I might have been present at your Aunt's gathering. Howsoever, seeing it in my mind's eye must be pleasure enough.

P.P.S. I am pleased to receive Colonel Fitzwilliam's letter and enclose my reply.

Letter Fourteen

Saturday 23rd May, Rosings Confessional

Dear Madam,

Firstly, please convey my deepest condolences to Mrs Collins, Miss Lucas and, when you may, all at Lucas Lodge.

Second, please accept my unreserved apology for any ill-judged remarks regarding said acquaintance. I am sure you are right, and you do well to remind me that anyone may make a truth out of anything - with due repetition.

If I may venture; you sound somewhat distressed. This circumstance is trying for each and all of us and you have borne through with infinite patience and humour. Do not give up.

You have my deepest appreciation regarding Georgiana. My last communication - for the present - was, as your elder sister's, all calmness and reassurance.

My answer to your new understanding of the unfolding of the Unmentionable is 'how could you know prior?' Or any of us. For my part, I would always rather hear of a resolute attention to the good or amusing, fanciful as it may seem, than dire portents aiding misery to spread. We must be kinder. Universally kinder. We all have differing experiences and, therefore, differing levels of understanding. Some will go through the entirety of lockdown without knowing what is now revealed to you. Others will come yet closer; know more. Of my acquaintance, few have contracted the actual illness. But I have heard of many who have succumbed to despair and the unnatural pain of isolation. For this, we are informed, the government is to blame. But how could they do better without the hindsight all have lacked? We must be kinder. Have more faith. It is always easy to imagine a better course, post incarnation.

This from my father, years ago, may bring you comfort; 'we cannot allow ourselves to view ourselves through any eyes other than our own, and those eyes must be ever loving and kind.'

In terms of forgiveness, I have an answer which may perhaps surprise you. We forgive others for our own sake first. I had a grandfather who was dear to me. Both dear to me, and not. And I to he. We fought through similarity and difference. For months we did not speak at all. But when he died, I felt only filiality, was left with only love. The disappointment I had felt at times, the disparity, the frustration, all evaporated in an instant and I knew only fondness. This left me many months experience of the most profound regret, which haunts me yet. Had I been master of myself, had I esteemed more and quarrelled less, been guilty of less vanity and pride, I might look back with greater peace. Had I forgiven him fully, completely, when I might; cherishing his humanity beyond all else.

(Your letters are the most precious moments of my day... I think of you... constantly... regarding what I might say... in correspondence. I...)

I thank you too.

Yours etc.

P.S. Enclosed is a further communication from the Colonel. I trust the news from home and town was all that you might hope?

P.P.S. I enclose what are left of Mrs Norris's Banbury cakes and hope they are to your taste. Lady Catherine has insisted on Anne's being placed upon a strict purge to counter any ill-effects occurring during her absence. Thus, we are to eat only Pease-soup, gruel and boiled turnips for the foreseeable future.

P.P.P.S. The Master of Ceremonies - a rascal? One would not think it to look at him. Of what vessel do you speak?

Letter Fifteen

Monday 25th May, Hunsford Place of Purgatory

Dear Sir,

I thank you for your apology, however unnecessary. The fault is mine for putting pen to paper in such a humour. I hope you will burn the letter, if you have not already done so.

I was saddened to hear of your Grandpapa, and of your remorse since. If it is of any comfort, I sincerely do not believe that resentments, large or small, live beyond our time here. Only love.

Yes, I thank you - satisfactory news from both home and town. Kitty has discovered a taste for baking and thus, she informs me, has had to let out each of her gowns. Jane sent a beautifully embroidered mask for each of us at Hunsford, carefully stitched by her own dear hand. She mentioned having received, at last, a brief letter from Miss Bingley *(in response to a far longer one from her)*. Jane continues brave and steady and, I am certain, as slender as she ever was.

Incidentally, the Banbury Cakes were delicious. Thank you for sending them. You must all have experienced great disappointment at their removal. I enclose, in return, some cheese cakes - made by Charlotte and I this afternoon. As they are a gift, they may not be sent back or redistributed. Guard them well.

My father writes that his unrelieved solitude palls and he is considering the commencement of a tunnel from his library to town. The thought exhausts him - especially having only access to cutlery as tools. I have responded that just because the completion of a matter may take 'a month of Sundays,' does not mean it should not be commenced. But as my father hates town, I do wonder if his motivation for said tunnel is misplaced. I confess myself compelled to encourage him, as he may reach town in time to stop Lydia from accomplishing something particularly foolish. But I grow delusional on both counts.

On the subject of my father, I am sure he would both agree with your thoughts on government culpability and disagree. Both most fervently. He has never had any faith at all in any governing body, believing that the very people most attracted to, or inheriting, such a path in life are the very last people who should ever be in possession of such power. He equally believes that the lack of foresight inherent in many - and the study of history leading, somehow, to the making of much the same errors again - indicates that no person should ever be in charge of another, let alone an entire governing body. When asked what we might have instead, by way of social structure, he invariably replies 'why, I've no idea, my Lizzy. But, thankfully, that is not for me to determine,' - and returns once more to his library. Really, I think he is mostly speaking of Mama.

I was moved by your words upon forgiveness. How often we may wish to forgive, but do not out of fear and pride. How often may we wish, privately, to be better than we are, only to then publicly fall short.

Grief is strange. Charlotte and Maria are intermittently beside themselves, then as if nothing has happened. Of a sudden I may come across one or other standing stock still in the midst of the garden, staring at the ground. There were letters of condolence, but not so many as one might expect - some offered comfort, others not quite so. All meant well, I believe. I do understand - what can one possibly say? But always better to say something of... affection, however brief. One, from a cousin declared 'I know not what to say. Thus, I send only love.' It is the one letter Charlotte has kept. Charlotte has asked me to stop smiling at her. 'Eliza,' she has said on several occasions 'there's that sad, half smile that is new between us. Put it away.' I wish I might embrace her... But at present, that is Mr Collins's privilege alone. Here it must be chronicled that while he may not always say what might be best, his actions - under this circumstance - are truly quite attentive, for he is often to be seen tottering nearby, ready to give his lady an affectionate - if awkward - pat.

How much I now look forward to. Such simple, vital things. The freedom to offer comfort to those I love. The freedom to express affection. The desire to vary my attire - not just on wash day. The freedom to go to Meryton; to see the dear, familiar faces. We are so attached to this life. There is much I can see in my mind's eye, of the world beyond Hunsford, but it will not do; I must have reality again.

Yours etc.

P.S. A rascal indeed. He has a small dwelling, by the Lea, at the farthest end of his estate, and has frequently been spotted casting off in a small punt from t'other side of said dwelling, whereupon he crouch-paddles his way to his mistress's house. As the river flows past Aunt Phillips's home, the whole village are aware. I confess, I was surprised as you. At local gatherings, he seemed all affability and devotion to his family. But Aunt Philips - ever alert - caught him passing 'notes' to Mary King at an assembly late last year and all was revealed - countless mistresses, of which his wife was all too aware. It transpired that, when first discovered, he had called her 'mad as old King George' and threatened not only to inform the whole of Meryton of her 'insanity,' but also to have her locked away 'for the good of the children.' Hence her dedicated silence. The man is clearly a follower of Fordyce. We all still hope he will find his way out to sea.

(Gracious, I sound like Mama...)

P.P.S. The swifts have arrived. I look forward to them every year, and this year they are more welcome than ever - their calls of joy announcing the summer.

P.P.P.S. My reply to the Colonel is enclosed.

Letter Sixteen

Tuesday 26th May, Rosings Sanctuary of Muffled Mutterings

Dear Madam,

I am most grateful for your letter and generous words *(I could never burn a letter of yours, but that is a secret between these walls and I)*. I am in complete agreement. I remind myself constantly of the same. There are no grudges yonder and regret, beyond reflection and resolution, serves no useful purpose and therefore must be set aside.

Regarding your father; a tunnel sounds a useful, if lengthy, proposition. We have two known tunnels at Pemberley. One from the kitchens to the stables. Another from the library to what was once the Housekeeper's cottage - such an obvious place for a secret door and passageway that it remained undisclosed for two generations. We have yet to learn its purpose, though all have the same suspicion.

Speaking of which, the Master of Punting would be, it seems, a man who perhaps should never have married. My father adored my Mother, and she he. I was blessed to have that example. My Uncle was less fortunately situated. He too exhibited a tendency to question the sanity of his wives, whilst taxing that sanity to the very limit. My father once said that he felt his brother, and all around him, might have lived far better and more tranquil lives had he not, originally, felt such obligation to be married. We are all so varied in our inclinations that a rigorous social structure to which all must adhere seems, often, to cause more pain than good. Thus, we return once more to kindness and allowance. If my Uncle had felt more harmony within, and was, thus, able to express himself freely and with truth, his ripples in the world would have been likewise of peace and truth instead. So too with Fordyce.

I am thankful to learn that all remains well with your family in both Meryton and town. Miss Bingley, as a favour to me, was employed in writing daily - and lengthy - greetings to my sister - now made impossible with the cessation of the post. This, perhaps, explains *(somewhat)* the brevity of her correspondence with Miss Bennet.

Anne, too, has been engaged in mask making. Hers, however, are for her own distinct use and seem, predominantly, to be a device deployed to infuriate her mother, who is now unable to discern a word she says. This gives my cousin the free reign you wished for her, to speak whatsoever she desires without fear of repercussion. Until recently, I had firmly believed that Anne's frustrations resided within her own conviction of having a weak constitution from birth, but it has since transpired that she feels - most fervently - that this is a notion wholly enforced upon her. My family, on my Father's side, are blessed with the most acute hearing, and I am thus - unfortunately - able to hear what Lady Catherine cannot. I say 'unfortunately,' because Anne has rather a ready wit and I dare not laugh before my Aunt or I will give my cousin away.

I am delighted to hear that Mr Collins rises in your esteem, somewhat. When my father passed, I felt profound grief, but also isolation. You are right - those of close acquaintance know not what best to say, so they depart, swiftly, and rather completely. At a time when liveliness might most be welcome, it is withdrawn - for fear too, I believe - a superstition that loss might be contagious, unsubstantiated as that may be. We do not need words from others at such times, for words will never do. But to be *present*, ready to offer affection, even humour, why *that* is of the truest, highest value.

I might add yet, that through such isolation, my sister and I grew deeply close. Thus, there is always light.

Yours etc.

P.S. I enclose further greetings from the Colonel.

P.P.S. The Rosings inmates were all most deeply grateful for the cheese cakes, which were exceptional. Thank you.

Letter Seventeen

Dear Sir,

Precisely! As a general rule, I do my best to not concern myself with that I cannot help. I have seldom found it to change anything for the better, but have likewise noticed that the successful deflection of my mind provides, at the very least, a strong sense of relief instead. When we sincerely love, we wish the very best for the objects of our affection - but, in the muddle of life, our petty concerns can confuse and misdirect our feelings. With the release of these concerns, love remains. But I repeat myself. You speak of allowance and kindness. As your Papa once said, you must give this to yourself and think only of the past as its remembrance gives you pleasure. Truly.

I would offer a suggestion, regarding Miss de Bourgh and her application of masks, which you are at liberty to take or leave. Your cousin seeks expression for her frustrations, but may not do so directly for fear of repercussion. I am certain that she will never find lasting peace or happiness while she believes your Aunt's approval to be the source of either. I fear she is unlikely ever to have Lady Catherine's compassion towards her will for, if readily available, it would have shown itself by now. Your cousin's self-compassion, however, is inherently assured, if she will allow it. When she is able to release her anger, privately, and to turn away from the past - which cannot be helped - towards the future - which can - then, I believe, she will find a place of lasting self-assurance; and should she find her mother still intractable, it will not matter so.

I appreciate your words on the Master of Paddles. A new perspective is always refreshing. Although I cannot offer sympathy with his behaviour, I may with the root of it. The questioning of the sanity of his wife as an aid to concealment, however, is a matter beyond my acceptance. On this, Mama and I are *(for once!)* in complete agreement. She was particularly shocked, indeed, to learn that such matters were discussed before his children. 'Does he not consider, Mr Bennet,' she has exclaimed to Papa on *several* occasions, 'that the children might *believe* it and then consider such their own *inescapable* future? I would not do a child of mine so *great* a *wrong* for *all* the *world*.' She can be quite wise, Mama, on the subject of children.

I have had cause recently, as you may know, to consider a path that did not feel my own, for the sake of others***. For the briefest moment, I felt the weight many feel almost constantly, to make a decision that does not accord with their idea of happiness, and desires for their *own* future. There is a stubbornness about me, however, which I cherish - for I will not be intimidated by the will of another. I allowed myself freedom, sanctioned by Papa. I am forever grateful to him. I know for certain now, what instinct alone guided me towards before. That had I bent to the will of another, looked to another for my own path in this life, my unhappiness would have been great indeed. We must allow ourselves choice. We must understand also, that where there is uncertainty, there is often no decision yet to make.

Now that Mr Collins has recovered fully from the Unmentionable, he has begun an intense investigation as to its originator. Mama behaves similar whenever she contracts a cold. The household is thoroughly interrogated, staff included, until she determines the culprit - usually Kitty - and holds them to account by grumbling. His current favourites are a household from Rochester, who moved 'lock, stock and barrel' last week 'in a cart with rusty wheels drawn by an *old nag*, Charlotte - and before the hallowed walls of

Rosings,' has been his constant lament (we hear his sobs at night). The fact that they should not have moved during lockdown has not escaped his notice. The fact that they were many miles hence when he contracted the Unmentionable, has. 'Charlotte, they have a bath in the garden!' He cries in despair. 'What a pleasure that must be, dear, in the summer months,' she responds without a pause. 'Charlotte, their eldest child plays the violin very ill indeed.' 'What a pleasure that will be, dear, when he is older and more proficient.' 'Charlotte, they are all so terribly loud all of the time.' 'Why, we are all louder than we know, my dear. Go into your study and close your eyes for an hour or so.' Upon investigation of my own, it transpires that Mr Collins has a dislike of those from the north of Kent - impossible to comprehend why.

It transpires that another near neighbour may, or may not, have been feeding Mr Collins's geese. It is no wonder really, as he has shown a tendency to tether creatures, that they might conspire to flee to more exalted ground. One must never underestimate the ricochet which occurs when attempting to force to one's will a being who considers itself inherently free.

Speaking of which, Felicity is once more fully at liberty. I had it arranged that as soon as Mr Collins caught and collared her again, either myself, Charlotte or Maria - indeed, whomsoever was nearest - would instantly free her once more. After many days' amusement, Mr Collins finally relented in exhaustion and is now furious with me. He has ceased all verbal communication and avoids me, but to leave letters upon the drawing room table or under my door referring to _his_, underlined several times, cat. Charlotte assures me that Felicity was always feral and that Mr Collins paid her no heed prior except for the odd kick, but he is not to be reasoned with.

Thus, I fear, you spoke too soon regarding his rise in my esteem.

Yours etc.

P.S. My reply to the Colonel is enclosed. I expect we might see you all, at a safe distance, on Sunday for Mr Collins's eagerly-anticipated missive from the church tower?

P.P.S. It is a long held and rather foolish belief that a man in possession of a donkey must be in want of a dog. I just thought you should know.

Letter Eighteen

Saturday 30th May, Rosings Temple of Concord (which may - I trust - fare better than The Hugh Temple of Peace)

Dear Madam,

I confess, I too am curious as to how Mr Collins came by the Unmentionable. Especially as both yourself, and the Lucas sisters have, thankfully, avoided the same. So too concerning we three miscreants and her Ladyship.

Unlike Mr Collins, however, Lady Catherine has no need to conduct an intensive investigation, having decided long ago that she most likely contracted the Unmentionable from either myself or the Colonel, being interlopers to Rosings. The Colonel, particularly, has been most unpopular since her recovery, although this may be as a result of his ill-conceived celebration dance.

Yesterday, Anne - owing to that extensive morning thunderstorm - returned early from outdoor exercise to discover Mrs Norris within her chamber, overseen by my Aunt, searching through possessions hidden within a trunk. Inevitably, to my Aunt's horror and dismay, these included several questionable books, two by notorious lexicographers Messrs Head and Grose. I am sure neither publication is known to you, so I will go no further. Suffice it to say, there were heated words exchanged, unhampered by any lack of clarity or volume.

In the evening, having had no clear platform yet to offer your ideas to Anne, I took it upon myself to act as mediator between my Aunt and she. I am now in a similar position to yourself regarding Mr Collins, for neither will speak a word to me; but there is at least peace, of a kind.

(Much to my incredulity) I am in agreement with your Mama regarding the protection of young minds. Indeed, I am furnished, it seems, with an example first hand; for Anne, having evolved beside a mother who never forgets the slightest slight, is herself - at present - completely immersed in every wrong ever done to her, whether intended or no. A circumstance most surely intensified by both our continuing confinement - with no clear knowledge of when it might end - and the dampness which has replaced the early days of blue skies and warmth.

The Colonel has been called away to attend to 'a ripple of unrest,' where - he was not at liberty to say, but he has given his full assurance that there is no cause whatsoever for alarm and nothing out of the ordinary (could anything at present be described as ordinary?). Thus, he wishes you to know - regretfully - that he will not be in attendance tomorrow morn and that the letter I enclose will be his last for a time. I may not hazard a guess as to where he is sent, or for what; indeed, it would be foolish of me so to do. We must be of good cheer and hold faith with his words.

Question: If you might steer change in the world in but three ways, which would you choose?

It may *(or may not)* amuse you to hear that Miss Bingley - having uncovered a pronounced aptitude for illustration in her brother's Valet - has commissioned the man, in addition to his present duties, to sketch her in a series of 'lockdown ensembles,' and then reproduce these to send to a multitude of correspondents. I have little idea why I am one such recipient, having not the slightest interest in fashion. Perhaps I might send them on to you?

Yours etc.

P.S. I thank you, regarding the dog and donkey. I am now much the wiser.

P.P.S. I fear my Aunt and Mr Collins are likely to have an agreement of the most violent kind regarding your recent neighbours. Mrs Norris first drew our attention to their freshly renovated dwelling at breakfast, informing her ladyship that in her (humble) opinion it was 'an abomination of the very worst kind.' My Aunt was out of the house and within her carriage before one might say 'multum stercora in parvum spatium.'

She returned pale and speechless.

Letter Nineteen

Monday 1st June, Hunsford Cove of Conciliatory Gestures

Dear Sir,

I thank you for your letter and, indeed, that of the Colonel, which contained many more reassurances. At this stage in lockdown, it is not difficult to imagine what might be the cause of 'unrest.' We are very fortunate here. You are right, we must - as ever - keep in the best of spirits and trust.

I am unsure quite how to respond to your news regarding your Aunt and Miss de Bourgh. Perhaps silence between the two is best, for the present. At times, there are simply no worthy words left to one.

Mama has a distant relation who does much the same in correspondence as Miss Bingley. Whenever a letter is received, it invariably contains a recent sketch of the lady, drawn by her sister. As accomplished as they are, Mama is ever baffled as to what to do with them – 'I simply do not understand, my dear Mr Bennet,' she will invariably say 'why she should think I need so many. I shall not thank her next time, and perhaps she will grasp the hint.' Adding 'I do so dislike people who force me to be rude.' At last count, she had three-hundred and fifty-one, and is yet afraid to dispose of them for fear the lady may, of a sudden, visit. Thus, to your kind offer and having, possibly, even less interest in fashion than you - I answer; no, thank you.

I must agree, I infinitely preferred quarantine in the sunshine with the bright blue sky. As refreshing as it is to listen to the wind howling round the house at night, rather than Mr Collins, I would welcome another long spell of clear skies and gentle warmth.

Actually, I *am* familiar with both Head and Grose. When I was but ten years old Papa loaned me - ever curious - a copy of Grose's 'Dictionary of the Vulgar Tongue' from his library. I spent many hours exploring its substance and thus, thanks to Papa and Mr Grose, I know expressions to this day that might shame a sailor. So, you see - impressionable. Mama was utterly horrified when she found out. For a year, she would not take me into town for fear I might forget myself. Papa also loaned me an extremely old book from his collection by Robert Greene entitled 'The Black Bookes Messenger,' concerning the exploits of one Ned Browne. I remember little of it now, although it was duly scandalous, excepting the opening expression 'read and be warned, laugh as you like, judge as you find,' which I adored and adopted.

Coincidentally, Mr Collins has engaged Charlotte's assistance in compiling a new dictionary of 'proper expressions,' fancying himself something of a lexicographer. While Charlotte is happy to have him engaged in so engrossing a project, she does cherish hopes that it may - in time and with the right encouragement - make for a more solitary pursuit.

In spite of previous weather bewails, it was well indeed that Sunday's sermon was so relentlessly, loudly wet, for it ensured that those who remained before their own houses and at a substantial distance from Mr Collins and the 'Lady Catherine Trumpet' (namely, all but we three women and, possibly, the Rosings carriage) were unable to hear his extensive missive regarding 'interlopers' and 'unwelcome guests.' Hardly biblical of him. I trust that your Aunt and cousin were comfortable within and found the rather sodden 'Lady Catherine' acoustically effective. Had it not been for the weather, his invention might have been something of a triumph. For our part, we did our best to divert our minds from the moment he cried out 'for aliens have entered, the holy places of the Lord's house!'

and pointed directly at the innocents from Rochester...

'Would you excuse me while I go and scream into a pillow?' murmured Charlotte, once we returned home.

This is now a common phrase of hers. It began, most particularly, when she endeavoured to encourage Mr Collins in the washing of his hands often and throughout the day. Although Mr Collins adheres to certain rudimentary cleansing rituals, he does not by any means consider the washing of hands as a necessity. Charlotte has an inkling that it is mostly through unwashed hands that infection is actually spread, but finds her husband resolutely unwilling even to consider such a suggestion. 'Why my dearest and then more dear than dear,' he says, winningly, 'you know as well as any that sickness is conveyed through miasma,' and with that he takes her hand, looks deeply into her eyes and speaks very slowly and gently. 'Let me most *patiently* and *infinitely* assure you that - when un-gloved - my hands are always rigorously perfumed with Truefitt & Hill's Freshman Cologne' (a gift from your Aunt, it would seem). Charlotte's most recent attempt to convince him was met with an upsurge of frustration 'do you think me a Pontius?' he exclaimed, quickly adding 'my dear.'

Charlotte, Maria and I have passed the greater part of this afternoon in conciliatory baking for those from Rochester, which we will leave upon their doorstep. I cannot imagine it is enough to compensate for such unnecessary unkindness. Mr Collins himself is not to be reasoned with, and although, as aforementioned, it is highly likely that they did not hear, they must surely have seen his gesture.

Answer: I have no great wish to change the world, only myself, as I may. That being said, it has been most amusing to consider, so these are my thoughts - first, dancing allowed for married couples to encourage continuing affection and vitality; second, no more entailments, or, indeed, Wills of any kind, only goodwill; third, infinite opportunity for all, no matter whom or where, teaching all to fish, metaphorically speaking... Oh, and no more disease, of course, compulsory handwashing, the rigorous vetting of clergymen for a reasonable level of personal appeal, all repetitive rascals to grow a moustache, that they might instantly be recognisable and deflected - may I really have only three?

It is Maria's birthday tomorrow, and we plan to surprise her with a small celebration. She has been rather anxious of late, understandably, and we hope to compensate in some small way for the absence of her full family.

Yours etc.

P.S. I enclose my reply to the Colonel's letter and ask that you leave it wheresoever he may swiftly discover it upon his return[****].

P.P.S. As a matter of very idle curiosity, where did you find yourself upon Sunday morning, that you were unable to attend Mr Collins's soaking?

Letter Twenty

Tuesday 2nd June, Rosings Residence of Righteousness

Dear Madam,

I thank you for your letter and wish to assure you, first and foremost, of my presence on Sunday morn. Stationed beneath a far oak tree, I bore witness to the whole. You speak the truth, had it not been for the weather I am convinced the Lady Catherine would have carried Mr Collins's voice to the very farthest reaches of the parish. Thus, we were blessed. Lady Catherine herself - who, unlike myself, was able to hear the sermon in its entirety - was quite delighted by it; both - I am given to understand from her jubilant retelling - the extensive portion referring to her astonishing resurrection, and that concerning your neighbours. It seems your cousin outdid himself, on both counts. Please accept my earnest pledge to add to your conciliatory gifts at the earliest opportunity. *(utterly inexcusable!)*

I would imagine there is right in Mrs Collins's theorising - she seems a regular James Lind - one of the few admirable Physicians of my knowledge. Perhaps Mr Collins might concede that miasma and transferral from hands are *each* likely causes? I must confess, it perplexes one in the extreme to imagine a person scrupulous in daily washing, who does not then - also - regularly cleanse their hands. It seems as much an oddity to me as a gentleman who endures all the rigours of formal dress, only to leave his home barefoot.

My father was an honourable man; broad-minded, and generous. When I was little more than four, I remember his escorting me on a tour of our estate, to show what one day would be within my care. He spoke at length of our immense responsibility to others, and what that must signify; 'to be placed at the head of... aught - a household, an estate, a country, even, one must always recognize the great gift of trust given, and repay that trust with kindness, with constancy and integrity,' he said. I have never forgotten it, and have done everything I can *(I hope)* to live by his words. You are quite correct, unrest has always the self-same basis.

When my mother passed, my father became suddenly less sure of himself. At times, he was susceptible to rather evident falsehoods. Not, I hasten to add, to the detriment of any within his care, but more to his own. Of that I will no further speak. I will tell you, instead, of his passing. I have never spoken of this to anyone. Not even

Georgiana, who was too young at the time, and then I never had the heart... When my father grew ill, I was advised to engage an acclaimed physician (for, as I now know, much credence for intelligence is given to those who speak freely of the ominous or grim - examine, if you will, our Scandal Sheets). The prognosis he gave was bleak. He had seen the case before, on several occasions, and was able to tell me, and most unfortunately, my father - how it would all fall out for him. This he did in immense detail and without my permission - for I was away one day on business that could not wait *(but one day!)*. When I discovered his action, I was enraged - more so than I ever have been, before or since. But the damage was done. This man was employed to tend to my father, to give him care - not to frighten and to leave him without hope. There can be no *care* in that! That he proclaimed would happen did so swiftly and with absolute accuracy. My father moved from moderate symptoms to the worst of cases, within a matter of days. I hope never to feel so *powerless* again. Had I hired a physician of lesser reputation, but greater humility, greater compassion, I am convinced my father could have lived.

You are right - utterly. You must not trust another to make a decision for your future; you must seek clarity within, that you may not be so easily affected by their *tutored* paradigms.

_____

Yes, only three allowed. Those are the rules! Dancing for married couples would not have occurred to me, but I must agree - indeed, it is the only dancing that truly appeals to me. A world without Wills might be somewhat chaotic. But Wills of goodwill only, I concede, would be preferable. How does one determine, however, what goodwill is exactly? What might be goodwill for one could easily appear not so to another. Agreed, regarding a universal teaching to fish; self-sufficiency is vital. Now, at the risk of appearing unchivalrous, if all rascals are to grow a moustache, how then are we to know a female rascal? A beauty patch might be an obvious suggestion, but I hear they are so easily removed or lost.

I too would eliminate disease, also unpaid labour - when all must eat, house and clothe themselves, it seems insupportable to expect a person to work for nought. Then I might lessen the penalties for petty theft, which are quite ludicrously harsh (especially among those who have little as it is), and introduce penalties, instead, for those who are careless with the hearts of others. But perhaps that is rather draconian of me.

I am most deeply, profoundly shocked by your early reading. One could not think it possible to look at you. I have never heard of Mr Greene's publication, but am tempted to seek it out that I might come to know more fully to what horrors you have been exposed. Your Papa is surely a most liberal guardian.

Yours etc.

P.S. I do hope your birthday celebration for Maria was as pleasant as possible. Is it usual to you to celebrate such an event? In our household, we might mark the anniversary with a small remembrance, but only Lady Catherine (depending upon mood) will have a gathering.

Letter Twenty-one

Thursday 4th June, Hunsford Parlour of
Impertinence

Dear Sir,

I am greatly relieved to hear that you were, indeed,
present on Sunday. It seemed most afflicting to
imagine that you might have had the good sense to
spare yourself, whilst the rest of us did not. I am
sure your conciliatory contribution will be greatly
appreciated by our neighbours. Of whom more,
presently.

The gardens seem to have exploded over this
recent week, passing from relative order to
abundant chaos. In frustration on Tuesday noon,
Mr Collins turned the goats loose to combat the
overgrowth, with - naturally - mixed results (that
could be his epitaph). Goats, it transpires, are
imprecise as to where they choose to mow and
seem all too taken with whatever Mr Collins
treasures most. Thus, I inadvertently won my way
back - briefly - into his good books, by glancing
early from my window and spying Evan and Tilly
both headed with unprecedented purpose towards
his prized artichokes. Having raised the alarm, the
household - in unity - ran outside and pulled both

extremely strong and stubborn nannies away and guided them towards greener pastures. Mr Collins was quite beside himself with gratitude at the preservation of 'so *modern* a vegetable, cousin Elizabeth.' Once he had finished weeping, he noticed - to his intense mortification - that Maria was still in her dressing-gown. He passed the afternoon locked within his study composing a sermon on the incontrovertible slide towards impropriety in unmarried women. I know this, because there was a new note upon the drawing room table expressing such.

This morning the goats had at the artichokes again, this time with pronounced success. A distraught Mr Collins stumbled the garden, wringing his hands, attempting to establish just how they had escaped their enclosure. It is true, a goat can climb rather well, but as a general rule these ones are rather docile, contented beings and seldom bother. After an hour or more he discovered, at last, the frayed rope to their gateway hung like bunting across the archway to our Rochester-neighbours' grounds. They had even draped wild roses delicately athwart.

'So, it begins,' gasped Mr Collins, having started it.

This afternoon was passed by the Parson of Hunsford, in the assembly of a grand sign on which was painted large 'TRESPASSERS WILL NOT BE TOLERATED.' He might as well have written 'NEIGHBOURS.' It was barely dry and hung where his adversaries might best see it, before an effigy of Mr Collins, stuffed with straw, was brought out and deposited in the aforementioned bathtub with a sign across his chest indicating 'BLOCKHEAD.' They had even fashioned him a small papier-mâché trumpet. The real Mr Collins was speechless.

'If only I could believe this might be an end to it,' murmured Charlotte to the sky.

My Papa is a liberal man, in many ways, you are quite correct. This he attributes to his mother, my grandmama, who was of so open a mind, so free a-tendency of speech, that Mama could hardly bear to have her in the house. 'People are changeable, dear Lizzy,' she would say to me, 'people are changeable. They mean well, most all of them, but do not pin your hopes on any one of them. Trust to yourself and all will fall out well. Trust to another (nodding at Mama), and you will find yourself at the mercy of their current whim.'

My father's present reinterpretation of her words seems thoroughly apt in terms of Mr Collins;

'human-beings, my Lizzy, have a tendency to censure one another in excess, only to weep with outrage and shout for vengeance when their turn comes,' adding, in case I had forgot, 'I want nothing to do with most of them.'

Mr Collins has spent the last three hours scything down any branches extending from our neighbours' grounds that have had the temerity to invade either our property or the green (you may remember that I have hidden his axe). He really is the most foolish man. It is now after ten and he is still without, though it is almost dark. He will be fortunate to return with all his limbs.

Maria has contracted a slight indisposition, we believe after Sunday's soaking, or perhaps owing to the dressing-gown extravaganza and ensuing humiliation. Thus, she spent most of her birthday within her chamber, wrapped in a quilt. When her condition worsened overnight, Charlotte administered warm wine throughout the next day, a Lucas family medication made from last year's elderberries. This proved quite the restorative. Charlotte and I are now rather more enlightened than we ever wished to be as to the contents of Maria's correspondence with my youngest sister, which she half-sang to us, and seems - at least in part - responsible for her recent anxiety. I thank heaven, after all, that the post was stopped. Lydia is most ingenious in covering a sheet of paper in minutely written tattle. If only women might seek employment (factories aside!), she would be assured of an infinite income among the Scandal Sheets of your mentioning.

With regard to your father, I am truly sorry. Yet you must not blame yourself. We are each of us encouraged to believe that those in positions of trust or authority are able to comprehend fully what course is best for others. You could not have known. With the temporary exception of Lydia, who does not seem to learn, I wish all might be easier within themselves for that which could not have been foreseen - and with one another. Shame and blame do make the most dreadful circle. Besides, at this time and distance, having no longer a clear and thorough memory of your exact feelings, the extreme level of duress you were most clearly under, who are you to act as judge upon yourself, to relitigate your case?

Regarding goodwill, I am inclined to think it not a subject for debate. I concede that certain beings might be unimpressed by 'sentimentalities' that they consider weakness, but that is up to them. Kindness is kindness, and needs no credential.

Over the identifier of a female rascal, I admit to being torn. Being, likely, so grossly outnumbered by her male counterparts, I feel she might be allowed to wander at liberty until the ratio is equalized. If not, then perhaps some foliage - evergreen. A pin made of laurel leaves, or spruce? A beauty patch is rather old fashioned and might send the wrong signal, don't you think?

I confess, you seem of a more liberal turn than I imagined (although perhaps not regarding dancing). In an attempt to commence the elimination of unpaid labour, I have mentioned to Mr Collins that he might consider a wage for Charlotte - not as his wife, of course (for that is of her own election), but as his... everything else. Should he ever make acknowledgement of my enquiry, I shall let you know.

I wonder when you might hear again from the Colonel?

Yours etc.

P.S. Respectfully, please do not refer to Mr Collins as my 'cousin' in future correspondence. If I myself have done so, then I apologise. It has been quite unconscious and unintentionally done.

P.P.S. Do you find your frustrations exaggerate in lockdown? I fear I become more and more like my cousin.

P.P.P.S. Oh bother.

Letter Twenty-two

Friday 5th June, Rosings Stockade

Dear Madam,

I trust that Miss Lucas is soon recovered. At least it is not the Unmentionable.

It seems that lockdown has now worn thin for my Aunt and she has decided that it simply must come to an end. The government cannot dare to argue, and will surely follow suit. She has - somehow - persuaded her Steward to leave his family and return to his duties, thus the last two days have been filled with the urgent - and unnecessary - rearrangement of furniture and, indeed, of all of us. It has been most bewildering. The Colonel is, perhaps, fortunate to have been called away. My Aunt has determined that the grounds will be next in her 'Maintain and Develop' programme, which might as well be called 'Wreck and Rebuild.'

I might mention that, regarding Anne, the most recent developments in the reassertion of my Aunt's authority have been rather unfortunate. After several days of quite fearsome silence between the two, Lady Catherine held her breath for an extraordinary (and slightly alarming) interval, then withdrew to her room and seated herself by a window, staring into the gloaming and refusing any attempts to restore her spirits, even by the favoured Mrs Norris. Although no actual edict of silence was issued, a dreadful hush fell upon the house and each felt compelled to move about on tiptoe. Anne was left rebellious, confused, vexed, then - of a sudden, it seemed - as though marooned. Sunken and filled with repentance, within an hour she was before her mother, almost upon her knees, promising a return to obedience and pleading for forgiveness. To this my Aunt spoke not a word, would not so much as look upon her daughter, allowing Anne a sleepless night to consider further, before sweeping downstairs the next morning with a written list of personal improvements for her daughter, to which agreement I was called upon both to proclaim and witness. Not as signatory, I hasten to add - for I could not have done so.

In order to restore my Aunt's good opinion, Anne must now devote two hours each day to embroidery. She _is_ to learn the pianoforte, but in theory only - no instrument is to be played. This for an hour each day. Also, drawing - using myself as subject - every evening. Outdoor exercise is confined once more to a circuit of the local area by carriage, or she may walk sedately about the grounds for an half hour daily, but only if accompanied by myself. She may read only from a selection of specifically chosen books. Only after a week of 'significant improvement' will my Aunt agree to commence actually speaking to her daughter once more. In the meantime, I am asked to act as intermediary. Also, we are allowed no more seasoning at meal-times.

To this I might say much, but it is not my home, and I must leave well alone. My Aunt has never been one to be easily reasoned with. Having witnessed first-hand the spirit that lies dormant within Anne, I have every reason to hope that my cousin will return in full force, once the time is right.

I would add that it has become apparent that the perennial coryza to which my cousin is prone, which has haunted her all her life and given rise to a suspicion of continuing ill-health, is actually caused by nerves exacerbated by her mother. For while she is at present, for most of the waking day, to be heard sneezing almost without pause; when she had determined to rise and demonstrate that unprecedented independence of spirit, I observed not so much as a sniffle.

I *have* enjoyed a dance, upon occasion. My previous objections, however, refer to an outrageous expectation of my participation, regardless of whether I would will it or no. Concerning surprise at my liberality, I would recall your attention to a request I once made not to early sketch my character. Indeed, I hope this correspondence may provide you with greater insight, greater clarity, than previously seemed possible.

You have my agreement regarding a beauty spot. Indeed, their previous and enduring popularity is a subject of bewilderment to me. Thus, yes to a laurel pin. Shall I suggest this to Miss Bingley, that she might endorse and circulate the notion? So too with the moustache. We must be fair!

Forgive me, but I find myself compelled to ask; is there truth in your Meryton Aunt having started a 'Tattle Paper' to provide the local area with 'news' whilst they may not hear directly from the lady herself?

Although I have, as you surmised, blamed myself for what happened to my father, it is the frustration over my lack of knowledge and experience, and the blind trust I had in the recommendation of another, that still holds sway over my remembrance. In the attempt by this man to assume a knowledge and authority that was expected of him, but which he did not truly possess, he neglected to consider that he was first and foremost called there as Protector. So too those in power and authority who oft forget their place as guardians. No, on reflection, this is not yet quite true; my greatest frustration is that I knew better, somehow, but did not attend.

That aside, I offer apology for sharing so very intimate a detail. It was inappropriate.

I am most interested to learn of your belief that a wife must have a wage. I confess to having never considered such a role as unpaid labour and thus in need of monetary exchange, although I do note your qualification.

Although it may seem that my Aunt has many and great demands upon her time, I am given to understand that she is engaged in frequent written communications with your Mr Collins. Her ideas for improvement extend, it seems, beyond Rosings and out into the parish. Indeed, I believe my Aunt to have penned the majority of tomorrow's sermon. To which, I presume, Mr Collins will add his own - aforementioned - views upon correct attire for young ladies - and effigies.

———

(I can put it off no longer)

I have this day received a messenger, sent by the Colonel, who is - he now confesses - installed with his regiment in Woolwich. He gives news of a small organised rally due, requesting the easing of lockdown, which he is charged to oversee. He was at great pains to assure me that every indication shows the intent to be peaceful and orderly. You see how little I am concerned, that I leave this information to the very last.

Yours etc.

P.S. As it seemed pressing, I took the opportunity to forward your recent letter to the Colonel, with my reply to his message. No doubt he will respond, when he may.

———

P.P.S. I am in agreement with your Grandmama *and* your Father.

Letter Twenty-three

Saturday 6th June, Hunsford Den of Ignominy

Dear Sir,

Thank you for forwarding my letter to the Colonel. You are quite correct, there was a matter of personal import raised by the gentleman to which I require, if at all possible, a speedy answer^{****}.

I am not excessively surprised to hear that the unrest of which the Colonel spoke lies within London. While we await the lifting of lockdown from our positions of privilege, others will find the need of generating income, of feeding their families, infinitely more pressing. I am most thankful the intent is peaceful and hope all goes well for them. Come what may, we must all have answers soon. I confess, I too long for reassurance of my family's well-being, and am certain you must be equally impatient for news.

If I seemed to lack compassion concerning your Papa, then it is most certainly for I to offer apology, and not for you. My frankness was inappropriate, and may perhaps be attributed to the informality achieved by a frequent written correspondence. It is easy to forget oneself, when not face to face; but that is no excuse. If I may, I simply wished to express - albeit it poorly - that whilst we might in the early days of what we consider a mistake, take some stock and resolution; to torture ourselves in later years, however, with that we cannot change, seems to me a misguided and painful application of our energies. Your intentions were clearly for the very best, now you must allow yourself peace. You are not my cousin - you do not offer kicks and demand love. So please, be easier with yourself *(that you might then be easier with others)*.

May I tell you of my Grandmama, as an exchange of confidence - to perhaps restore your faith in me? Like you, I have never mentioned this happening to anyone but Papa. It has always felt too private, and - perhaps - more than most might wish to know. I was present at her passing. My Papa was nearby, but had retired to his room after two day's vigil. I had been holding her hand for some time, talking over precious memories and giving thanks for the many gifts with which she had blessed me. At first, her hand would squeeze mine gently in acknowledgement, but the pulses grew gradually fainter until there was no further answer - although I knew she heard me still. At last, I knelt upon the floor and began to sing to her. My voice has no great merit, less even than my playing of the pianoforte, but she was always fond of it. For an hour, I sang through every favourite of hers that I could think of. At times she lay quietly with a slight smile upon her face. At others, she became animated, her eyes - though dimmed - would open suddenly wide and I could feel her joy. At last, I sang the one I knew she loved the very best of all. An expression of utter radiance broke across her face, she lifted her head a little from the pillow, I was yet holding her hand, and I brought it up to my face and held it against my cheek. Then she yawned, closed her eyes... her head dropped gently. For the briefest moment I believed she slept, but in that instant of passing I felt a deep, quick pulse in my heart and I knew...not that she was gone, but rather that she would be with me always - in the way that you know for sure what you never can explain, what never can be proven. It was like light, like love, as though all the true goodness inherent in each and every one of us, existed in that pulse. I knew too, from that moment, that there can be nothing ever to fear. That we leave our cares behind, but keep our loves. That we are here to grow, throughout our lives, as she did - and beyond. If you find this remembering too fanciful, I ask you to say nothing - for it is precious to me *(I share it with you knowing - hoping - you will treat it as the treasure that it is)*.

We were graced, this afternoon, by your Aunt and cousin who arrived unexpectedly by carriage, and for whom Mr Collins dragged nearly every piece of furniture from the parlour, to arrange at designated distances upon the lawn that his guests might sit and refuse tea for fear of polluted crockery. Each wore beautifully intricate masks which we were given to understand were painstakingly embroidered by Miss de Bourgh herself. Clearly, one may accomplish much during two hours of embroidering a day, although - as I conveyed quite firmly to your Aunt - I would not personally know, and have absolutely no intention of finding out. May I discreetly ask - do your Aunt and cousin truly believe it best to wear their masks below their noses? Mr Collins himself uttered a queried blunder in this direction, which was met first by frosty silence and then, after he had offered many compensatory bows and pulled his mask beneath his own proboscis, your Aunt at last declared that 'Anne finds her nasus greatly irritated by a mask, thus - clearly - it is best for all not to cover.' After many *subtle* gesticulations from Mr Collins, which we first professed not to comprehend, Charlotte and I also reluctantly lowered ours.

After an half hour, we were encouraged to go our own ways, leaving your Aunt and Mr Collins to discuss the improvements to Hunsford of your supposing. Your cousin was also there. Try as I might, I cannot seem to stop my mind from ruminating upon what they will be. Masks below the nose for everyone, I imagine. Outdoor visiting rights, perhaps? Although that may be still an aristocratic privilege. Perhaps the village might gather within their gardens, wearing masks as aforesaid, and stand mutely without food or drink while Mr Collins speaks. Oh, yes - that would be Sunday.

I was sorry indeed to see your cousin once more subdued. I had lately formed a rather different picture of her in my mind. I trust that, as you suggest, she is simply biding her time.

Charlotte and I took the opportunity to have a quiet walk together, our first since the Edict, Maria being still indisposed - although a little better, thank you. It was all the more pleasant for being unexpected and long hoped for. Charlotte, it transpires, is more greatly concerned than I realized by her husband's ongoing feud with our Rochester-neighbours. 'Whilst wishing to be a good wife,' she told me 'I had not considered truly what might be required of me. Thus far, I had thought to let him have his way as much as possible, for the harmony of our relations. Now I wonder if I have rather wronged him instead. For the sake of a moment's peace, I have allowed him continuance along an imprudent path which, while clearly evident to me, was not so to him.'

She is in rather an impossible position.

Yours etc.

P.S. In answer to your question, it is not a 'Tattle Paper,' specifically. I believe this may be a name given by another. Early in lockdown, my Aunt Phillips had certainly assembled a copied sheet of news, and a scheme that this may be forwarded - once read - to (designated) others within the village. Why do you ask?

P.P.S. Respectfully, I do not recall referring to 'wives' regarding unpaid labour. Only Mrs Collins.

P.P.P.S. *My* Mr Collins! Why, that really is the worst of all.

Letter Twenty-four

Tuesday 9th June, Rosings Atrium of Archetypal Alteration

Dear Madam,

I could wish for the ability to convey within a letter my tone and therefore my intent, for both may be so easily misread. I required no apology, although I do thank you. Also, for the description of your Grandmama, which I shall treasure indeed.

I hope I have given no offence regarding the miscommunication received regarding your Aunt Phillips. News is greatly different to tattle. I assure you those were not my words. I enquired after, I confess, many weeks' hesitation - simply to have the information disproved or clarified by one whose testimony I trust. I am now satisfied.

I may only offer apology for my Aunt's unexpected visit. As I am sure you know by now, it was hardly out of character. I believe my Aunt intends to visit all within the parish over the next several weeks 'out of necessity' *(or belligerence)*. I am reliably informed that such a freedom is not, however, extended to me. I wonder, however, whether any or each of us may be welcome at any time in the future, after Sunday's sermon.

I took notes on the day, that we might enjoy its content again. To my slight shame, I was subject to my Aunt's approving eye for so doing, supposing that I did so out of admiration. Although generally I disapprove dissembling of any kind, under some circumstances it does appear essential; especially as a guest whose welcome has long been over-strained. Thus, I felt it best not to enlighten her.

To begin with an encouraging aspect, Mr Collins was acoustically faultless. Even without the Lady Catherine, his voice rang out far and wide. I had no previous suspicion of his ability to achieve such volume and clarity; my Aunt was truly delighted by his performance. Naturally, she was quite markedly alone in this, but cared not - a security which stems from an unassailable belief in the Divine Right of de Bourghs. Thankfully, her intentions for reform do not stem from a desire to extract unreasonable sums of money from those less fortunate than she, but more from a sustained assurance that whatever she believes best should be instantly adopted by all beneath her. Namely, everyone.

'Quintessential & Universal Reformatory Improvements for ALL Residents of Hunsford,

WITHOUT Exception & To Take IMMEDIATE Effect'
(the title alone).

First, to remedy a quite alarming lapse in personal care, almost the entire populace being quite unforgivably grubby and dishevelled, residents are to bathe once a week, wash daily, brush their hair, scrub their clothes, clean their shoes, sponge their teeth in brandy (an old idea, favoured by my Aunt), the use of birch or liquorice as a tolerable alternative, if they must. Boils to be lanced and, my particular favourite, all - again without exception - to eat less, that their clothing may better fit.

Gardens to be immediately maintained. Then, dwellings to be cleaned from top to bottom, clothes and bedding laundered and aired (the order specifically suiting my Aunt, who has been displeased during her daily drives to see gardens turned all to unpolished wildernesses).

Drowning spirits in potent portables to be frowned upon. Uplifting spirits instead through the partaking in regular exercise, the reading of suitable material - an approved list to be provided by the Rev. Collins - and the playing of instruments, if suitably proficient.

Wholesome games within the family may be allowed, but no wagers of any kind - lottery tickets and whist to be immediately banned. Ah, yes, quilting to be adopted by some, knitting or crocheting by others, dependent upon standing within the village. I do hope this latter does not apply to me.

With spirits as they have been, we are fortunate there was no riot.

Regarding the use of masks, a demonstration given by Mr Collins as to how best to wear same (under the nose). Also, a demonstration to show that one should not wear a mask around one's neck, one's ear, one's ankle, or, indeed, one's arm. It may here be noted that I have witnessed no such infractions, but clearly my Aunt and ~~your~~ Mr Collins, believe it necessary to cover all possible contraventions.

Next, while Mr Collins (and Lady Catherine) appreciate that many may not understand the specific distance of seven feet, designated by the government for social distancing, he would be delighted to offer a demonstration for each and every member of the parish. (Demonstration then performed amidst bafflement, especially as clearly underestimated).

Finally, any with produce to sell may do so now on alternate Friday afternoons, with due care taken to adhere to all aforementioned measures. Coinage must be cleansed in lavender water before exchange, no exceptions.

The detached congregation did well throughout, I felt. In retrospect, it would have been better, perhaps, for Mr Collins to cease while ostensibly ahead. As it was, I was able to take only few notes concerning his consecutive lecture calling for greater decency in unmarried women, as the disruption in the - no doubt - already fraught crowd, drowned out all he had to say. Indeed, so potent and unified was their wailed chanting of 'my artichokes, oh, my dear artichokes,' that it took until late this morning for the echo to entirely leave my head. Evidently, news of Mr Collins's renegade goats has somehow spread, in spite of isolation.

I do hope that Miss Lucas is now much improved. My cousin noted her absence on Sunday and, I believe, has sent a recuperation gift via Mr Collins.

As soon as ever I hear more from Colonel Fitzwilliam, I shall let you know. As you suggest, news of our loved ones is also long overdue.

Yours etc.

P.S. Regarding Mrs Collins, you are right. She has my sympathy concerning the dilemma inherent in raising an unwitting indiscretion with one unlikely ever to take kindly to comment, no matter how well intended.

P.P.S. Regarding *'your* Mr Collins,' I may only wholeheartedly apologise.

Letter Twenty-five

Wednesday 10th June, Hunsford House of
Convenient Protocols
Dear Sir,

Does any one of us take kindly to comment, I wonder? However well intended. I know of none who - while politely accepting a kindly-meant critique publicly, do not privately bite upon a chair and think the person wholly untruthful in private. We must all take our own part first, yes?

It is most generous of you to call Mr Collins's most recent indiscretion 'unwitting.' I could think of another word, similar, but with different meaning, which might better apply *(witless)*. Mind you, I confess I have a firm intent myself for a new leaf. It may not be entirely possible, whilst I share a lodging with... my cousin, but for the future I should like to say to everyone 'you did your best' or 'do what you will.' And mean it. Even Mr Collins. It is somewhat uncomfortable to be so censorious, even in jest. That being said, I am seldom so in as widespread or extreme a fashion as our respective relations were on Sunday morning. But there, I excuse myself again, as if I have no responsibility for my thoughts and words. I am grateful to have no pulpit, nor inclination towards.

My sister Jane has the best heart of any person I have ever known; she speaks no ill of anyone, and always speaks as she sees. At times I fear of her meeting with misuse in the world, but then I remind myself that her goodness will always attract like, her loving nature, love *(in time!)*.

'Let that be an end to it, my dear,' said Charlotte gently to her husband, as we reached the house. He nodded slightly. I do sincerely hope by that he will abide - even considering the continuing presence of the bathtub effigy. Although I was at first amused by Mr Collins's oration, it became truly painful to see him humiliated to such degree; and yet, he made his private grievances a matter for public consumption, so it was no wonder. Life is fraught with complication. Too far in one direction and the opposite thought comes to meet one in most compelling fashion. I pitied my cousin, for what he had created. It went too far too fast, and he was quickly overmuch immersed for clarity or, indeed, reasonability. Now he must rise up again on Sunday next, knowing most certain now that a cassock and the patronage of your Aunt will not ensure respect. I believe Charlotte intends in future to assist her husband in his sermon-writing. I know my friend well, and the set of her mouth indicates a firm purpose to intervene.

Maria is much improved, I thank you. She did indeed receive a rather beautiful paintbox from Miss de Bourgh and was utterly delighted by the attention. I know Charlotte and I are most grateful for the diversion it has given her. She is of a gentle and impressionable disposition and thus the perfect vicarious correspondent to Lydia's written escapades, for she is both suitably shocked and horribly compelled all at once.

I am not offended by your question regarding my Aunt Phillips, I wondered only from whence - of a sudden - it came. Indeed, in this case, perhaps, news and tattle are close relations. To give an *(unasked for)* explanation, my Aunt considers her role within the town as 'Merchant of Information' to be of great import. While she is, perhaps, sometimes ill-advised *(or indiscriminate)* in the news which she conveys, she is most conscientious in her visits and many are relieved of loneliness by her presence and inquisitive exuberance. Thus, in an awareness of present and ongoing isolation within the parish, she has taken it upon herself to continue in her duties. As far as I am given to understand, once a week my Aunt amasses news upon a sheet of paper - both sides. This she copies out five times and personally delivers to five households on an approved list. Once read, these households each convey their copy to another previously stipulated home, and so on and so forth until the sheets return to her. Each household is invited to add approving comments, should they wish; in fact, it is most decisively encouraged. If the militia are at all aware, they must surely turn a blind eye; perhaps because spirits are truly lifted by her efforts, or, more likely, because they realize it would be folly to try to stop her. The only matter not really to her credit, as I understand it, is that if even mildly offended by anyone within her circulation, they are suddenly - and without warning - removed from the list. Although I would not accuse my Aunt of deliberately looking for offence, she certainly does seem to discover it easily enough.

Goodness, it is warm, is it not? We are all in hiding. I write even later than usual, that I might sit undistracted in the cool.

Question: how does one cease to feel anger, whilst still believing it just? How does one forgive? How may one release the essentialness of being right, and, in letting go of that, must one then be wrong? Why are we so afraid to feel we have erred, even slightly, that we will insist upon right and perpetuate something that might have faded long ago? Why are we so fearful of blunder, when our blunders are a necessary part of who we are, part of our growth?

Which leads me neatly to another query, which you may well refuse to answer, that being your right. I have it on reasonably good authority... well, authority, no. I have it from Mr Collins that Lady Catherine has suffered an 'a most grievous and quite outrageous outburst' from her nephew?

Can this be true?

Can this be you?

Yours etc.

P.S. Since writing the early part of this letter, I have heard from Charlotte that her husband has already completed another sermon - without her proffered assistance - on the subject of oppressors and the oppressed. He being victim, of course. Energised by outrage, he has also been out at all hours, digging a ditch around the perimeter of his estate, that 'trespassing neighbours' might swiftly tumble 'neck and crop.' We do not have the heart to tell him that the rope from the goats' pen was clearly easily removed by a long arm or crook reached through the hedge, without need for a toe to touch upon his grounds. Watching him at work, it strikes me as quite astonishing what may be achieved through vehement indignation, and remarkable how futile it frequently transpires to be.

P.P.S. Charlotte is to sell her goat's milk soap at Lady Catherine's market tomorrow. Maria and I are not to assist, as it would be 'inappropriate, indecent and unfitting.' Mr Collins concocts rules as swiftly and conveniently as my sister Mary does superstitions.

It is a matter of private amusement to me to consider that every 'official' rule by which we are asked to abide was originally invented by some person or other. Often for the good of all. Sometimes for the good of only them. Imagine if, in four hundred or five hundred years' time, female descendants of Mr Collins are still to do (or not to do) all manner of silly things, just because *he* once said so. Thus, we must always think, before we pass something on.

Letter Twenty-six

Friday 12th June, Rosings Rooms of Musing Contemplation

Dear Madam,

Your question is one which I have frequently asked of myself, but I have yet to find a determined answer. When feeling, as you say 'just cause,' I have found that over time and with due diversion, my anger naturally abates, my *cause* becomes less insistent. Yet if circumstance draws my unmastered attention once more towards he I consider perpetrator, I discover all again, almost as if no time has passed. I would conquer this, for I feel it an aspect of my character which places me at tremendous disadvantage. To be so rapidly affected by events long passed is to find oneself continually weakened by that which may not be changed and, as you correctly observed in previous correspondence, how might we be certain that we remember justly? There is a state of mind open to all of us, from which no good can come; and anger gathers fuel as it is fed. I would surmount it, be master of myself, if I knew how.

I have finally submitted to the grooming of my locks, and Mr Shakespeare's beard has gone. I half miss it. My face seems strange to me now.

Having decreed that Anne's conjectural expedition to Coventry is at an end, and having rearranged every item (and person) which she - at present - may, my Aunt has taken to amusing herself by calling her daughter constantly and throughout the day, from the foot of the grand staircase. This is something of an annoyance, not only to Anne - whose responses grow increasingly irritable - but to those who room nearby. Being Her Ladyship, the summoning does not stop until Anne makes an appearance - at the very least at the top of the stairs - better yet, as close as possible to where my Aunt is standing. Naturally it is done out of a continuing insistence upon authority. But, as Mrs Norris knows, one may overcook anything.

'Never fear,' muttered Anne to me, upon a recent descent. 'When this is over, I plan to commit a minor felony and be transported to the new world.' Adding firmly, 'doubt it not.'

It is always good to have a clear objective.

I have, I believe, rather heartening news, having heard once more from the Colonel, although -

unfortunately - without, as yet, a reply which I might forward on to you. The anticipated protest took place last afternoon, commencing in St Giles - and moving west. Only forty marched, each masked, each holding extended - ahead and aside - either end of a broom, to ensure a good distance from one another as they walked. The Colonel tells that all walked in silence, without slogans or cries for change. When they reached the Green Park, they presented a scroll of paper on which was written the names of all who had been lost to hunger, all to fear, and sorrow. This was calmly received, and the men and women allowed to go upon their way. The Colonel - who seems deeply moved by the whole experience - states that this action appears to have been all the more effective for being so greatly unexpected. Whoever led must be really quite remarkable.

I agree completely regarding the handing down of laws unchecked. Also, furniture. At Pemberley we have quite the most unfortunate set of cabinets which have been horrible heirlooms for several generations. Although no one within my family enjoys them, they are not to be disposed of, nor even placed out of sight. It is written. I do not understand it, yet - as their current owner - I have not the heart to be rid of them.

I can assure you that reports of my 'grievous outburst' have been grossly exaggerated. I simply - and gently - requested that Lady Catherine allow the village to go on as they pleased for a while, that Anne be free to pass her time as *she* thinks best, and that if my Aunt still wishes to impart wisdom to anyone, then Mr Collins might - as a willing candidate - be advised to treat everyone (cats included) with greater consideration. Finally, I asked that we all be released at last from this quite ridiculous dietary regime. I might add that at no point did I raise my voice, or employ a tone that was other than completely reasonable; though the thought of another portion of Pease soup was a fearsome provocation. Not one of my requests was accepted, and I felt no better for their airing. Thus, it goes.

Yours etc.

P.S. Mrs Collins's behaviour does her credit indeed. To be neither a fury on her husband's behalf, nor a fury towards her husband, is deeply admirable.

P.P.S. Your description of your elder sister aligns with what I too observed, an equality of consideration with all she meets.

P.P.P.S. Proprietary as she may be, I am not convinced of my Aunt's fully appreciating the notion of a market being named in her honour.

Letter Twenty-seven

Monday 15th June, Hunsford Shelter for Truculent Clerics

Dear Sir,

I must offer a hasty correction to my words regarding my sister *(or perhaps your interpretation of such)*. Jane's sentiments are emphatically not of absolute equality with all. She has a true, affectionate heart, this is quite correct. However, although she is generous and amiable with all whom she meets, there is a deep wellspring of feeling reserved for her family and certain very particular others *(other)*. She may not be indiscriminately expressive of such with these particulars *(particular)*, but she is, I feel, all the better and truer for such lack of extravagance.

I am delighted - even amazed - to hear of so temperate a protest, especially when under such duress. It seems progress indeed. To have so profound an impact through so gentle and calm an undertaking is entirely admirable. Beyond admirable. I wonder now, what is to follow?

On the other end of the broom, as it were, I need not go into details of Mr Collins's sermon on oppression yesterday. You were there. Surplus food was thrown; the target attained with formidable accuracy. To see him upon the floor of his study afterward, propped against a wall, why, I confess to an experience of absolute compassion for the man, sunk now so low. I do not believe he has been allowed a thought of his own in his entire life. Every action he commits is, in truth, on behalf of another, to impress and ingratiate himself. In spite of tremendous speeches to the contrary, he seems to have absolutely no internal perception of his own value, believing such to be wholly dictated by how he is externally perceived.

Consequently, in what may only be described as a state of utter imbalance, and at the time unbeknown to we who were all abed, Mr Collins stumbled out late last night with his storm lantern and made his way in the direction of our Rochester-neighbours' home, with what objective only heaven knows. He now declares his intention to have been 'to go and have it out' with the head of their household, and remind him that _he_, as preacher, knew best for his flock, or something of the sort. Indeed, it was a challenge to comprehend his words. All the candles being out within, he hesitated next the old ash tree in the garden, to relieve his feelings, we think, he was reluctant to say. After this momentary pause, he decided to proceed, but - forgetting - tumbled headfirst into his own ditch, flinging the lantern upwards as he went. On its descent, it instantly caught the hedge alight. By the time all were awakened and water procured and thrown (how grateful I shall be not to have to draw from a pump ever, ever again), the entire perimeter hedgerow was gone, not to mention the goat enclosure, the goats being removed to safety by Maria and Charlotte at the earliest opportunity. Now there is not only nothing to stand as physical barrier between Mr Collins and his neighbours, but he is also at the mercy of their goodwill to believe the fire an accident.

That Mr Collins began the feud is undeniable. That his neighbours have continued it is also quite correct. Where will it end? What must yet occur for one party or other to call it over, when each have gone too far? How does one respond to such as my cousin - without becoming almost like him? Certain he is a man of decided patterns of behaviour, so regular in his thoughts, so determined in his righteousness, that any event out of the ordinary throws him into a chaos of letters and sermons in an attempt to control what he may not. He does not intend any cruelty, I believe that. He has simply been raised never to question what once was learnt. But there, you see, I attempt to understand him, when I may only understand myself. Is the answer simply to go one's own way, as if he does not exist? That in no longer attempting to persuade him otherwise, one is able to release oneself from the awful need to have him _be_ something beyond his reach? And yet, the fire is an all too cogent expression... of what? He is often foolish, frequently witless, daily careless, but never a man to commit a physically destructive action such as that.

Thus, it remains for his neighbours to decide which way to proceed. Do they persist in painful acrimony, loathing Mr Collins not just for what has transpired, but for what might have happened had the night gone ill (or iller)? We are all faced with such choices at one time or another. Do we continue to think poorly of another, to frighten ourselves at 'evil-intent,' rather than to think it simply petty foolishness, or an unfortunate lack of foresight? Do we proceed along a path where only further misery for all awaits? Tell each of our acquaintance of the wrong done to us, exaggerating a little as our reach extends? Or do we stop, while we can, bear our parts as best we may, then move forward graciously, knowing better what we would have in the world, what we would be?

I confess, I like the Rochester-neighbours. There is something buoyant and joyful about them. I have every faith in their forgiveness.

It must be a relief to have your Aunt once more verbally engaging with her daughter. Mama frequently ceases to speak to, well, most of us, at one time or another. But never for an entire week. Actually, she seldom manages more than an afternoon before she forgets herself and resumes communication - and that is only supposing that during that afternoon we, or she, is away from home. Otherwise, she is speaking again within moments.

There is something in the air, at present (other than the Unmentionable) for Maria of all people has this day had at Mr Collins. I think she took her chance having seen him so humbled after the fire. For this I cannot blame her; she has borne through the last few months with barely a whimper of complaint concerning her new brother. I was not there and did not hear, but - as I understand it - she presented him an itemised page of frustrations, front and back. To hint that he did not receive it well would be a quite colossal understatement. In history, it is ever thus - a small group of people, often related, at loggerheads.

On that theme, I offer humble apology for dubbing the Hunsford Market in honour of your Aunt, it was most inappropriate of me. From what I understand, it was a very quiet affair and poorly attended. I suspect the additional provisions anticipated for sale had been set by to throw at Mr Collins in the future.

Yours etc.

P.S. Could you consider gifting the cabinets to someone of whose friendship you would rid yourself? My father was given a ring by a Great Great Aunt who found him 'insubordinate and troublesome.' Having few fond memories of the lady, he one day presented the ring to my Mama, in the first year of their marital bliss. She was most underwhelmed. 'Why you should think I would be delighted by some old relic is quite beyond me, Mr Bennet,' she declared - she tells the story herself to this day. 'Why, supposing I wear this and then am destined to live the same life as the personage who owned it first? I would not wish that under any circumstances.' She was vastly less impressed when she discovered a lock of the lady's hair within the ring, of which Papa had been - hitherto - oblivious. My father, on the other hand, was rather gratified and keeps the ring yet, comprehending in the gift a fondness of which he had been previously unaware.

P.P.S. The awful irony that while in London so many go hungry, but in Hunsford food is thrown, is not lost upon me.

Letter Twenty-eight

Wednesday 17th June, Rosings Bastion of Filial Fortitude

Dear Madam,

Colonel Fitzwilliam returned this evening, quite exhausted, but in a humour of the most tremendous relief and optimism also. He sat within the dining room for the briefest period, supping quietly while we three inmates looked on, suppressing a thousand questions. Even my Aunt remained quiet, a handkerchief pressed to her lower face. It seems the Colonel has had little recent opportunity for sleep; or indeed a bath. We are all deeply curious to hear fully of his experiences, but must restrain ourselves a little longer while he recovers. He was abed before the first candle was lit.

I sincerely regret that we at Rosings knew nothing of the parsonage fire, for we would have offered every possible aid. Thank heaven it was no worse. You must instruct me as to whatsoever I might offer by way of assistance or appeasement. Having laughed at the fringes, I cannot deny my part in the co-creation of this... spectacle.

Speaking from my own experience[*]... No, I may not... In the case of this manifestation, it was clearly commenced as a simple exchange of insult for insult, mounting in recklessness and severity. Mr Collins began it, no question, and without reasonability, rationality or benevolence on his side; but with my Aunt instead, which doubtless felt the same to him. Reprisal followed, humorous as it was. Had he not felt such pride and righteousness in his post, he might have stopped. Had your neighbours not retaliated... he would certainly have continued anyway. What, then, were they to do? Or anyone when faced with such absurdity and intolerance? Mr Collins has surely been directed along this path since he was old enough to walk. Try as I may, I cannot solve it, unless we are to shut him away for a year and bombard him with alternative configurations of thought? But then, and without doubt, he would resent such an action grievously and simply bide his time to return to old behaviour with even greater verve and vendetta.

From personal experience[*]... But, no. I cannot... I might only say that I have found myself *wishing* to excuse another, *believing* I had done so, only to find my trust once more and soon betrayed. Yet, may I truly, objectively, speak of forgiveness? Did I indeed, in actuality, set out to forgive? Or did I simply offer readmittance; a weary, weakened trust and then lie in wait, certain of its being broken? In attempt to guard ourselves from further hurt, do we simply dig more pits wherein distress dwells?

It does appear that Mr Collins lacks the truest freedom of all - to think as one will. When so much from our earliest years is under the scrutiny of others, to find, yet, that still, quiet place of private truth, of particular preferences, is of paramount importance, and must be constantly reached for as something attainable by all.

Indeed, coincidentally, such has been the subject of recent lengthy consideration on my part; in light of what I have witnessed at Rosings, my own more personal experiences at both school, the university and at home, and the intense relief that finding myself unable to look at a newspaper has given me. Aware as I was, that whatsoever I was reading had been constructed by another human being, and therefore influenced by their own particular point of view, however impartial their intentions, I confess to finding myself still deeply, often most unfortunately, influenced by aught to which I gave my attention; with the added vexation of little true power to offer assistance or alteration in each depicted circumstance. I was often angered, at the very least frustrated. Seldom to any purpose.

If all might keep to their own trust, could each then - more readily - let one another be? Or is the interest and engagement we have with one another part of the rich pageantry of this life? Each answer offers only more questions.

It seems that Mr Collins is now known locally as 'the Prince Regent.'

It amused me to hear of your Mama's attempts at silence with her offspring. I could sincerely wish my Aunt might be so unsuccessful. She has taken, recently, to calling Anne 'an oddity.' Also 'strange' and 'distinctly mad.' That word, once more. To the last, Anne suggested - quite calmly, I would add - that she might seek employment for herself as a governess or chamber maid, thus securing a lasting independence from her mother. The horror at her daughter lowering herself to such, and thus lowering the name of de Bourgh, was enough to render my Aunt pale and without retort. Anne was quite delighted.

Yours etc.

P.S. I can think of several who might enjoy said cabinets. An excellent suggestion, thank you. Perhaps we might part with them after all.

P.P.S. Regarding Anne once more, you may be interested to know that she and Mrs Norris have formed an alliance. Whether it is friendship or not, I may not speculate. Certain, there is trade. Anne - unlike my shamed self - noticed that Mrs Norris alone was left to wash for the household without assistance. Although most are altering attire less than usual, it is - as you once observed - a considerable task, especially for one. That we might have extra and more tasty rations without my Aunt's knowledge, Anne has offered help, for which Mrs Norris appears sincerely grateful. My Aunt is, thankfully, yet to notice the state of Anne's knuckles. I have considered offering my own assistance, but readily admit no inclination towards such. Thus, if I am asked, then I shall roll up my sleeves - but not until.

Letter Twenty-nine

Thursday 18th June, Hunsford Parsonage - A letter of Gratitude (Ultimately)

Dear Sir,

I can hardly contain my delight at receiving news of the Colonel's safe return. I confess, I am also deeply curious to hear his detailed report of the happenings in London *(and other matters****)*. I wonder if he knows aught of whether quarantine might soon be at an end?

I find myself both patience and impatience personified. I have never known such a time of contrast. I am glad of it. If I allow it, allow the growth.

I have decided at last and after long deliberation that if I *were* able to effect one change in the world, it would be that all thought truly well enough of themselves to be sincerely happy. Imagine all the trouble it would save. From my observations, it seems clearly apparent that most of the 'bad' behaviour in the world could surely be accredited to an abiding feeling of personal lack, satiable only by attempting to pull others along with you. I do not - *cannot* - believe this to be congenital. It must surely be enforced, then perpetuated.

I have heard of Mr Collins's new moniker and while I confess it *did* amuse me, I do consider it slightly unfair. My cousin may be many things, but he is certainly not a profligate. Quite the opposite, in fact. Mr Collins himself heard of his new title this afternoon, and now accuses all and sundry of the most profound disloyalty. Including the goats.

Prior to this discovery, and - indeed - to his credit*(?)*, he attempted to make every amend within his power. A verbose and *quite* sincere apology from a proper seven foot away. Digging and clearing the remainder of the hedges and planting new ones, transposed from part of your Aunt's estate - and with your Aunt's *(withering)* permission - in the very cart by which his neighbours moved, not so long ago. We three women have baked and baked these last days, and all has been most graciously received. Your Aunt, as I understand it, is furious with her Clergyman. The greatest punishment imaginable for the man.

It does strike me repeatedly that our new neighbours are predominantly joyful people, and that Mr Collins - in all truth — is not. I wonder, did he set about their reformation out of a genuine belief that they required reform or because he in some way wished them to be less happy, that his own lack of joy could be less evident. In which case, what foolishness to turn all his attention *towards* them, rather than away.

On the subject of penance, Maria's has now begun in less-amusing earnest. Charlotte was dispatched to arrange a room for her with a trusted woman in the village, that her husband may not be forced to see or hear from his sister again. He has decried it a spousal duty to remove from his presence any person whom he deems intolerable (quarantine or no) and is, it would appear, absolutely not to be persuaded otherwise. I am greatly surprised at the immediate compliance of both sisters. Maria is repentant at the 'trouble' she has 'caused' and anxious to go quietly, although I do believe this to stem – in partiality – from an irresistible sense of ensuing freedom. Charlotte is resigned, even hardened to her present course. During our very brief discourse on the subject, Charlotte intimated that she has faith in her husband's wrath being short-lived. I am less convinced. Indeed, I confess to feeling deeply unsettled by the course Mr Collins insists upon for Maria, for Charlotte, and for the entire Lucas family, if this really is allowed to perpetuate. Perhaps I am overly mistrustful, but it bodes ill that having caused so much offence himself, he would then make so little effort at reparation, allow for none on the part of Maria, and hold the sibling bond to be of so little value. It feels almost as if he has found an excuse to be rid of her; although I cannot imagine why he should wish it. Yet, if Maria is pardoned within a score of years I shall be deeply, deeply shocked.

You have my agreement: as tempting as it may seem, if you were to shut Mr Collins away and engage him with newer, warmer ideas, he would simply resist with all his might, deeming them false and wicked. We all are prone to frequent blunders. Perhaps the desire truly and universally inherent is to reclaim clarity within - or to simply feel... better! I have no doubt that Mr Collins's anger is really more intense towards himself than to anyone else, for all the bluff and *(ahem)* smoke. If he might allow himself an error or... ten, accept this as natural and that our growth is of more value than all else, then step forward afresh, knowing more firmly where best to tread - would this not be a conciliation of a kind?

We are not meant to drag the past behind us. It is too heavy. The more we chew on our wrongs and woes, the more they trouble us. What if we grew more skilled at leaving them aft? Ah, how freely and freshly we might skip through life, were it not for what *she* had said or *he* had done twenty year ago!!

As if oblivious to familial upheaval, my testing cousin has found the time to create a device, consisting of a tiny, hinged mallet, and a small piece of wood which, when brought together, creates a resonant and repetitive rapping sound. With this he attempts – several times a day - to call the free cat to his will. There can be few undertakings, I imagine, more futile than the attempt to train a cat. Thus, he has simply conceived yet another device with which to infuriate himself. Charlotte has suggested that a place in the garden is constructed, especially for him, where he might go and spend an ample portion of his time in peaceful contemplation. Sheltered, of course, for the winter months. He is persuaded that this will be a good and healthful thing for him. Also, a new enclosure for the goats.

I am all amazement to hear of the bourgeoning friendship between your cousin and Mrs Norris. The Unmentionable makes for the most unlikely of fellowships. I was under the impression that Mrs Norris was supported by three other members of staff. Are all now dismissed?

Yes indeed – Mad - *that* word again. Just three letters and so easy to use regarding another without care or forethought. I hold yet that it is employed as a distraction by those who cause the most terrible pain to the accused and refuse to account for it, even privately.

We all deserve a second venture; I do believe that. A multitude of ventures. Our misconception is that these must be bestowed upon us by others, rather than gifted by ourselves. Every day is a new opportunity. Every moment. If we are sensitive, we know when a situation does not feel right to us. Must we remain confined, standing by old decisions that no longer serve? Or do we heed the call, do better next time, according to our own true nature? When we stay for the endorsement of others, or even their forgiveness, we often find ourselves in a limbo of sorrow, not understanding - perhaps - that others may only forgive and approve according to their own practised beliefs. Thus, it is no condemnation to remain unforgiven as it is simply an indication of another's progress through life, deserving only our brief compassion. We must look forward, reaching for life in all its fullness. We must allow one another to be human – even Mr Collins, and the Master of Paddles; and even if we find it best to leave them far, far behind.

These are the thoughts that cause me sleepless nights now. Sleepless nights! An entirely new concept.

I hope we are near the end of this... epoch. Valuable as it has been.

Yours etc.

P.S. Please remember me once more to the Colonel.

P.P.S. It is a strange fact of letter-writing, in a desire to amuse one becomes a bearer of tales, and as one knows 'tale-bearers are as bad as the tale-makers.' Within society, I simply ask questions and let others tell the tales. Within a letter, that will not do. I would emphasise - I am truly grateful for this time and for all I have learned... for our correspondence... to have found so willing a counterpart in my quest for amusement... I appreciate... but am eager - oh so eager - for life to return in all its vibrant richness.

P.P.P.S. On revisiting an earlier letter, I find I have a pressing question. Who was Hugh, and how and why did he come to have a Temple built in his honour?

Letter Thirty

Friday 19th June, Rosings Refuge of Reprehensible Aunts

Dear Madam,

Ah yes, the Hugh Temple of Peace. Well, I must confess, there was – as far as I know - no Hugh. It was a misunderstanding of mine from childhood. My father had told me of the vast temple's destruction, attempting to explain to my four-year-old self the meaning of 'vast' or 'huge.' It was many years before I realized my mistake, and I am now rather fond of the sobriquet.

Regarding the servants of your mentioning, they have indeed long-since departed. Two at the urgent request of Lady Catherine, and one of her own, equally pressing, volition.

I am powerless to offer solution concerning the unprecedented behaviour of Mr Collins with regard to Miss Lucas. I may only prospect that it arises as a consequence of these uncertain times and will, thus, be remedied in due course. Nothing on earth could induce me to behave so to my sister. It is quite simply beyond my comprehension.

I am obliquely put in mind of a second-cousin-twice-removed who would join us for the Christmas festivities when I was very young, Georgiana being not yet born. The man was partial to the imbibing of large quantities of liquid refreshment and, on each visit, there would unfailingly come a time when it seemed quite correct to him to tell my father and mother exactly what he thought of them. It was seldom complimentary. In the morning he would have no memory of the incident, leaving my parents at a loss as to how to respond to such persistent and unflattering indiscretion. His father, who generally accompanied him, suffered equally from fleeting amnesia or, if pressed, would become suddenly irate and accuse my parents of a 'deeply disappointing and selfish over-sensitivity' to his son's 'humour.' After the fourth occasion, my father took it upon himself to speak gently and sincerely to both. They left immediately and in high dudgeon, refusing all subsequent invitations.

Miss Lucas has always struck me as a mild, good-tempered person. If she tendered complaint, I do not doubt it was well-founded. Yet conscience compels me to proffer that her written-rebuke was a fraction ill-judged, especially considering her subject. If Mr Collins has proven anything over these past weeks it is that he is inherently, profoundly incapable of withstanding criticism, no matter how much he may personally distribute. We must not allow ourselves to become recriminatory puppets, however powerful the provocation.

———

My mother's cousin made a most unfortunate match. She was an exceptional woman, independent and full of spirit. Yet she married a man who was... unkind. Never in public. In fact, to this day, he remains largely revered. For many years my mother was her one confidant; naturally only by letter, for the lady in question was kept far apart from extended family and friends. In time, the frequency of the letters dwindled to once or twice a year. She lived in isolation, wandering the halls of their home, unable to remember her own name and, eventually, distanced from her daughter who, after countless attempts at assistance, could no longer bear to witness a circumstance of such sorrow without solution.

———

Do you know, I believe my Aunt not so dissimilar from her gracious subject as once I supposed? I wonder, have I been rather too blinded prior by an *awareness* of her 'nobility' to notice. Or perhaps our correspondence has shed some much needed - long-desired, even - light. For whatsoever her

Ladyship most urges, flies - almost invariably - as swiftly as ever it can... away. She fights. She is used to fighting. She believes that conquest will give her what she wants, speaks proudly of being 'a Formidable Foe.' Yet when one examines carefully, it is never long before the latest tenacious passion slips once more from her grasp. I wonder that she cannot see. Lady Catherine is, I understand, widely feared and, sadly, engenders the affection of few. Indeed, she does not allow affection, but instead demands it; an oxymoron.

I never considered my Aunt to be one for superstition, but she too has - of a sudden - acquired an unexpected penchant for assistance in warding off ill fortune. In this case, she has accused Anne of 'giving her the irksome eye,' and called upon a woman from the village to investigate her suspicions. I was not present for the rituals, but am given to understand that they involved clove-buds, a candle, and were inconclusive. Thus, she remains 'all a-jitter.'

'If I knew how, I most certainly would have done it,' murmured Anne.

My Mother once told me that Lady Catherine wished, many, many moons ago, to be a dancer - a Marie Sallé. It was not possible. My Uncle spent many, many years attempting to compensate for this loss. That was not possible either.

In truth, I cannot counter the irresistible inkling that my Aunt is almost certainly at the root of Mr Collins's decision regarding Miss Lucas. Lady Catherine requires almost constant intellectual stimulation and, in its absence, finds regrettable amusement for herself in fidgeting among the affairs of others.

Please forgive the open expression of my frustrations. I am steadily compiling my own itemised list, yet — taking heed of Miss Lucas — will have to make do with burning it, upon completion.

Of course, the origin of the word 'family' lies in the Latin 'familia,' which translates as 'household servants.' But I expect you know this.

————

Now to Colonel Fitzwilliam, and London. It pains me to relate that news arrived this morning to subvert his aforementioned good humour and optimism. The peaceful protest of which we spoke was not, as initially thought, well received by the powers that be. Indeed, late last night, each protestor was taken from their home and all are now incarcerated, awaiting trial for 'the execution of an indisputable attempt to incite civil disruption.' Cover of darkness, naturally, had no effect upon the information reaching far and wide. Those who reported the original event factually are now documenting the injustice; those, less factual, herald the 'necessary protection of the public from dangerous insurgents.'

I confess, I have long wondered why quarantine was not implemented with swifter efficiency. Had they locked the ships down sooner, would all have transpired as it has? I am no stranger to wisdom in retrospect, yet this is hardly the first time in our nation's history that such a circumstance has occurred. How much misfortune might have been spared if, in the very first instance, the ships had immediately been held at anchor and lazarettos established? Do we employ the teachings of the past as well as we might? Grudges are held on to, but lessons remain unlearnt.

Yet while we might blame the government for what has been poorly managed, we give all external power to strangers, and not ourselves.

Know that I have more information than I am at liberty to disclose. Would that I could. As an extensive reader, like yourself (though you deny it) I have observed that in novels, as in life, responses to challenging events are generally rooted in these factors – a desire for power, a desire for love, for monetary gain, or a wish to be seen as hero or benefactor.

The existence of the Unmentionable _is_ undeniable, yet in every trial of body and spirit there are those who will do their best to overcome, bring aid and as swift an end to suffering as possible, those who seek the greater good; and then those who seek personal advantage, personal gain, and are indifferent to the collateral destruction.

I would like to be of service in some way; observing now how much distress might surely have been spared with foresight. Yet I fear my own background of privilege is hardly conducive to sufficient understanding of the desperate plight of an existence rooted in poverty and deprivation. To live from hand to mouth, with the terrifying anxiety of knowing not how to provide from one day to the next... I may imagine, but that is not enough. Like the so called 'mad' women of previous discourse, are those in privation not additionally, in truth, quite deliberately stifled and diverted, for want of a better word, by the constant propagation of loss, of fear. Much of import may be ignored while chaos reigns. Thus, it is essential for each of us to question what we are told.

The Colonel has this instant informed me of his immediate departure once more to London, following an urgent communication.

A scandal has erupted in our parliament, our Primus Inter Pares betrayed by one he appeared to trust, the government in disarray and lockdown abruptly at an end. The Colonel has heard of a London in absolute confusion, almost the entire city taking to the streets in either celebration or protest. I must away directly. The Colonel has assured me that he will look to my sister's well-being as soon as ever he may, but I cannot leave this to him alone. Thus, I depart immediately and heaven help any who stand in my way.

We are not here to watch.

Yours etc.

P.S. I am now able, most belatedly, to enclose Colonel Fitzwilliam's reply to your urgent query. I do hope you find it satisfactory.

P.P.S: Please be assured of my swift return. I hope that I... may... call upon you... in the future. I hope...

Glossary

Are the trees in the field human, that they should be besieged by you?	Quoted from the Book of Deuteronomy 20:19
Asclepion	Referring to Healing Temples located in Ancient Greece.
Aurelius, Marcus	Roman emperor from 161 to 180 AD and a Stoic philosopher. 'Meditations' is a series of private reflections and ideas by Aurelius, never intended for publication.
Banbury Cakes	A spiced, currant-filled, flat pastry cake, made in the Banbury region to secret recipes since 1586 or earlier and still made there today.
Bastion	A fortress or stronghold.
Beauty patch	Known as 'plaisters' in England, covering scars and pockmarks. The French called them mouches (flies) as they resembled small insects. Often fanciful shapes, such as heart and stars.
Bennet, Elizabeth	The spirited protagonist of Jane Austen's Pride and Prejudice. Frequently known as Lizzy or Eliza by her friends and family. She is the second-eldest of the five Bennet sisters.
Bennet, Jane	The eldest Bennet sister. Beautiful and kind, she tends only to see the best in others. She falls in love

with Charles Bingley, a rich young gentleman recently moved to Hertfordshire, but he is persuaded that she does not care for him and so, reluctantly, jilts her.

Bennet, Catherine 'Kitty'	The fourth Bennet sister, very much under the influence of her younger sister Lydia.
Bennet, Lydia	The youngest Miss Bennet; a tremendous flirt, careless of others, wilful and imprudent.
Bennet, Mary	The middle Bennet sister; earnest and studious.
Bennet, Mr	Lizzy's Papa, who feels tremendous affinity with his second-eldest daughter. Well-read, with a very dry wit, rather tired of his wife and younger daughters. His estate, Longbourn, is entailed to the male line.
Bennet, Mrs	Lizzy's Mama. Prone to nervous fits and tremors. Her entire focus is upon marrying off each of her daughters to wealthy men. Often heavy-handed and socially unskilled.
Bingley, Caroline	Mr Bingley's vain and snobbish sister who has set her sights on becoming the wife of Mr Darcy.
Bingley, Mr Charles	Darcy's close friend and suitor to Jane Bennet. Handsome, kind and wealthy, but easily persuaded away from his own true inclinations. Darcy has mis-

	observed Jane's modesty when around Bingley, assuming that it denotes a lack of feeling. He has used this to persuade his friend not to pursue his courtship.
Birthday celebration	Although Birthdays were marked during the Regency period, they were not celebrated as such. The King's Birthday would be widely celebrated, however, as a national holiday.
Blockhead	An idiot
Breeches	Breeches, or short pants, were worn just below the knee.
Brummel, Mr	George Bryan 'Beau' Brummell; a fashion icon of Regency England. For a time, close friend to the Prince Regent. (1778 - 1840)
Cassock	An ankle-length garment worn by members of the Christian Clergy.
Catalani, Angelica	An Italian opera singer (1780 - 1849) with an incredible three octave range, who performed at the King's Theatre, Haymarket, London 1806 - 1807.
Cheapside	A street in the historic and modern financial centre of the City of London.
Cheesecakes	Rather different to present-day cheesecakes, Regency ones were more akin to the modern Danish: a puff-pastry filled with custard.
Collins, Mrs Charlotte	Recent wife to Mr Collins, daughter to Sir William Lucas and

	Lady Lucas, and Lizzy's closest friend. At twenty-seven, believing her marital prospects to be hopeless, she agrees to marry Mr Collins, thus gaining financial security and relieving herself of the fear that she is a burden to her parents.
Collins, Mr William	Mr Bennet's distant second cousin, a clergyman, and the current heir to the estate of Longbourn House. He is a pompous, wearisome man, fawningly devoted to his patroness, Lady Catherine de Bourgh. On visiting Longbourn, he set his sights on marrying Jane Bennet, but finding she was soon to be engaged to Mr Bingley, proposed to Lizzy instead. When she rejected him, he proposed to Charlotte Lucas and was accepted.
Coryza	Catarrhal inflammation of the mucous membrane in the nose.
Coventry, expedition to	To send someone to Coventry is an English expression meaning to deliberately ostracise someone from their family or community. Typically, this is done by not talking to them, avoiding their company, and acting as if they no longer exist. This possibly originates from the English Civil War, when Royalist prisoners of

	war were taken to Coventry and then shunned by residents.
Dancing allowed for married couples	In Austen's time, dancing in public with your spouse - although not unheard of - was generally frowned upon.
Darcy, Fitzwilliam	The romantic hero of Pride and Prejudice. A wealthy man who owns a large estate in Derbyshire called Pemberley. Initially, he appears to be unpleasant and haughty, but - as the novel progresses - he is revealed to have a noble heart, capable of tremendous love and loyalty.
Darcy, Georgiana	Darcy's sister, younger by a decade. She is gentle and accomplished, with a dowry of £30,000. Mr Wickham persuaded her to elope with him when she was fifteen, but she was saved by the intervention of her brother.
De Bourgh, Anne	The only child of the late Sir Lewis and Lady Catherine de Bourgh. She is heir to the de Bourg estate, Rosings Park.
De Bourgh, Lady Catherine	Aunt to Mr Darcy and Colonel Fitzwilliam. A difficult, controlling woman, used to having her own way.
Denny, Mr	An officer. Friend to Wickham and Lydia Bennet.
Fitzwilliam, Colonel	Nephew of Lady Catherine de Bourgh and Lady Anne Darcy

For aliens have entered the holy places of the Lord's house	(Darcy's mother); cousin to Anne de Bourgh and the Darcy siblings. Jeremiah 51:51
Forced Strawberries	Cultivating strawberries in a greenhouse/orangery for fruiting and consumption all year round, rather than for a season.
Fordyce, Rev James	A Scottish Presbyterian minister and poet, best known for his collection of sermons published in 1766, Sermons for Young Women, or Fordyce's Sermons. (1720 - 1796)
Gardiner, Aunt & Uncle	Mrs Bennet's brother and sister-in-law. He is a successful tradesman, which earns the scorn of Caroline Bingley, even though - or because - her own fortune comes from trade. Both he and his wife are kind and level-headed and close to their nieces Jane and Elizabeth.
Gracechurch Street	A main road in the historic and financial centre of the City of London. Home to the Gardiner Family.
Gray, Thomas	An English poet, letter-writer, classical scholar, and professor at Pembroke College, Cambridge (1716 - 1771). Lizzy is referring to

	his 'Ode on a Distant Prospect of Eton College.'
Gruel	A thinner type of porridge, consisting of cereal boiled in water or milk.
Grose, Francis - A Classical Dictionary of the Vulgar Tongue	A collection of rude words and slang, first published in 1785 by Francis Grose.
Head, Richard - The Canting Academy	A slang dictionary written in 1673.
History of Little Goody Two-Shoes, The	A children's story by John Newbery, published in 1765.
Hunsford	A Parsonage near Westerham and the home of Mr and Mrs Collins
Joseph as Vizier of Egypt	Gen 41:41-52. Joseph was betrayed into slavery by his jealous brothers, but rose to become appointed Vizier, the second most powerful man in Egypt, after the Pharaoh.
King, Mary	A minor character in Pride & Prejudice who inherits ten thousand pounds from a distant relative. She is courted by Mr Wickham and then taken out of harm's way to Liverpool by an Uncle.
Lazarettos	A quarantine station for maritime travellers. Can refer to ships permanently at anchor, isolated islands, or mainland buildings. The first lazaretto was established

	by Venice in 1423 on the island of Santa Maria di Nazareth in the Venetian Lagoon
Lea, The	The River Lea, also spelled Lee, originating in the Bedfordshire part of the Chiltern Hills, and flowing southeast through Hertfordshire and then Greater London.
Lind, James	A Scottish doctor and the pioneer of hygiene in the Royal Navy. By conducting clinical trials, he discovered that citrus fruits cured scurvy. (1716 - 1794)
Lock, stock and barrel	A popular saying for many centuries. Based on the three main components of a flintlock gun: lock denoting the firing mechanism, stock the wooden shoulder-piece to which it is attached, and barrel, the conduit through which the bullet is fired.
Longbourn	Hertfordshire residence of The Bennet Family.
Lottery tickets	A game of chance played with cards/tickets and fish/tokens.
Lucas Lodge	Hertfordshire residence of the Lucas Family.
Lucas, Maria	Younger sister to Charlotte (Lucas) Collins, sister-in-law to Mr Collins and daughter of Sir William and Lady Lucas.

Lucas, Sir William & Lady	Neighbours and friends to The Bennet family.
Sallé, Marie	A French dancer and choreographer, famous in the 18th century for her emotive, dramatic performances. (1707 - 1756)
Mad as Old King George	Referring to George III, father to George IV. In later life, he suffered from frequent periods of mental illness, leading to the establishment of a Regency in 1810. (1738 - 1820)
Master of Ceremonies	Responsible for supervising every aspect of a ball, from room arrangements and adherence to dress codes, to musicians and the order of dances. He would also introduce prospective dancing partners to one another.
Master of Paddles	Nickname for the Master of Ceremonies by Lizzy.
Master of Punting	Nickname for the Master of Ceremonies by Darcy.
Meryton	A fictional town in Pride & Prejudice, located near Longbourn and Netherfield in Hertfordshire.
Miasma	Bad air, or night air. A now obsolete theory that diseases were caused by a miasma, imparted from decaying organic matter.

Militia	A military force of civilians, raised to supplement the regular army in case of emergency.
Multum stercora in parvum spatium	Translates roughly as 'a lot of rubbish in a small space.'
Nasus	Latin for nose.
Neck and crop	Originally used to describe a spectacular fall from a horse where the unseated rider flies past the horse's neck and throat, crop being an archaic word for throat. Came to mean 'entirely, completely.'
Pantry	A small room or cupboard in which food, crockery, and cutlery are kept.
Pay your taxes	A cheeky reference to the fate of Aristocrats during the French revolution, who were largely exempt from paying taxes. It is suggested that Darcy is a member of the old Anglo-Norman aristocracy, as indicated by his own name and that of his Aunt, Lady Catherine de Bourgh, although he does not possess a title.
Pease-soup	Also known as Pease pudding and Pease porridge, it's a savoury dish made of boiled legumes, typically split yellow peas, with water, salt, and spices, often cooked with a bacon or ham joint.

Pemberley	Derbyshire estate owned by Fitzwilliam Darcy.
Phillips, Aunt	The sister of Mrs. Bennet and Edward Gardiner, and Aunt to the Bennet and Gardiner children. She is widely thought to be rather vulgar.
Piano Forte	A fortepiano is an early piano dating from around 1700 to the early 19th century. During Pride & Prejudice, Lady Catherine states to Lizzy of music that 'there are few people in England, I suppose, who have more true enjoyment of music than myself, or a better natural taste. If I had ever learnt, I should have been a great proficient. And so would Anne, if her health had allowed her to apply.' She encourages Mrs Collins to play the piano forte in Mrs Jenkinson's room (Anne's companion in the novel) where she will be in 'nobody's way.'
Polemoscope	An opera glass or field glass with an oblique lens and side aperture that allows the user to discretely see what is happening to their left or right. Known also as 'Jealously Glasses.'
Pontius	Referring to Pontius Pilate, fifth governor of Judaea 26/27 to 36/37 AD, under Emperor Tiberius. Well-known today as the

official presiding over the trial of Jesus. In Matthew's 27:24, Pilate, 'seeing that he was getting nowhere, but that a riot was starting instead' took some water and 'washed his hands in front of the crowd, and said, 'I am innocent of this man's blood. See to it yourselves!''

Portent — A sign or warning that a momentous event is likely to happen.

Potent portables — Alcoholic beverages.

Pottle — A sort of conical basket used to carry produce.

Poultice — A soft, moist cloth, containing herbs, bran or flour, which, when applied to the body, relieves soreness and inflammation.

Primus Inter Pares — Latin: a first among equals. The Prime Minister.

Prince Regent, The — Later George IV. The eldest son of King George III and Queen Charlotte. From 1811 until his accession, he served as Regent during his father's final illness. He was known among the people as a profligate, thanks to a careless and extravagant lifestyle. (1762 - 1830)

Quizzing Glass — A single magnifying lens on a handle, held up before the eye to enable close scrutiny of an object or person.

Greene, Robert	A prolific English author and dramatist, who enjoyed popularity during his lifetime. 'The Black Bookes Messenger' details the villainies of one Ned Browne. Today, he is best known for a pamphlet believed to be an attack on William Shakespeare entitled 'Greene's Groats-Worth of Witte, bought with a million of Repentance.' (1558 - 1592)
Rosings	The palatial dwelling of Lady Catherine de Bourgh, located in Kent. Hunsford Parsonage - home of the Collinses - shares one of its boundaries.
Sanctioned by Papa	While Lizzy's Mama is adamant that her daughter accepts Mr Collins's proposal in order that the entailed estate of Longbourn may remain within the family, her Papa allows that the match does not go ahead, appreciating just how much it would be against Lizzy's wishes.
Scandal Sheets	A newspaper or magazine specializing in scandalous stories or gossip.
Sesquipedalian	A long and ponderous word, polysyllabic.
Shakespeare & Goldsmith both agree	Shakespeare - 'The better part of valour is discretion.'

	Goldsmith - 'He who fights and runs away, may live to fight another day.'
Shuttlecock	A predecessor of modern badminton, played with rackets and a feathered 'bird.'
Spying Fan	Also known as Monocular Fans. A lady's brisé or cockade fan with a miniature spy-glass added to the rivet or centre, so that one might peep discreetly at one's surroundings.
St Giles	The Seven Dials area of central London, close to Covent Garden.
Stockade	A barrier constructed with upright wooden posts or stakes as a defence against attack.
Sugar nips	A large pair of pincers designed to cut sugar from a block or sugarloaf.
Tale-bearers are as bad as the tale-makers	As said by Mrs Candour in R B Sheridan's 'School for Scandal' (1777).
Talisman	An object (such as a rabbit's foot) thought to contain magical powers, protect from ill will and bring good luck.
Tattle	Gossip, scandal, tittle-tattle.
Teaching to fish	Proverb: 'Give a man a fish and he will eat for a day. Teach a man how to fish and you feed him for a lifetime.'

Temple of Concord and The Temple of Peace	Both located in Green Park, central London. The Temple of Peace was destroyed in 1749 during a firework display, as was the Temple of Concord in 1814, during the Prince Regent's Gala.
Timon	Darcy is referencing Shakespeare's (and possibly Thomas Middleton's) 'Timon of Athens' (1607).
Truefitt & Hill's Freshman Cologne	The world's oldest barbershop, established in 1805, St James's, London.
Whist	A common card game in Jane Austen's era, played between four players (two opposing pairs).
Wickham, Mr	The infamous rake of Pride & Prejudice; extremely charming and untruthful. He befriends Lizzy and relays a false history of his acquaintance with Mr Darcy, encouraging her prejudice towards him to develop further. Later in the novel, he seduces Lydia Bennet, exposing the Bennet family to potential ruin.
Wollstonecraft, Mary	An English writer, philosopher and advocate of women's rights; far ahead of her time. Today Wollstonecraft is considered one of the founding feminist philosophers, being best known for 'A Vindication of the Rights of Woman' (1792), in which she

argues for equality, education and imagines a social order founded on reason. (1759 - 1797)

With gratitude to: -

Jane Austen

Austen Authors
Jane Austen Centre
Pemberley.com
Randombitsoffascination.com
Regencydances.org
The Jane Austen Wiki
Vic Sanborn - Jane Austen's World
Wikipedia

'Lizzy & Darcy in Lockdown' is also available
to view via YouTube on Summer Light
Theatre's Channel.

Lizzy & Darcy Unleashed

A sequel to 'Lizzy & Darcy in Lockdown'

*For all the Readers
who wanted to know more*

Key

(Bracketed and written in Italics) = thoughts that are not sent

* = Referring to Mr Wickham

_____
= Indicates a pause in the letter, during which the writer collects their thoughts.

A letter from Colonel Fitzwilliam to Miss Elizabeth Bennet

The 19ᵗʰ Day of June at Rosings Park

Dear Madam,

I must apologise most profusely for both the inevitable brevity of this letter, and the very great delay in response to yours preceding such. Please accept my sincere assurance that this has been no matter of intentional discourtesy, but rather as a consequence of the many and most urgent demands upon my time.

You will recall in previous correspondence my repetition of an idle thought I had of Mr Charles Bingley being perhaps 'indebted' to my cousin, Darcy having once briefly congratulated himself on having latterly saved 'a friend' from the inconveniences of a most imprudent marriage. I gave confirmation of my cousin having mentioned no names, being sensible to the indelicacy so to do, not least for the sake of the lady's family should it become known. Also, emphasising it were only mine own conjecture that the person could be Bingley.

You have asked what 'arts' my cousin employed to separate the couple. I would resolutely answer 'none'. I need utter not his profound artlessness, for you can be in no doubt of such, his character speaking in full eloquence for itself. Concerning 'what reasons' my cousin might give for this 'interference,' I would answer that there were, as I understand it, some very strong objections against the lady.

This is as much as I know. Would we might speak in person, for I fear my poor epistolary endeavours have by some means lessened the honourable purpose of my cousin's endeavours in your eyes, bequeathing a discomfort which would otherwise not exist. For this, I may only apologise.

I would only assure you once more and again that my cousin is a most loyal, most devoted friend.

Yours with great sincerity,

Col. Fitzwilliam

Seven weeks later...

Letter 1

Friday 7th August, Rosings Park

My dear Madam,

Having written and sent a score of letters without return I confess I am at a loss to comprehend your continued silence as response. I am aware that you suffer no ailment, for I have seen you twice at a distance and, on both occasions, having clearly seen me, you have hurried away in the contrary direction. Restrictions aside, I do not understand. I sense I may have caused you some offence, yet know not how this can be. Having read and reread our correspondence, I admit myself utterly confounded. Whilst having no wish to coerce a confidence, yet valuing your friendship as I do, it would be remiss of me to make no final endeavour to restore our communication.

Very well. Hitherto I have constructed only brief epistles. Perhaps a more detailed account of the last two months will somehow prove a restorative incentive *(for I find I cannot do without it)*.

You will recall, no doubt at all, the circumstances under which I departed Rosings upon the nineteenth eve of June. My expectations then of the disruption in London led me to believe I might be absent a month or more at least. My intentions were to return Georgiana to Pemberley at the earliest opportunity, re-open the house and then, in due course, to leave her there settled once more in safety and some freedom. This was not to be.

I know not how much you may have heard concerning the London riots and deposition of our government's First Lord, nor whether this might be carried rumour, rather than actual fact. I trust, therefore, that you will allow me to impart the most faithful account I can muster from my own experience. Naturally you will keep in mind that eyes may be blinkered and sight restricted – even mine – and a mind troubled may not bear the most accurate witness.

I departed Rosings almost in the midst of night, taking with me Anne's mare as spare and riding hard towards London. Though my main aim was to find my sister in Grosvenor and remove her with all due haste, I had allowed myself the faith that I might delay the securing of mutual transportation until I had arrived within the city. I initially wished not for the encumbrance of a carriage, knowing it would slow my passage. This was the first of many unfortunate decisions on my part.

Although the Colonel had been most emphatic as to the gravity of the situation, I had misled myself to believe that by the time I likely achieved the London perimeters, the army and militia must have all contained *(stultus!)*. Reaching the city, however, it became apparent that all was yet alive with noise and dispute. I confess, in my continuing naivety I had thought to attend your family in Gracechurch Street upon my way, then diverting with ease westward upon securing their safe passage towards Hertfordshire. This was utterly impossible. Never in my life have I seen so many people together all at once; London Bridge was simply unreachable. Shoulder to shoulder they stood, flooding every street, some with torches still lit though it was by now fully light, thousands upon thousands crying out in what might either have been joy or anger; somehow impossible to tell. I later heard that many warehouses and businesses had been looted in the east of the city, but was party to no evidence of this at the time. I am compelled to add, however, that as advantage will oft be seized when eyes are averted, I do not doubt the truth of it, yet for the sake of clarity must insist that I may not attest as actual witness here.

It is passing strange, nevertheless, what later springs to mind upon remembered reflection; the enterprising who sold pomanders and baked goods, the usual spiritual divide casting a canon-scatter of discriminatory blessings and curses upon the heads of the random, the angry who ripped masks from the faces of others, the released who tore masks from themselves. Windows were broken, bricks hurled like missiles, buildings vandalised and set alight. Everywhere were screams of sudden terror, then also voices raised at once in chants of peace, hands that beckoned strangers to safety, men and women tending tirelessly to the injured. Such is our diversity; a maelstrom of varied emotions. Yet I digress.

Riding west, horrified to find myself still south of the Thames, I discovered the bridge at Blackfriars to be equally encumbered. My horse by now utterly exhausted, I was forced with great reluctance to leave him tethered to a tree near Nelson Square and there to mount the most reluctant mare. She was grievous out of condition having had little exercise this many a month, for Anne cares not to ride with any frequency finding it a 'nonsensical, twisting, giddsome-making exercise in discomfort and futility.' Thus, after half a mile of wheezing and hacking (she) I was forced to proceed on foot, tugging the valetudinary Bessy aft. We made a fine and grumblesome pair, I do assure you. I attempted then to forge a path through to Westminster, but this proved equally impossible, the throng being far too densely unyielding and myself too impatient to remain inactive in the hope that we might pass in time. My frustration I need not describe, for my sole remaining alternative was now to go around on foot by Battersea! This I did, cursing my own folly as I went. I pause incidentally to remark upon this bridge's enterprising Tollkeeper, for there he stood resolutely collecting his fee from all who would cross, in spite of almost universal fury and threats to his personal well-being. His obstinacy, however, was my saviour, for this bridge was not near so over-burdened as the others, each traverser being forced 'on pain of sword' to pay and cross in muttering single file. Having paid my and Bessy's due, we crossed the Thames at last only to be faced with more and absolute confusion. I expect you will laugh to yourself at my pitiful expectations of the west of the city being a-riot in a more civilised fashion than the east? Brevity being the soul of wit, I will adapt my tale to some necessary economy. Against my better judgement, not to mention schooling as a gentleman, I found that I must needs push and force my way this time. Thus, I once more mounted Bessy and she and I bucked and wrestled with one another respectively to, and then, across the length and breadth of Hyde Park, affecting not to notice any caught rabbit-startled in the path of our cavorting. For this I am not proud, although I must state that we harmed no one unless to galvanise is to harm; yet it was most necessary for the sake of my sister.

I found my way to Georgiana at Grosvenor at last, where Bingley, it transpired and at the first sign of unrest, had at once departed his domicile with his sister to secure the safety of mine – the Hursts choosing to remain within their house for reasons undisclosed *(and unsought)*. Georgiana being in residence barely a street away and Bingley's nature being what it is, this was no real surprise, yet in my apprehension I had not once considered it as a possibility. It was something of a revelation then to discover that Georgiana had – out of a natural but rather disobliging reluctance – adamantly refused to depart. Nothing, it seems, could be said nor done to persuade her, and short of lifting her out, which would hardly have been proper, they had all been compelled to endure within and hope for assistance, though only one servant of the four had remained to protect. I am thankful that Bingley had then the presence of mind to organise the closing of shutters at the front of the house to feign a lack of occupation for, ultimately, they were safe enough, yet I confess I did private wish my friend this once possessor of a more persuasive, more forceful nature, efficient as he proved himself at closing boards. There are times when his natural diffidence does him no credit, for it put my sister at potential risk. That being said, I too could not persuade her. It is the first I have ever known her to be in the least obstinate. After many more attempts to encourage her out of doors, Georgiana at last confessed herself possessed of a deep, immobilising fear that she might be left with only the gown in which she stood to wear for many days, should we depart immediate as Charles and I had wished. Well, this was easily attended to and I felt she might have mentioned it sooner. Without my having to speak a word of command, the aforementioned remaining servant offered to accompany our party and carry with him whatever garments my sister most desired. True, I would immediate have bid him thus to do, yet I appreciated his willingness and spirit. Thus, Georgiana having reasonable swift selected what she most wished to bring, we were at last free of the house, Miss Bingley complaining most fervently that she had not been likewise urged to think upon such very great necessities and demanding that we might call upon the Hursts once more to remedy this flagrant oversight. I freely disclose that both Bingley and I affected most diligently not to hear her. The lack of suitable future clothing, however, paled to insignificance when it was realised that walking was de rigueur, and she chuntered most vociferously for nigh an hour. We allowed it without attempt to intervene, for it seemed to invigorate her and she strode ahead for quite some time, barely issuing complaint at all regarding Bessy's having made it plain that she would carry none but Georgiana.

Thus, we made our weary way once more across the bridge at Battersea, where by now the toll I previous paid had doubled. I pause here briefly to mention news we received the very next day that a lady and gentleman fleeing the city by commandeering a small vessel to which they were unused, set an unwitting course straight for the aforementioned bridge and rammed it hard, substantially destabilising one of the piers. No doubt the night's income – which might otherwise have purchased a country estate – must now be spent upon its restoration. So much for profiteering enterprise!

Not long aft, we were relieved to discover an inn near the common, where thankfully there were reasonable clean rooms enough and arrangements swiftly made for warm wine and baths for the ladies who were quite exhausted. Miss Bingley in particular had suffered prodigiously during the walk through her quite ridiculous footwear. Whosoever designs a slipper or a boot in which a lady may actually walk some distance without being both blistered and tortured will win my everlasting patronage; poor Charles had been forced to throw her across his shoulder for the last stage, for she had become too weak to continue and begged most piteously for assistance.

Having seen them safely settled and been, naturally, quite prodigiously over-charged by the landlord, I commissioned a rather inelegant cart and driver and set off once more for Blackfriars where I reclaimed my horse, by some miracle left undisturbed, and finding him now tolerably rested, rode at last through the swift dispersing crowds by London Bridge with the ungainly cart jogging behind. Upon reaching the residence of your Aunt and Uncle, I discovered the house shuttered and abandoned and upon enquiry determined with intense relief that your Uncle had early and with great presentiment secured their safe passage out of the city. But you should know this from my first communication. You will also know that the house was yet intact, no signs at all of unnatural disturbance or e'en rifle fire, and all were witnessed to be in quite the best of health as they departed. Would I could have done more. As luck would have it, returning to my horse upon the finalisation of my enquiries it was revealed to my weary eyes that he had, this time, indeed been stolen and I was forced to chase the young heel who had hold of his reign and administer quite the hearty clip around his ear. I assure you, I had run and walked enough this day for twenty year and those final steps were almost more than I could tolerate. But I exaggerate. I returned in darkness to the inn and there collapsing slept until midday.

We remained at the Horse and Bugle near a week, each morning's breakfast commencing with the self-same bewailing of Miss Bingley as she grieved the despoiling of Rotten Row in her mind's eye for good and all. Fortunately, Georgiana had bestowed her with a pair of her own boots and a gown, with which she seemed unprecedented pleased – though both did fit her rather ill, so she was not out of humour entirely. On the twenty-sixth we heard, as all did, of the reconstituted government's decision to proceed with further quarantine and, after a brief disagreement, decided to return with all immediate haste to Rosings.

Accordingly, we made use once more of the landlord's cart and pitched and juddered our way back into Kent. Naturally this was not necessary, for there were carriages a-plenty acquirable by then. Yet Bingley and I agreed it would be good for the development of Miss Bingley's character, in particular, to travel such a distance thus, and she was none the wiser. Yes, there is something very levelling about a state of crisis, is there not? How fortunate we were that it did not rain.

Accordingly, as you are aware, I am once more incarcerated with my Aunt. Within an hour of her arrival, Miss Bingley had commandeered Mrs Norris's exclusive services, removed the absent Colonel from his own room citing that the one designated to her was 'drafty' and 'distinctly fusty,' and appropriated seven of Anne's gowns to wear without fully seeking her approval, whilst criticising the shape and style of each in detail.

'I wonder, is she widely liked?' mused Anne to the ceiling.

I affected not to know, for wealth may oft produce a friend where none might otherwise have stood.

Naturally the monopolising of Mrs Norris lasted only as long as my Aunt required to discover and remedy the situation. Lady Catherine is not one who considers servants to be 'people' exactly, yet she knows enough to realise when a good one might be overstrained and like to leave.

To my genuine surprise, I found Georgiana to be less than eager to endure an enforced and protracted sojourn at Rosings, refusing to leave her room for many days. I have yet to quite account for this rebellion, even allowing for the natural feeling some do harbour that a brief stay with one's family is as good as a feast. It will not astonish you to learn that Lady Catherine has always had the most emphatic opinions regarding the raising of Georgiana. Indeed, she seems generally to forget that it is I who am appointed guardian, and not she. I agreed to conceal my sister's unsociability by emphasising to Lady Catherine daily that she was fatigued to the point of ill health, having suffered greatly with her nerves through the riots and rescue. Naturally, our Aunt's patience wore thin with such antics within a day, but I am nothing if not persistent and saw no sense in reintroducing my Georgiana until her good humour was once more restored. For the first month, she took meals only in her bedchamber and exercised out of doors once night had fallen. She is barely more sociable now. Most odd, but there we have it. I have seldom known her so out of sorts. Could the journey in the cart have lasting unsettled her nerves, I wonder?

Colonel Fitzwilliam has this week at last returned, his arrival producing quite the stir, for in his arms was coddled a ragamuffin of a small dog whom he discovered wandering alone and frightened by West India Docks. Naturally, opinion was instantly intensely divided as to the welcomeness of this little creature. Anne was immediately enchanted and volunteered to bathe the 'filthsome article' (Lady Catherine's words) and see if she might tempt him to some food. It is well that it were she, for the little chap has thus far shown no incline at all to any other and barks most fierce and constant towards the rest of us. My Aunt was not as fully disturbed by him as might have been expected. Oh, she pays him no mind, calls him 'dog of some sort' if she must make reference to his presence and has decreed that should a caller of note arrive in future he must be instantly and completely hid, but beside that he is not unwelcome in her eyes. Miss Bingley, on the other hand, feels quite a strong repugnance for his origins and has taken no more to him since he has been spruced. If he is allowed to enter a room, she instantly climbs upon a chair and cries 'vermin!' until he is removed. Upon reflection, this may indeed be why he often barks without cessation for it is quite clear that he has no comprehension whatsoever as to why he might be so disliked, and every desire to prove such disinclination wrong.

'That is quite enough,' declared Lady Catherine to no one in particular. 'If I wished for such excitement, I would simply pour my tea the opposite way around.' I have never once known my Aunt to lift a teapot, so that in itself would indeed be a consequence of some note.

This morning at breakfast, my Aunt saw fit to remind my cousin once more of his dependency upon marrying a woman of fortune. I doubt it had slipped his mind. Such are our familial obligations. As you know well, my Aunt delights in relieving her feelings of boredom by being quarrelsome, and she has been very bored of late. I am surprised that she misses society as much as she seems to, for she was always full of complaint when such diversions were open to her. I expect, like all of us, the frustration lies more in what is denied one, rather than a sincere wish for the company of others.

Yours etc.
P.S: I hope most sincerely that you are in good health *(and might respond at last).* How do you fare with the Collinses in this second lockdown?

P.P.S: Bessy's name had me wondering, have you been known at all or ever as 'Bess'?

P.P.P.S: Knowing well the restriction upon our movements, I will look for any reply *(you might deign to pen)* as ever, within the old elm, where you have no doubt found this.

Letter 2

Saturday 15th August, Hunsford Parsonage *(even yet!)*

Sir,

I thank you for your letter and the lengthy description of events provided, although it was not requested. You are fortunate indeed to have escaped the London riots unharmed and to enjoy the peace of mind of having secured the well-being of those you love.

I will begin by boldly declaring that I could not agree with you less, regarding the company of others. I have little sympathy with the sentiment expressed that one might wish to see no one at all, unless it is suddenly denied one. It speaks of a character almost completely preoccupied with having one's own way, that the society of others – with their differing opinions and tastes – becomes altogether objectionable. We must be challenged, sir, either to stand by our own thoughts in the midst of contrast, or to have them dusted off and replenished with fresher material. Certain, if we do not, then we become without fail that unsocial creature who is so unused to the art of conversation that – when finally forced to attend a gathering — is either taciturn to a fault, or so alarmingly loquacious with the little activity of their lives, that they become readily avoided that the same tale may not be repeated far beyond the realm of courtesy. A fait accompli.

('My dear Madam!' I am not your dear Madam! I note you do not care to ask direct the reason for my silence. Heaven forfend you should, for I would surely answer and then you might be forced to take responsibility for your actions, rather than sweep them aside like the newly appointed servant who, unaccustomed to your particular 'taste,' over-fragrances your handkerchief and is instantly dismissed for ruining your whole week!)

(Yet how impossible it almost seems to reprimand you with integrity, when clearly you went to such lengths in attempting to secure the safety of my sister and the Gardiners. What contradictory creatures we are! I cannot think why you would make such efforts when you imagine my entire family quite beneath your contempt. What may I say, then, to thank you and yet not perjure myself, nor allow my dearest Jane to continue maligned and undefended?)

(No, I will not be deflected by a little sweet that masks a host of sour.)

I am grateful, Sir, for your efforts regarding my sister and extended family; it bestowed me with a certain peace unhoped for in the circumstances, to be secure in the knowledge that they had escaped the city in good health before the worst of it began.

Notwithstanding my appreciation expressed, I confess I find myself in all the awkwardness one might expect as the possessor of information regarding my sister that in my eyes does you no credit.

To spare each of us from the confusion of poorly constructed repetition and the conjecture of hearsay, I enclose the Colonel's letter forwarded to me prior to your departure to London, in which he responds to my most urgent request for information concerning a matter to which he had (inadvertently) hinted in an earlier communication. I had pressed him for clarity, believing the subject to concern the happiness of a person whom I love dearly. It has caused me no small amount of unease that in writing so to you I break the confidence of the Colonel. Although I doubt not that you will find his description of your involvement all that is loyal *(and subservient)* to you, I still trust that what may be perceived as an indiscretion on his part will not be cause of dissonance between you *(although why I should be disturbed, I know not. Yet I am fond of the Colonel... Oh how complicated it is to issue a reprimand to anyone, however much they might deserve it.)*

I am not yet as clear as I wish to be, thus I will speak frank and ask that you take my tone as civil as possible, under the circumstances. There is little doubt in my mind the man of whom the Colonel writes is indeed Mr Bingley, and the woman (*well, here courteous words near fail me*) my most beloved sister, Jane. I therefore simply ask that, for now, you confirm my summation to be correct.

(I have no wish to communicate further with you, no wish at all.)

Yet I have felt myself so deeply, fearfully alone these past months... No, I am resolute. For Jane's sake I will bear my solitude.)

(Yet Jane would not wish me to go quite stark out of mind. She would understand, my most dear and loveliest of sisters. She would not reproach me, surely, under such circumstances as these?)

(Oh, I must speak to someone!)

You ask about the Collinses? Very well, I will tell you. Naturally, at the first issue of the latest curfews, Mr Collins restricted Charlotte and I to the parsonage, even though I am certain it was writ that we might be free to spend a limited amount of time within a garden. I abided by his law a week. Thankfully Mr Collins is a man of such stringent routine that his behaviour is predictable to the moment, thus I am able to achieve some liberty each day. You will doubtless be shocked to learn that I have found a way to climb from my chamber window and to the ground via the wisteria. Thank heavens it is such a long-established and robust tree, for it holds me admirably. I am able to spend an hour out of doors from a half-past three until a half-past four each day, when he takes his tea alone within his study. This small escape is a source of the most tremendous relief. Indeed, it is through the remembrance of the day's adventure that I can abide each evening in the parlour before bedtime.

I made a pact with myself during that first week of imprisonment, that when I was free once more, I would endeavour to think as little as possible of what perturbs me. Indeed, I have irrevocably realised how health-some it is to direct one's thoughts always towards what is pleasing — something I once did naturally as habit, but now must reinstruct myself with due rigour, for it is no easy matter to stop one's mind from dwelling upon miseries once it has become used to so doing.

Mostly, of course, I simply look at and exist in nature. It is so unrivalled soothing. The more I look and listen, even from before the window in my chamber, the more I feel our ancestors to be present; those of old who sought so much inspiration from our natural world. Last afternoon I stood to watch the clouds move fast across the sun, saw the rapid change from golden-yellow to orange-red and back, followed the trickles of rain which caught the light in rounded droplets upon the panes and, much later, the moon in crescent shape and the stars visible then lost, visible then lost, amid the cloud. I hope it is always appreciated so. I hope that each generation will know it's unparalleled import. A city is a pleasant place to visit for amusements; I confess I have been suitably diverted when in London, yet I would not wish the city to encroach too far. All should have land, I believe that. A place to live which cheers the heart that one may call one's own, and a garden to wander in. Those are, I believe, the most basic requirements and all should be entitled to have such.

When the nights draw in, I shall still find my way out of doors. Indeed, I have e'en been known to wander out at night, when Mr Collins is a bed (he goes promptly at a half past nine).

(But I ought not tell you this, for the world is not so changed that a woman may wander out alone at night. Yet I will not cross it through, for I hope you are shocked; it will do you good you pompous creature.)

Speaking of pomposity, Mr Collins' general frustration during the first lockdown with our neighbours, Maria and myself, were nothing to his current humour. What power has been bestowed upon him as the 'grand pater' of this household (his words, of course) has gone entirely to his head. I am certain that were I a year or four younger he would be schooling me daily. Doubting that I would be a receptive student, we may thank goodness for small mercies. Yet it is an immense lack of humility and self-absurdity, surely, that encourages a person to believe that they may be appointed ruler of another? To have all at one's disposal! Who of substance would require or desire such a thing, and by what right should they enforce it? Ever I bewail the lack of humour in my cousin, for it would redeem him where nothing else may.

Indeed, if you would seek proof of the inappropriate nature of those who decide to seize such control of another and, upon their own warped judgement, determine and direct in what manner said other is to be happy, one need look no further than the Collinses, for Charlotte has become a changed woman in the last month or so. I confess, I hardly know her. She will take her husband's part in everything (no matter how shudderingly foolish), has all but lost her sense of self, her humour. It frightens me. Of Maria, she speaks not a word and will not be induced so to do under any guise or ruse. It is as though she has forgot her altogether, although of course this cannot be so. She has insisted that Mr Collins take over the care of Felicity, and when he called me 'liar' for having the temerity to affirm my affinity and nurture of the dear little being, Charlotte simply nodded in sage agreement and would not look at me. The first day of his latest custody he took the largest of his miniature bell collection, which was cumbersome and heavy enough, and fixed it with a rope around her neck, that wherever she went it might ring loud and mournful and he would know where she was. The weight of the bell pulled her wee head down sadly and for several hours she simply took to a corner beneath the stairs and sat crouched in a shaking heap. As soon as my cousin was at his supper, I took it from her neck and flung the offending article from the front door with a resonant clang. He then attached a lighter bell and spent a week almost fully occupied with her whereabouts which near drove us all, he included, to distraction. I am thankful that within that time Felicity discovered how to move about the house free without causing the bell to ring. I wish she would not cry for me, nor try to leap upon my lap. It only makes him angrier.

Indeed, my cousin and I are further from friendship than ever we have been, which is quite something to say. This continued lockdown makes the most appalling inmates of us all. I have felt and thought in ways I believed impossible. You know enough of my character to conceive that I do not suffer fools, that I have – indeed – a temper of a sort *(more than you know)*. Most unfeminine, perhaps, but there it is and I admit it. Yet I will tell you that the odd phrase of frustration hurled at Mama or Lydia is nothing to what I experience of late. At times I am so angry I almost may not breathe. It is foolish; I am not a marionette, and yet I act as though I have no choice. I had a moment, even, just a moment *(oh I can hardly believe that I could confess this to anyone, least of all to you – I must tell it though, I must speak of it to someone)* where I might have throttled Mr Collins with my bare hands and enjoyed it *(there, it is said and I will not take it back)*. More than a moment, in truth.

We live in a world that tells us that animals have not souls. Who first decreed such, heaven knows! It is as ridiculous as so much else. But I will tell you this, although you have not asked and likely give not the tiniest of jots. That cat from whom I am so completely restricted is compassionate, loving, intelligent and loyal. She would sit with me for hours on end, coveting nowhere else. She would lay her little head upon my hand and give me intermittent licks. She would greet me every morning, every evening, she would talk to me and never tire of being nigh. No soul! I have lost her now, it seems, but I will not forget how she had made this time that was so unprecedented hard so infinitely more bearable than it might have been. Every single day she showed me how to be present and happy. I am disgusted at myself for knowing not how to rescue her from the clutches of dogma and possession without love. You see, because she was found by my cousin and tethered upon his property she is, without apparent question or argument, his possession to do with as he sees fit. How am I to believe this possible? That we have such foolish laws that decree an animal or a person the 'property' of another. How very convenient that is. These laws, they are fictions are they not?

Self-serving nonsense that must be enforced by fear and violence that we dare not laugh and turn away.

Speaking of which, you mentioned Lazarettos in your penultimate letter. I too have been somewhat confounded at the way in which the Unmentionable has been 'contained.' Although I attended no school, I know others who have and they were not strangers to illness and epidemics. I may tell you that the moment typhus or any other were detected, those who could were sent immediate away, and the rest of the school secured that none might leave or enter that it be controlled as swift as possible. Yet you will know this, of course.

Out of very idle curiosity, do you happen to know what became of our First Lord of the Treasury?

We were paid a visit last week by our Rochester neighbours who have fallen heavily upon hard times. Mr Collins naturally reprimanded them first of all for leaving their home and placing him at risk, then gave as little concession to their plight as he might reasonably do; yet where Charlotte would once have quietly steered him direct to offer more compassion, she did not. I wonder, is my friend now lost altogether? She avoids my society, agrees with everything her husband says as if she were a parrot, I even hear them in discussion of my character while at breakfast – my faults, it seems, are abundant and pressing. Perhaps the very worst of all, she sings no more. Is it possible that my friend, one who has been another sister to me, could be now so altered that she has forgot our shared bond altogether? It is as though she is altered from within; all the warmth and kindness in her eyes is changed to – how best to put this? – almost a conceit. That is not quite it. Yet it seems to me that she enjoys the feeling. Before my very eyes, the Charlotte whom I knew who was warm and kind and practical and bright has vanished to be replaced by a person who seems both hunted and huntress. On occasion, seeming friend once more, and I being fool enough to trust, I find that whatever words have passed between us are then shared with her husband and used to my detriment. I am confused between wishing to shake some sense, some *Charlotte,* back into her, and wanting to flee as far from here as I may. I know it is our restricted circumstances that do create this situation, yet I cannot help but wonder if it has simply expedited what would, in time, become inevitable. How could Charlotte, as the years go by, not have found her very spirit compromised by the match that she has made?

How could she not find herself divided as his influence prevails? My heart will break, I think.

There is a fear that is borne of unreasonableness that increases in the breast of another who finds there is no way to respond with impunity. That, indeed, the answer to the conundrum is that you cannot please them, nor may you fight them. There is no argument that may be broached, no word or action that could make the slightest difference. It is a mild relief when one accepts this, for the mind may leave the puzzle be at last. Yet one is still left unable to change what is most unpleasant and, lacking the freedom to leave, one must needs go in circle upon circle.

Yet these are not new thoughts. We may only look at history. Thousands of years of battles and raising statues to 'conquerors' as if that were a good thing. Often what is unkind is most vigorously enforced, in families as in institutions. If it were good, surely, there would be no need for force? We raise statues to villains in bronze or even gold that the glitter might distract our minds from their deeds. Why may we not respect one another, love one another, even?

(But I confide too much. I do not trust you.)

How do we stop our mind from turning over and over at injustice and uncertainty? Why does it prove so hard to think of something better? Why not accept that others will do what they will and it has little whatever to do with us? We ruminate endlessly; yet why must they be changed? Because we fear them and the harm they seem to do. Because there is no compassion, flexibility or commonality in their thinking. Because they hurt the people we love and we know not how to rescue them. Yet we are wrong to fear them, for it weakens us. We must learn to think of other matters; the sky at its most blue, the leaves unfurled, the blossom abundant in its exquisite beauty; we must think of those who love us and whom we love, we must remember the birdsong, the soft, warm breezes, the ripples of water upon the river shore, the ducks, the swans, the geese that fly in troops honking, the leaves as they whisper among the trees, the warmth of the sun on our skin; there is so much to think of and be thankful for if we only will decide and, having decided, suddenly unlimited avenues will spring forth and our questions be either answered or unnecessary. Incidentally, the river is quite the most effective place to ensure concealment, for Mr Collins – fearing miasma as he does – will go not within a field's distance of the riverbank.

Returning to less philosophical matters, have you heard aught of the government approved tonic? It seems my cousin with his potion-tinkering prowess has been commissioned to mass produce this remedy to distribute to the village. I wonder, do we have your Aunt to thank for this latest distinction? The postal service runs for the government, it seems, if no one else, for my cousin has been supplied with both recipe and ingredients with which to begin. Being the dutiful wife she is, Charlotte has been the first to test each batch. I cannot attest to it curing anything, but most thankfully neither did it kill. Thus far she has had a rash which spread across her face and neck exactly in the shape of Africa, a blurry vision and weeping eye which lasted three days and nights and stuck one lid fast down, puckered knees, elbows and chin, and a tongue swollen to amusing, yet not dangerous, extent. Tomorrow, she is to test the final batch. Upon such evidence, I have adamantly refused to drink as much as a droplet and, if nothing else, I shall be resolute upon this until absolute proof attests otherwise. Charlotte has been set at semi-liberty this afternoon and is instructed to distribute official notices around the village advising everyone to partake of the tonic for the duty and care of their loved ones. How the villagers are to see these notices when no one is to go out is anyone's conjecture. We may hope though, may we not, that this tonic will ultimately prove effective and we may all be dosed and liberated before Michaelmas?

Ah yes, regarding the Colonel, it is a most unfortunate feature of our society that a younger son may have no opportunity to marry for affection, saving the happy circumstance that a woman of suitable fortune might also be gifted with attractions beyond her dowry. It serves neither husband nor wife.

It is not my business and you have not asked my opinion, yet I would venture that it is perfectly natural for a young woman like your sister to resist leaving an environment in which she has enjoyed a certain autonomy, to be placed instead in another where she has none. We are not the sheep you seem to think us. We enjoy our freedom and have not the desire you imagine to be constantly tutored and advised. Alternatively, have you at all contemplated the possibility that she might have felt truly isolated in Grosvenor Square, and therefore feels both resentment towards you for allowing her to be left in such circumstances, and a genuine uncertainty when in the presence of others, being long unused to company? I speculate, of course, and you will forgive my impertinence, yet where was Miss Darcy's companion, I wonder?

I am not ashamed to confess how much I envy your peace of mind, that you may now daily look direct upon the faces of those for whom you care. Yet I must wonder at you in that peace. Knowing what it is to fear for the safety of those you love, be it either physical or psychological security (for both are equally potent), I marvel that for these many months you have continued a correspondence with me, knowing all along how you had hurt my sister.

I await your reply with interest.

(not) Yours etc.

P.S: Our Father always raised us never to treat a servant poorly. They are hard-working and to be respected. It is strange, though, is it not, what we ask of them and how they are seen by many as 'beneath' them? If one is unable to dress one's self without a servant's help – naturally I refer to none in my own family – then who is the dependant, really? Why, the very idea of a paid companion, for example, is in my opinion, a most absurd attempt to replace a far more valuable friendship based upon mutual connection, resonance and humour.

How much is missed when one must buy everything.

P.P.S: Is not the Colonel also guardian to Georgiana? 'The raising of Georgiana?!' Why, it sounds as though she were a ship!

P.P.P.S: Why, of course you would imagine the west to be more civilised. I would expect no less of you. It is the wealthy side, is it not, where most were perhaps frustrated and inconvenienced within their townhouses, but none were likely starving or fearful for their survival? Yet I would comfortably have wagered beforehand that many an early rioter over in the east wore fine clothing and an attitude of absolute prerogative. What, miss an opportunity to roister careless of others and add to their coffers? Surely that is a matter of simple daily habit?

P.P.P.P.S: No, I have not. Do you compare me to a coughing, bucking, wheezing mare? Or to good Queen Bess, perhaps?

Letter 3

Monday 17th August, Rosings Park

Dear Madam,

I thank you for your letter. I am relieved indeed to know that you are well.

Your assumptions are in part, at least, correct concerning your sister and my friend. It does appear to me most foolish, however, that I must be induced to explain my intervention after so long an interval during which much of far greater import has evolved.

Concerning the Colonel, you may set your mind at ease. I am not ashamed of my actions, therefore his reference to such matters not. I am somewhat surprised that your persistent enquiries did not alert his instinct to your intimate connection, but I fear that is how he can be. Thus, he had no inkling that the woman to whom he referred was your sister, and is therefore most entirely blameless *(if a little loose of tongue)*. Clearly, I had no wish nor intention that this information should reach your ears and thus no desire to cause pain either to yourself or to your family. Yet I do feel that you might yourself have been more immediate frank with the Colonel, and also with myself.

That is all I have to say, except perhaps to answer the charges levied at my integrity that having wilfully caused your sister 'psychological' pain I then participated in a – what would one say? – dishonest, perhaps, correspondence with your unwitting self? I have no wish to offend you, truly it pains me so to do, yet I must in all conscience express my bewilderment that you consider your sister to be the recipient of so deep a hurt after so very brief an acquaintance with my friend. I cannot consider myself dishonourable with regard to our communication, because I do not consider my intercession a matter of any great injury or import. Bingley was easily persuaded and all swiftly and most satisfactorily resolved. That is all.

(Yet that is not all)

Our opinions differ and that must be expected. Yet I would counter that a decision to marry seldom, if ever, belongs to one man alone. It is naive in you to imagine such. Bingley has not the most necessary guidance of a father to turn to. Knowing well how that is, I gave him counsel. Counsel, I hasten to add, that he himself sought. I trust we may now say no more about it. The matter and the feelings of which you speak with such indignation are long since passed. It is futile to continue so.

You are very fanciful upon nature. I imagine you hear not the night-time cries of rabbits as they are hunted or, should you see the pheasant skitter blithe across your path, imagine him not stuffed upon your plate? *(No, that is cruel. I need not be as ruled by my emotions as you. I will strike it out. One must not write aught that may be sent when out of humour. It is imprudent so to do. Yet how tempting it is. I will have a glass of wine.)*

You ask about the fate of our First Lord of the Treasury? I am indeed party to information concerning his well-being, some of which I am at liberty to share.

You will have heard, no doubt, that contrary to original claims via the Colonel of the First Lord (let's call him 'Filo' for the sake of economy, shall we?) having been betrayed by a good enemy and the riots then begun by protestors and celebrants in unison following his deposition, that he was instead really dragged from St Stephen's by rioters as the Great Bell of St Paul's boomed midday across the city; then mocked through the streets, put within a pillory for a week, forced to wear the plague mask of old, and finally imprisoned. While this latter account is certain rag-writing, it transpires that neither report was truly correct.

First and foremost, it is utterly impossible that our dear Filo might be dragged from St Stephen's at the midday chimes for, indeed, no member of the House of Commons worth his *sal* has ever deigned to rise up from his bed by then, let alone be washed, dressed, breakfasted and away from his residence before three at the most early.

As far as we now know, the riots themselves were actually begun in a tavern near Limehouse at around four in the afternoon, resulting from a discourse over those self-same protestors lately unreasonably imprisoned. As I understand it, the deliberations concerned not only how the prisoners might best be freed, but were also in response to rumours that certain members of the government – led by this good enemy, it seems – were intent upon the absolute prohibition of any such future expression of civil opposition, however peaceful. Tempers grew fast, as they are like to do when faced with a bewildering engulfment of regime over liberty; insults, accusations and liabilities augmented, so in most no time at all what had begun, surely, with the best intent, flew fast beyond control in quite the opposite direction. How torches came then to be carried west towards the Docks, and warehouses set alight, is neither yet disclosed nor explained. I remember your once speculating in correspondence at what may suddenly be achieved through 'vehement indignation' and how 'futile' this accomplishment will generally transpire to be. Yet in terms of their momentum, it seems a quite distinct digression to turn west at all, when to a man and under oath their unified intent was wide declared to take their grievances direct to Westminster. Confusion of detail and timing notwithstanding, I am reliably informed that the majority of these instigators reached the lobby of St Stephen's Chapel at not long after a half past five, gaining considerable support along the way. From my previous letter you will know something of the chaos and destruction wreaked as they progressed and have some impression of how they had unprecedented multiplied in both size and indignation.

Now again to Westminster within, where I have it on reliable authority (yes, the Colonel) that upon that very afternoon Lord Batty-Bathurst had been speaking, thus most of the house who had assembled just before five were deep asleep by a half past, the required social distance between each within the Chapel allowing most to lie stretched out upon the benches. Taking advantage of the peace and general indolence, the betrayer (the name of whom is suspected by me, and known by the Colonel who is under oath not to reveal it) stood and – in a choking whisper – denounced our Filo as an 'incompetent, deceitful and poorly-groomed buffoon who was a disgrace to our fair empire.' This was nothing unusual. What *was* unprecedented, however, was the immediate arrival of a band of 'soldiers of fortune' consisting no more than ten rifle men, who had been personally commissioned by said rival. In their stockinged feet, so as not to wake the slumbering inmates, they stationed themselves at strategic points within the Chapel, taking aim towards the Primus Inter Pares and Lord B. Being a man possessed of reasonable good sense, readily available for emergencies and celebrations alike, the esteemed Filo calmly offered to remove his own person and to resign his tenure. This he clearly did with fingers crossed behind his back yet, notwithstanding this, for that present moment he allowed himself to have an old plague mask stuck square upon his head and then to be led contrite away (while a rifleman encouraged Batty to resume his lullaby). As fate would have it, it was just as he was led into the lobby, which had previous been deserted, that it filled completely with the front-line mayhem of the Limehouse crowd. Seizing his chance, the wily Filo fell at once upon his knees and crawled his way between and round the legs of all, and out escaping into liberty where he disappeared unheeded within the throng. At this, the good rival, seeing the simmering mass before him, and being in favour of keeping his skin as a priority, ordered his riflemen to fire as one into the air, which startled the crowd quite, yet not enough to subdue entire. Another like shot was ordered and then a third threatened towards the rioters. That second woke the Serjeant within the Chapel and he at once sprung to action, ordering his men to take up arms. (It may be noted here that all but one of the tavern instigators were later found to be unarmed, mentioned to no avail in their defence as proof that their original intent had not been one of violence.) While many of their gathered supporters had joined armed with bricks, brooms and, in some cases, pitchforks, these were clearly no match for firearms. Thus, they were swiftly subdued. Without their leaders, the crowd outside knew no longer what to do, and the resulting many hours of rioting and destruction were evidently a result of an energy and anger provoked to the point of anarchy that must find outlet somewhere, I suppose.

It was not until many days later that Filo's whereabouts and well-being were confirmed. It transpires that once he had trotted forth, he made his way as fast and furious as he might far out of the city. After a heartening supper and a good night's sleep he set about slowly gathering his supporters over several days, then returned well after the rioting had been contained, regained control within the Commons and had his rival immediate locked up (though as I understand it, he has since been released for 'acting heroic under the circumstances' and will now serve out the year for the sake of 'cabinet stability.' A noble and interesting idea. It was well done in the end, I suppose, for Filo had been but ten days in office before he was removed and it might have set a bad precedent for another First Leader to be deposed so soon. (In actuality I regret the flippancy of that last remark. Perceval was a man of predominant integrity, deserving of my greater respect.)

It is an irony indeed that while the betrayer will soon enough face an ignoble, yet certainly rather privileged, exile, those alleged to be the instigators of the riots were arrested and brought to trial within a week, found guilty to a man then dispatched the week subsequent. So goes justice for the Commoner. It is of interest to me to note that lockdown had been forcefully reinstated once more before sentencing was served. I know not what you have heard regarding Mr Bellingham, yet

I will tell you that although all did not go well for him, he did engender the most tremendous support for his cause nonetheless.

There, now you know all I do. Would I prefer to have told you once again of peaceful folk, engaged in calm but necessary civic queries – for none should just accept their lot? Yes, I would. I abhor savagery, as you know. Whatever the provocation or injustice felt, there can surely be no excuse for the maelstrom of anarchy and fear unleashed upon a city already overwrought? It was ill-conceived in the extreme.

Yet, in this case I wonder – what could the government expect having thus unjustly acted in response to so peaceful an initial protest? Why must we accept time and again that those in so called 'power' overbalance and forget their vows of service? In families, schools, universities, factories, we find those who must exploit, insult, demean, misuse. These are not benevolent leaders seeking a fair and just world, but ego-driven over-lords who have clawed their way into a tenuous security, believing its sustenance requires the almost constant striking out at those whom they perceive to threaten their strong-hold. It is not for the common good, but for their own good entirely. They hide – often behind a well-publicised philanthropy – which means nothing save that they might continue their ignoble deeds without discovery. They will broach no competition; they will not play fair. Why should this matter? They are just one man, or woman, even, are they not? My answer, it should not. Yet they are so generally and ably supported by those who believe they might gain from their benevolence. A crumb dropped here and there. Fools! Worse, there are always those who enjoy and endorse the subjugation of their fellow man. Yes, it will out, will it not? Months of repression, fear, starvation turned all to anarchy, unleashed and unbridled. Retrospectively, I was fortunate to pass unheeded.

I had a friend at university who was quite convinced of an elite power that controlled our kings, our queens and politicians. His theories were far-fetched and oftentimes he was the earnest recipient of much mirth at his expense. He had penned a novel for which – and in spite of ample connections – he could find no publisher. I was asked to read it, and I did so. It was well-written indeed. The story of himself as hero within a world so bleak, so without any freedom or joys that one could hardly bear to turn the pages. A world where friends were turned enemy through fear, encouraged to report upon one another for the slightest infringement of an endless set of rules designated 'for their own good.' Most were kept in a poverty of spirit, deprived of literature and art. The least educated of the population were cleverly sustained by a fairly constant supply of undemanding entertainment, inexpensive alcohol and food. Thus, they were, he felt, unrousable. His hero attempted a small rebellion, almost immediately quashed, and he swiftly dispatched to Elysium. Finis. It was a hopeless tale indeed, but yes, well-written. When asked to give an opinion I told him true that while I admired his workmanship, I failed to comprehend why he had not sought to give the reader hope. 'Because I saw none,' he replied. It is that which does not help. There is always hope, for there will always be change, always a striving for balance. There will always be new desires and those with energy enough to see them through. Yet we may not sit idle and plead for a world of freedom and joy in which we have no input. We must be that we wish to see. I lost a friend that day. He desired my help to publish and I refused it if he would not change the end. He would not. Yet I stand by my decision to this day. The world may oft be disposed to a petty ghoulishness which many a lowbrow novel will easily supply, yet we are always in truest and most earnest need of hope to cheer us forward, and there is a responsibility to be met in this.

To continue upon a theme, my Aunt and Miss Bingley do not do well together. I am unsure as to why I thought they would; a similarity in character, perhaps. Evidently this does not necessarily a natural friendship make. It is amusing enough to witness I suppose. Almost every evening Lady Catherine will ask Miss Bingley to describe how her father came upon his fortune. As her guest, Miss Bingley is naturally obliged to answer, as well my Aunt knows, and she does so with increasingly evident annoyance, which only encourages Lady Catherine further.

Miss Bingley then invariably asks my Aunt with great concern if she is 'in good health?' To which Lady Catherine raps back 'how else should I be? I am always in excellent health.'

'Oh, I am sure of it,' declares Miss Bingley with all due sincerity. 'It must be the candlelight gives you that unfortunate pallor.'

A silence usually follows, broken only as Bingley nervously cracks his knuckles and is stared down by his sister.

Then, 'how is your dear Mama?'

'She is gone these several years your Ladyship.'

'Ah yes, I do remember now. My condolences. How she must have suffered.'

Miss Bingley keeps her eyes upon the tablecloth.

'I lost my own dear Mother when I was considerably younger than you. That was much worse, I assure you. I was sixteen. That is no age. You are more fortunate than I was.'

Here Bingley will attempt to intervene, but to no avail.

'Yet I bore through with stoicism, I assure you. As I do everything. Had I been but five it would have made no difference.'

'Indeed, your Ladyship is all that is most singular.'

A further silence. The Colonel shuffles a little in his chair.

Then, 'how is your dear husband, Lady Catherine?' They stare at each other for a moment. Lady Catherine almost smiles, but returns instead to her soup.

'My condolences,' continues Miss Bingley. 'How he must have suffered.'

'Not at all!' Barks Lady Catherine. 'That man was blessed each day of our union.'

'Indeed,' seizing the advantage in a ringing voice. 'I hear he was a saint.'

Silence reigns again.

'Oh, for heaven's sake,' mutters Anne to the centrepiece.

'Yes, yes,' continues Lady Catherine as if anyone had asked. 'It is a most terrible shame to make one's fortune from trade. Oh, I understand it, money must be acquired somehow. One must not let one's family starve, I suppose. Yet it is so very shameful, so against the natural order of our world.

We must accept where we are born, must we not? Not try to force ourselves upon our superiors and buy our way into their kingdom. You see, my dear Miss Bingley we, those of our ilk (gesturing at her relations, both seated and in portraits), know how best to order this world. Without us, our tenants would starve or become utterly feckless. Most people, you see, are foolish and not to be trusted. That is why they will always need us.'

Miss Bingley bites her thumb.

'Do you not agree?'

Of course she does, yet her confusion and fury makes it nigh impossible to concede to my Aunt.

'What was the business to which your father leant his 'skills,' pray?'

'I do not think it good to dwell upon the past, Lady Catherine. My brother means to purchase an estate, it is only a matter of time, and when he does...'

'Yet I do hear that many 'trades' have been most grievously affected by this lockdown. Some will not recover.' Says Lady Catherine, taking a mournful sip.

'Yet to us that matters not.'

'Indeed? How so?'

Miss Bingley's spoon clatters to her bowl and she stands up hurriedly. My Aunt dabs at the corners of her mouth with a napkin and affects not to notice. One might think the napkin is used to quell a smirk.

Bingley reaches swiftly for his sister's hand, declaring 'I have often thought, indeed, what a very pleasant thing it will be to own my own land.'

'Why do you not do it then, young man? Idleness, perhaps?'

'Oh undoubtedly, Lady Catherine. Yet it also stems from a sincere desire to find the right property. I have not the temperament to settle upon simply any estate. It must be a place with whom my heart agrees. I am sure you feel so here.'

'I have no idea what you mean young man,' snaps my Aunt, sensing the slip of her victory and turning in the direction of greater sport. 'Your brother may not vote, Miss Bingley? Nor your father before him? It is my certain belief that no man who cannot vote should ever be allowed to own land. Anne, do not stoop! If I had my way,' she continues 'I would return all merchants to their proper place. They must give back every last coin of their ill-acquired fortunes and return to the position which God decreed for them in life.'

While Bingley simply laughs quietly and gently pulls his dispirited sister to her seat, Anne of a sudden slams her spoon upon her plate.

'What utter nonsense Mama!' she cries. 'You are so old-fashioned it makes my head ache.' This is a new addition to the evening conversation, and we are all a little taken aback. 'What you speak of is a cruel, regressive order which binds the many in poverty while the few…'

'Good heavens, calm yourself child,' her mother interjects smoothly. 'Does she not sound the very likeness of a French peasant?'

The Colonel clears his throat. 'If I may…'

'No.' She does not take her eyes from her daughter. 'Oh, do go on, Anne. Do share your opinions. We are all fascinated, are we not? No doubt they are amply well-conceived. Speak up! You approve La Révolution?'

She would not dare. The interruption has done its work. With a slight shake in her voice Anne continues in half a whisper. 'I…well, no. N-not quite. Yet they were driven to it. Fear is a terrible thing, Mama. It urges people to commit the most hideous acts.'

'Ah yes! Decapitating others? You applaud that do you? La guillotine!' Lady Catherine is prone to a rather copious imbibing these days which encourages a certain loquacity upon subjects of which she would in general refuse to speak. 'You would have it so?'

'No Mama.'

'Liberté, égalité, fraternité? You wish for it?'

'I-I do.'

'She does! Oh, the irony. She believes she would not be the very first upon the scaffold!'

'N-not the beheading.'

'What, then? Give up your life of comfort? I do not think so.'

'I would not. Yet I believe...that all...should live in peace and...security.'

'She believes! Foolish child. You cannot give these reptiles equality with us. They would abuse it, that I can tell you. As for security, why, it is a dream told to infants and idiots alike, for only they would believe a moment in its prospect.'

Miss Bingley laughs nervously, out of relief, one hopes, that the onus no longer rests upon her. Anne's eyes dart towards her and, evidently perceiving this a slight upon herself, loses all remaining self-assurance and lowers her head.

'But are they reptiles?' Muses the Colonel, as tactfully as he may. My Aunt quells him with a look. I would speak, yet for the life of me can think of absolutely nothing that might be of suitable diversion. It is at such times as these that I remember how formidable she once appeared when I was yet a child.

Anne inhales audibly, which her Ladyship chooses to observe as the commencement of the vapours.

'Ah, here it is! She always was an emotional child. We could do nothing with her, try as we may. A handkerchief Mr Bingley, you are closest, do not let her use a napkin for heaven's sake, it is so uncouth.' With the utmost compassion, Bingley passes the requested article.

'Where Wav'ring Man, betray'd by vent'rous Pride, To tread the dreary Paths without a Guide,' cites Lady Catherine sadly. 'Poor child. You are quite simply out of sorts through a chronic disobedience and lack of duty. A structured life is what a person requires, far more than – what was it she said, nephew – 'peace and security?' Good heavens, what an idea! That a daughter of mine should speak such nonsense! Our rights are taken, and then held on to. That is how it is. Is it not so, Miss Bingley?'

Another slight laugh and the thumb is bitten again. 'Good grief, do stop shaking Anne; you make an ogre of me.'

Miss Bingley clears her throat softly and ventures:

'A suitable match would be just the thing. So very settling. Why, you are *quite* attractive Miss de Bourgh.'

'Yes, yes, her features are not unremarkable, yet she has her father's hands and feet.'

'Oh dear,' Miss Bingley nods in unqualified sympathy and a moment of affinity flickers between the two, then goes out as quickly as it came.

Anne nods, almost to herself it seems, and without another word departs the room in haste.

The Colonel stands almost immediately, murmurs that he must retire to his room. He never has been one to endure a scene.

Another silence as he awaits permission, then Lady Catherine flicks a hand towards him.

'Go after her will you. You alone seem proficient enough to handle her tantrums; I confess, it is beyond me.'

The Colonel remembers to bow, and departs swiftly enough. 'Stark raving mad, is she not Mr Bingley? Well, however your father may have made his money, I would not wish you such a wife for all the cotton mills in Lancashire.'

Lady Catherine then drums her fingers upon the tablecloth, darting accusatory glances at each of us in turn, before fixing her eye upon me.

'Where is your sister, nephew? Are we to have two renegades together in this household?'

I affect not to hear and those of us who remain return to our cold soup in a silence of self-conscious discomfort.

I admit freely that while I am indeed and in general grateful for the presence of my sister and friends, like yourself, whilst I weathered the first lockdown well enough, I have found the second enforcement a far greater challenge. My faith has been sorely tested; my powers of reason confounded. So much of what I hear matches not entirely what my senses do reveal. Perhaps this has ever been the way, yet it seems heightened in our second isolation. Moreover, I feel less myself than I have ever known. I am beset with thoughts of freedoms past of which I did not full partake. Contrary to a previous implication, for which I received a most just rebuke, I find I have not danced as much as I would wish, nor even conversed as freely. I have never taken the waters at Bath; I have no wish to, yet I should like to know I could should the impulse come upon me. Yes, that says all. It unsettles to imagine that existence may continue so, that our freedoms could now be far behind us with much of life as yet unlived. I do not believe it possible. No. This is the last brief burst, I am sure of that. We will be free again, and soon, and this present time will seem but as a dream.

(Courage, man. Would you have the lady think you a milksop?)

How do you find the constant mask-wearing within?

If the tonic to which you refer is that which is government endorsed, then your cousin's appointment is not courtesy of her Ladyship, but instead, as I understand it, a 'voluntary' matter, although all gentlemen of the cloth are 'strongly encouraged' so to do. The Colonel has hinted that it was devised by a close relative of one within the House of Lords and he is extolled now within the highest circles as a hero, though by report it seems little more than a violent expectorant. I speak not against nepotism per sae, for without it I would not enjoy my own position. I am certain, also, that I would wish to increase whatever opportunities I may to advance my own future children in their lives. Yet it is not guaranteed that a person of strong ability, character or intelligence will produce a like offspring. You may only look at the vastly different nature of siblings, even, to illustrate my point. Incidentally, Miss Bingley, rich in the feeling of benevolence it seems, has also volunteered and is producing bottles with a red velvet bow tied around the neck of each and her name signed upon the label. Having a mind for business, she is also charging for them.

With what else may I regale you *(in the hope of diverting your attention from a determination to be irked)*?

I do not disagree regarding the fate of the younger son, yet it is evident that what is a Shibboleth to one or many, may suit another and just as many well. I may not concur with the arrangement of an entailment, for example, yet it is evident that those who stand to benefit might well consider such a very fine agreement.

This second quarantine has proved too much for many within the village and they struggle to sustain themselves. My Aunt has risen to the occasion and designated duties to us all of alms-giving. This has become something of a rivalry between Anne and Miss Bingley who are often to be found these days crocheting furiously in the drawing room. Anne has also made a series of pomanders with hot-house oranges and cloves. I could not help but wonder if the underprivileged might, instead, prefer to *eat* an orange than hang it in their home, but must say nothing out of deference for her efforts. You see, I learn to hesitate to speak my mind, in case of offence.

I did not ask your opinion regarding my sister, this is true, but I am grateful for your suggestion that she may indeed have endured some loneliness in London. I am seldom troubled by such myself and had not thought of it, so will find a way to gently enquire. As regards a companion at Grosvenor, indeed she had. Unbeknown to me, the woman fled within a fortnight of lockdown, in spite of promises to the contrary and a considerable gratuity. Georgiana did not inform me of her absence when she should, having 'no wish to alarm me.' Naturally I will speak further to her on this matter, for deceit of any kind is not excusable, but I await a suitable moment.

You mentioned the risible friendship contrived by a person of wealth and a paid companion. Although I have gathered no evidence, I believe that it is not always as you suppose. Many a genuine friendship has prospered between a Queen and a Lady in Waiting, I imagine, or a gentleman and his manservant. A governess and her charges, even, might find an enduring bond beyond childhood.

Contrary to which, my cousin's companion Mrs Jenkinson was one such mentioned in earlier correspondence who left my Aunt's employ at the beginning of lockdown, and could not be prevailed upon to stay under any pretext, be it financial, out of the oft referred to (by my Aunt) gratitude for the placement of her nieces, or for the sake of Anne. In fairness, she was quite clearly terrified at the prospect of being taken ill, and determined that Anne would be the most likely candidate for transmission. Needless to say, my cousin was inconsolable. Quoth she, 'Jenkinson was a tiresome old bore who made herself indispensable by insisting there was something wrong with me when there was not. Naturally, she and my mother were in accord. I do not miss her and am glad to be rid of her.'

In considering the joys of actual friendship, Miss Bingley tries whenever she may, I have noticed, to encourage a confidence with Georgiana to the exclusion of Anne. I am happy to say that this Georgiana does not allow. Yet is this behaviour usual within feminine circles? I do not admire such exclusionary schemes; it does the inceptor no credit. Nor do I admire what you convey concerning your treatment by the Collinses. You are their guest. It is not correct to school, interrogate or insult you.

You cannot – must not – await approval or agreement by the world (or your relatives). Far more important that you are in agreement with yourself. This is Anne's great misunderstanding, for she must needs persuade her mother to her point of view and thus casts herself within an endless loop, painful to witness.

Yours etc.

P. S: I am sure you are quite correct concerning roisterers! Yet, it is passing strange to me, for you write as one from deprivation, or so it seems.

P.P.S: Neither. It simply struck me just how many names by which an 'Elizabeth' might be known. Have you a preference?

P.P.P.S: You spoke of the presence of your ancestors. Is this, indeed, a good thing? I was raised surrounded by portrait upon portrait of my own, and may attest to it being a somewhat dubious blessing.

P.P.P.P.S: Incidentally, considering the considerable information to which I am party, it would seem, upon reflection, that the Colonel might well be accused of being rather indiscreet. Yet as he is all affability and consideration, we must surely allow for this small failing?

Letter 4

Monday 24th August, Hunsford Parsonage

Sir,

I write from my exile in the Hunsford kitchen, where I have been sent that my 'scratching' pen doth not keep his lordship awake. Once I have finished this letter, I fully intend to take the miniature gong from his study, creep my way up the stairs and clang it booming loud before his door. This will, I hope, give a clear indication to you of the temperament in which I am inclined to make reply to your most recent communication.

How very convenient it is for you to write thus. In one breath you both admit culpability regarding my sister, and refuse to accept responsibility for the harm you have caused; for I am the petty one, am I not, for yet considering an event of months ago that while having reached no satisfactory resolution in mine own eyes, is long since passed in yours? How typical it now seems to me, that you should feel no shame *(yet how greatly I am private saddened and perplexed, for in our correspondence you had seemed so altered. So capable of broad-mindedness, of humour and compassion).* I am grateful, at least, that you saw fit to give the slightest consideration to my family in terms of our reputation and feelings, yet I would remark that in boasting of your 'triumph' to anyone – however close a confidant – you risked both repetition and discovery. The secret being out, I will give my emphatic assurance that you will cause no (further) pain to my family, for nothing would induce me to repeat what I have heard. That is how poorly I think of it!

I wish you to understand that whether you trouble yourself to explain your motivations to me or no, I do yet comprehend them perfectly *(how characteristic that you imagine I may not)*. Yet I would argue that *you* do not fully comprehend your own actions. You have utterly misjudged what you have witnessed, of this I am certain, not least in your conviction that my sister has sustained no 'deep hurt'. How do you dare to make so outrageous a supposition, or claim to comprehend the inner-most feelings of another? You have misrepresented my sister shamefully and you have taken upon yourself a determination that should have been your friend's alone to make. I do not doubt that he is used to such governance in you, yet that does not make it proper. I would further venture that you counselled not in the interest of his happiness, but rather to facilitate your own *(and that of Miss Bingley, no doubt, for what more perfect arrangement could she possibly imagine than herself as your wife, and then a union between her brother and your sister).*

You criticise my lack of frankness? Again, you distribute blame most freely. I had no wish to render an accusation for which I had no proof, therefore I waited until the Colonel might either clarify or deny my suspicions. For many months indeed, it was Miss Bingley to whom I attributed the dubious credit of their separation and it was not until the very end of May that my doubts were entirely roused. Nevertheless, if you truly believe it 'futile' to offer a reasonable justification for your actions *(for, of course, you cannot)* then I will press no further. Know that you have done nothing to dissuade me from a grievous low opinion of the standards of behaviour which you have set for yourself concerning this matter (and others*).

You speak of 'exclusionary schemes' as being a bafflement to you, another mystery belonging solely to the domain of feckless female-kind? Is it possible that you can see no irony in this statement? The exclusion of my sister notwithstanding, I am astounded that you, of all men, should make a claim at such naivety*.

I am not fanciful, I refute that *(how characteristic that you imagine a single striking out of words on your part will decide the recipient not to read them)*. I appreciate the natural world in all its variety, wonder and magnificence. Sometimes, yes, I must think as you say, who can help it? Of course, I like it not, yet I accept that nature will do as it will and there seems a certain order to it, hard as that may be to comprehend. It is we who might do differently, with more compassion, consideration and, frankly, less greed.

(Regarding your opinion upon nepotism and the dissimilarities between parents, 'offspring' and, indeed, siblings, I may fair safe assume that it was not Jane's own sweet nature which engendered your objections. An impossibility if ever there was one. Therefore, no doubt at all, it would be your judgement of our 'low' relations — in spite of contrary and clearly fanciful declarations of 'broader views' on Cheapside — and, worst of all, may heaven help me, my own near and most dear. With a sigh I must in private concede a slight, a very slight, incline to my understanding of a reservation concerning, perhaps, my youngest sister and — forgive me — my Mama. Indeed, were I disposed to think more kindly of you I might feel obliged to

blush yet at the discomfort of that particular evening. Yet why this should be used as cause to overlook Jane's own countless virtues, I cannot comprehend. Mr Bingley must be of weak character indeed, to be so easily persuaded. Well, I care not how Mama recommends herself to you. It seems there are few capable of meeting your criteria. How Mama recommends herself to <u>me</u>, however, is all that is of matter. Therefore, I shall be sure to mention her, indeed all of my family, copiously in the future, as an antidote to both your prejudice and how aching much that I do miss them. How I wish the post, at least, might be allowed to resume.)

The other day I thought of music and it dawned upon me that I have heard none (Charlotte's past singing aside) since that last evening at Rosings *(and that of a shocking poor standard)*. How I wish the thought had not occurred to me, for now I think of music constantly and long to hear my sister Mary play. She is quite proficient, you know, yet I have ne'er full appreciated her diligence till now. I was happier before I missed it, I believe.

You will indulge me, I hope, for I find that I must speak at length of my family far away in Longbourn, for I do miss them sore. I will begin by enlightening you, as much as ever I may, to Mama's dear nature. I will speak frank, that you and she be better acquainted *(and to enlighten you concerning that which you so determinedly misunderstand).* She is a lover of music yet a quite abominable singer, her voice being always off-key, yet her enthusiasm knows no bounds and one cannot help but love and admire her for it, albeit through a veil of tears of suppressed laughter in church. Likewise, dancing and the opportunity to dance is almost irresistible to her. Were it not for her daughters and the priority she designates to us as our Mama, I am certain she would always be the first up and afoot. At home, she will oft appear at a skip within the drawing room when Mary is persuaded to play a gig, full of gladness and irrepressible rhythm. On each and every Christmas she will make for every one of us small bags of cloves and lavender, beautifully embroidered; thus, now in Hunsford, I have a jar of cloves set by within my chamber to open that I might be reminded close of home. Although, officially she does not cook, she is an accomplished and affectionate baker of cakes – her Twelfth Night cake is rightly famous and we all look forward to the making of it each year, and the anticipation of the accolade of 'Queen of the Celebration' to whomsoever is fortunate enough to find the bean. She has a vast collection of bags and bonnets, but can seldom find one to hand, therefore before she leaves the house, we must all hunt for whichever bag and bonnet is the current favourite. It is seldom, if ever, where last it was seen *(in truth, that is often somewhat frustrating)*. What else may I tell you *(that you have no wish to know)*? Mama loves animals and greets all canine and feline residents as the dearest of long-lost friends whenever she, or they, return home.

Mama's childhood was rather different to ours. Her father was a cheerless man. Of an evening they would all be forced to sit in silence upon hardbacked chairs while he ate sweets that he shared not. He seldom worked, although naturally he owned property, and money was always rather scarce. Her own Mama was present and yet somehow absent, though kind enough. When Mama was but six years old her little legs were so thin that she got one caught within a gap in an old wooden bridge and remained there for an entire day until her absence was finally felt and a rescue achieved. When Mama and Aunt Phillips were of age and late home from a ball, their father insisted that they remain out of doors all night to learn the value of punctuality, though it were bitter cold — they slept at last in a stable and covered themselves with straw. They had no dowry, yet were expected to care for their father as he aged. When he passed, it was discovered that he had willed every penny of his estate to a distant relative whom he had never met. Thankfully our Uncle Gardiner had by then achieved much advancement in his profession and always professed to 'care not' at his exclusion. I have ruminated much of late how very fortunate I am that our household is, instead, warm and loving, albeit it chaotic. Oh yes, when I had scarlet fever at fifteen, Mama stayed with me throughout and slept upon my chamber floor each night so as to be near to me, yet not disturb my rest.

Papa, as you may know, prefers a quieter life of peaceful contemplation. Mama is often irritated for he takes 'so little interest in the vast majority of our children,' yet I have often thought his lack of interference perceivable as quite the kindness, for we have lived in a most enviable freedom, I should think, and – importantly, you will agree – with opportunities abound to expand upon our minds by extensive reading, if we should wish it. Papa's library is substantial and delightfully diverse, with books that overspill to many different rooms (and stairways) within the house. Of course, I am aware that it has often been remarked in Meryton and among our acquaintance, that my father is somewhat 'detached' within his own family. Yet I find it very fine that he need not remind himself of his own masculine 'superiority' by domination.

Besides, it amuses me that any of his critics imagine he might have the slightest say where Mama is concerned, even should he wish it. She is quite the tornado when she desires to be, nothing less. It is important, though, for a mother of five daughters to have spirit, do you not think?

I wonder if you could comprehend this, being a man of your station. Or simply, being a man. You see, Mama is afeard that she will be without a home in time. So much so, that oft she can conceive of little else. She has come to think only of bricks and mortar. She pushes all of us onwards, regardless of how we (or she) may truly feel, for she must have an assurance that her home will somehow remain. I wish I could persuade her to treasure what she has, but the entailment of our estate afflicts her grievously. How could it not? Through Mama I have come to understand (previous to the Unmentionable) what it is to live in fear for one's future well-being, even if to all other eyes one has nothing at all to be afeard of. She suffers cruelly with her nerves, and although this is something of a fond *(trying)* amusement within our home, it clear seems very real to her. It should not be thus. So many of our systems are Shibboleths, as you say. Why do we not question more? You witness 'impropriety' perhaps, and do not question the necessity which may drive a person reckless forward. If you did, perhaps you could be kinder.

Yet why must we fret so? Felicity seldom does. She lives within the present moment – sleeping when she wishes, washing regardless of whom she offends, ignoring whosoever holds no interest for her. Mama worries almost constantly; Papa, as if he is some ancient and pre-ordained opposing force, worries not at all. It is not, I hasten to add, because he inherently believes that all will be well, but rather that he noticed in his early years that worry is 'most ineffective and solves nothing,' therefore he saves his energies. I may tell you too, that Mama also worries incessantly about who may have noticed or passed judgement upon her behaviour. This manifests itself as a sort of constant sense of defiance. For his part, naturally, Papa worries not one bit concerning how he is perceived. 'I never have been all that troubled, Lizzy,' he told me when once I enquired. 'Yet had I been so, your Mama's stalwart efforts to draw attention to the error of my ways would either have made a wreck of me, or a non-believer in the value of an externalised perception of one's qualities. To my mind, the more self-conscious we are, the more insufferable we become. Thank heavens you always say what you mean, child.' I would hasten to add that I do not 'always' speak with absolute freedom, for I might offend when it is far better to hold my tongue and laugh in private. Besides, I am certain that there is very much of the ridiculous about my own person, and I would not be such a charlatan as to publicly laugh at others, whilst imagining no faults of my own.

I find a sleeping cat or dog the most peaceful of sights. How completely they repose, with such commitment to the delights of relaxation. I envy it, particularly now. I am suddenly unable to sleep a night through. I wake and worry, wake and worry. This morning, before it was even light or the first bird had chirruped, I was absolutely wide awake with a mind so full of concerns for the future that it took the most violent of internal wrestling not to shout aloud as a relief of nerves.

Did you ever experience a feeling of fear so intense that you thought it might engulf you? In recent years I have studiously developed the ability to appear calm when I am perhaps not quite so. It is a necessary factor for one who must enter society, is it not? We must all pretend. Hardly an original thought. Do not misunderstand me, I have the greatest respect for the evolution of etiquette (the artful Earl of Chesterfield notwithstanding!). Yet I cannot but wonder whether we do ourselves harm in the suffocation of our feelings for fear of impropriety. We are a nation designed to be repelled by ungainly displays of emotion, are we not? Yet these sensibilities are a part of who we are. What must we do? Are we to be in an inner-conflict perpetually, so that Great Aunts throughout the land may remain unflustered? I say again, I have become a master of repression, yet the feelings remain – they are not conquered, not dissolved. One matter is certain, it seems a harder task to repress these stifled finer feelings for the sake of our close society within this second, more stringent quarantine. Nothing makes sense but the longing to taste freedom once more. If he were able, my father would tell me to 'shake up, Lizzy, shake up,' and he would be perfectly right. I am not used to these doldrums. Four siblings will stir the misery out of you in no time at all, I assure you. How I miss them all. *(Even Lydia.)*

I believe I am afraid that this is how life must be now, forever and a day. That we must all get used to it and, worse, *will* get used to it. I do not enjoy this feeling of helplessness. I wish I had left Hunsford when the riots occurred, made my own way back to Longbourn. I know not why I hesitated; I would not do so now.

(Pull yourself together Elizabeth! He will not care! Do you wish him to think of you with pity? Besides,

you do know right well why you hesitated; you paused several days to pack and say your farewells, did you not? Well, you are wiser now. No person who wishes to achieve a full and effective escape may possibly pause to pack first. They must leave immediate with the clothes in which they are dressed. I am sure of this.)

These days, Charlotte is constantly cleaning and moving furniture. While Mr Collins is greatly in favour of the former — for cleanliness is next to Wesleyness — he is most decidedly disturbed by the latter. His wife's alterations to the arrangement in the parlour caused him so much consternation, indeed, that he who lifts no finger but in the service of God (and Lady Catherine) betook himself down the stairs an hour past his bedtime (creak-squeak-sneaky-creeeky-squeak) and turned it all around again. Seemingly his outrage was stronger than his memory, for it yet looks nothing like it did before. Prideful creature that he is, he will not own the difference and has twice this evening sat upon a chair that was not there, whereupon we both must look away, affecting not to notice as he flails upon the floor. Ridiculous are his ways. The first posterior-bounce surprised me so I almost laughed aloud, yet timely choked instead. May I assure you that within my chamber I have laughed a-plenty, so bug-like did he look. I am thankful for a cause to laugh. Thankful to that Slubberdegullion, is it possible? I would add, incidentally, that it is quite incredible to witness how very little God seems ever to ask my cousin to actually *do*.

We have a rather lively badger who admits himself into our grounds at night and rampages about to his heart's content, digging extravagant holes in the lawns and uprooting wherever he sees fit in search of grubs. I do not begrudge him. He has a right to go as he pleases and I am rather fond of the little rolling rogue. Naturally Mr Collins — amateur naturalist that he is — believes the holes to be somehow dug by our Rochester neighbours and is all a-fluster. I am resolved not to undeceive him, for fear he decides to forcibly remove our new friend. Tempted as I am to feed and encourage the little chap further, I resist. He is clearly more than capable of foraging well for himself and I have no wish to create a need that is not there.

I am well aware of the sad circumstances within the village, for I hear Mr Collins saunter forth each alternate day to benevolently distribute your Aunt's bounty. If it has not added to his popularity exactly, then neither has it hurt it. He returns with quite the beneficent glow, for indeed there is nothing quite like giving other people's money away. Incidentally, and somewhat inappropriately, it may be noted that Mr Collins chose to donate several of Miss de Bourgh's intricate pomanders to himself, eating the fruit in quarters of an evening and then cramming strips of the peel into his nostrils to ward off further ailments.

Regarding the constant mask wearing, I confess I do not take to it at all. Perhaps if it extended to the winter – heaven forbid – it would feel of some benefit, increasing internal warmth so greatly as it does. I will admit freely that when I am away from others, and alone, it is removed. I would also add that there is much about the rules of when a mask may or may not be effectively worn that I simply do not understand. On this I will say no more, except to tentatively suggest that perhaps such a small piece of material may seem rather flimsy to offer much protection from a disease that 'vengeful sweeps the globe seeking out the unrighteous' (Mr Collins, who has convenient forgotten he was among the first to have it). Yet I am most grateful nonetheless not to have contracted my cousin's latest summer cold. Rather than a handkerchief, which I regret to relay is, according to the Law of Collins, only to be used for blotting one's forehead or perspiring philtrum, certainly not one's nose, my cousin has taken to sneezing repeatedly within his mask and this does seem to have proved, somehow, protector.

I see your 'Supper at Rosings' narrative and raise you 'an Evening at Hunsford Parsonage'. The scene is set in the parlour. A fire is lit in the grate, with one log only for the evening (which begins promptly at six and lasts until the chime of a half past nine). Later, the candles are lit with reluctance and an eye upon their cost. Mr Collins reads ponderously loud from a small selection of possibilities that might all be entitled 'Upon the Inherent Inferiority of the Female,' carefully surveying both Charlotte and I for irrepressible yawns (or snores). These are greeted with tuts and extravagant throat-clearances. No window may be opened, even though the walls close in upon one quite and – were one less refined – one might feel quite desperate to spring up and yell, or pound one's chest. I am not to read; I am simply to sit. Charlotte is permitted to darn, being in less dire need of reformation than I. Mr Collins must have quite the heavy tread, for he wears through his socks like no other. Or perhaps his perspiration is so bile-some that it dissolves wool. Worse yet, we are expected to nod and give assenting murmurs, that he might feel secure and encouraged in his endeavours. Thankfully he seems impervious to my inner mutiny and his inherent vanity prevents him from discerning the irony with which I utter 'hmmm.' Sometimes I wonder if my night-time anxieties are truly as a result of the Unmentionable and our currently uncertain future, or these tortuous evenings during which my heart pounds to pain throughout, most fervent for escape. I may yet throttle him.

Concerning my evening reformations, I am given to understand that my cousin is most vehemently afraid that I will run amuck as Maria has done. Indeed, his fear of Maria has become almost extraordinary. While he will not tolerate her to be mentioned, even indirectly, he yet speaks often and at length of 'wicked temptresses' in 'gardens of licentiousness' who 'futile endeavour to tempt' him by being 'shameful under-dressed.' On earlier occasions, when I yet would try to speak of her, he would at once turn to Charlotte and cry 'you know what I have suffered!'

Oftentimes, I cannot help but glance at Mr Collins and think 'this is the man to whom my friend belongs.' Belongs. She is his property. How is it possible for anyone in these modern times still to 'own' another person? Is this not slavery? Yet you will say, 'Mrs Collins gave her consent freely,' I believe, and I would answer 'as free as a woman of past six and twenty might do in our society.'

An idea propagated, that a woman – or indeed any creature – is of a lesser value than another, deserving of cruel treatment, or censure, or demeaning circumstances, is to carry forward the most wicked of notions. Must we continue to teach that women are play things to be trifled with? That we are here only to be as ornaments or trinkets, easily used and discarded? It is a wrong to us. It is a wrong to men to raise them such cruel fools. Thank heavens there are those of your sex with heart enough to find their way through the maelstrom of miseducation and fundamental irksomeness. There is hope yet.

(Still, I must marvel more, that we exist in a world so entirely at the mercy of men. That we are, by law, their possessions, to do with as they will. This cannot endure, I am certain. If I perceive this now a wrong, then others must do also. I cannot imagine that in two more centuries women could still be raised without autonomy of their own person, to feel despised or outcast if they are not wed, or to have their every youthful thought directed solely towards their physical allure, the better to captivate a wealthy man. We will be as equals then, I am sure of it. It cannot be otherwise.)

Whenever *(if ever)* we are finally, truly, free, I am resolved to waste not a single other moment of my life in idling, out of courtesy, with those with whom I have no sympathy. I will take back these hours and days with a diligent and watchful eye, choosing careful where I deem it best to make the very great investment of my time. I need not be rude, exactly, yet when this or that irksome person or other – whom I would infinitely rather avoid, yet out of obligated courtesy hitherto have not – when they sidle-slither up to me to make some distasteful remark upon my choice of gown, perhaps, the lineage of my shoes, my family, or my general appeal, I will simply look them in the eye, say nothing and then depart their company. I have been practicing before the glass. I will waste no smart remark, but simply turn away. This is not what is expected of ladies, you will say, but I care not, for these rules are clearly made by gentlemen with no intent to mind their characters. Oh, you know not, sir, what we are forced to endure at assemblies and balls. The hanging hand, that somehow does not rise to level of a lady's waist quite swift enough, the claw-like grasp which clings on to point of pain, the one with irksome breath who with a manoeuvre all their own will sudden turn and seize one by the chin. Oh, let us not forget the men who say that 'no' will not be 'tolerated,' the ones who, while possessing neither rhythm nor grace, will blame and criticise their partner for the very faults that they themselves commit. How can they wonder, then, why a gentleman of good-nature, courteous, of smart attire, attendant to his personal fragrance, his conversation and his manners, who steps in time and with a light foot and happy heart, is so very much admired and coveted? Such a person knows well that what may not be freely bestowed is never worth possessing.

(Good grief, with what ease do I now rile myself.)

Almost everyone returned to lockdown will, I believe, be faced with the same dilemma. Having tasted freedom once more, however briefly, how may we now go on with the lack of it and − I imagine this is quite common − in the company of some household despot who must have all their own way. I wish not to think of Mr Collins, yet it is almost impossible. His presence is so unfortunately dominant. I go out, of course, and as you know. I hide within my chamber. I have even started sketching, though I am prodigious poor at it. Yet as soon as I do hear his voice or find myself within sight of the house once more my heart begins to pound within my chest, my throat constricts, my fists clench. It is worse now that Charlotte is abruptly so devoted. I miss her wry little glances in my direction in the midst of his pontificating. I miss her kind nods and amusing asides. Most of all, I miss my friend. It comes to a point where I can no longer bear to watch.

I wish I might chastise you indeed, for failing to rise to the defence of Miss de Bourgh. Yet I may not, knowing well how little I am at liberty to say within my own present environment. It would have astonished me to point of horror once to believe I might ever be reduced to quite so tongue-tied and restrained a little mouse.

I was ruminating about politics and the tendency, as I understand it, to vote continuously with one party, and therefore — theoretically — one set of ethics, often because one's father and grandfather have. It seems a perilous idea. Surely, we should be looking afresh each time with our own eyes? The son or daughter of a bad king might be, themselves, a tremendous leader. An elected official in the same political party may have very different ideals to their predecessor. In this household, Mr Collins is king. This is not a good thing for he is both foolish and utterly self-orientated. I am certain he cares not at all for any other than himself, and your Aunt *(and that only because he may gain from her)*. Yet on the rare occasions when he goes forth leaving Charlotte and I to our own devices, the atmosphere within the house shifts almost immediately. As one, all relax — it is as though birds begin to sing again and dark clouds move away. Of course, this cannot be, but it seems so – truly. If we (or rather, you – for I may not) elect an official because of his lineage without considering his character, our world will grow the same as Hunsford Parsonage. I hope to remove myself soon, though I do not know how. I throw the desire out into the universe, holding faith in its being heard.

Filo is a wily man indeed. I admire his sense of self-preservation, I suppose, for it enabled him to return in force and restore order; although to what end, I am no longer sure. Perhaps I do not admire him after all. It is most confusing. I feel such sorrow yet to think that in such time as ours a peaceful protest went unheard.

Sincerely,

P.S: Perhaps the thought of Mrs Collins being given permission to occupy her one place of privacy for pianoforte practice was too much for Mrs Jenkinson?

P.P.S: How hard it must be *(I hope)* as a brother to 'discipline' your sister. It must seem rather absurd, surely?

P.P.P.S: I wrote much the same to the Colonel when he made complaint at being a second son. Yet concerning roisterers, I have eyes, do I not? Wit enough to form an opinion? I am a gentleman's daughter, yes, and have known no deprivation of home, or food, or clothing, it is true. Yet I am deprived a higher education, should I wish it. I am denied an occupation, a vocation in life beyond that of wife and mother and, should I not 'find' a suitable husband before I reach a certain age, I may well be denied that too. I may not vote, nor own property. Should I marry, I will belong to my husband, as will our children. Need I go on? I have no sympathy whatever with those who exploit others, nor with those who use their 'high' birth to persecute and do harm. I may not speak plainer. Why, you yourself express opinions that are not what one might expect from your ilk *(and how I once admired you for it)*.

P.P.P.P.S: A genuine friendship between a Queen and a Lady in Waiting? Now who is the fanciful one? There is no freedom in such a bond. It must be impossible, almost completely so, that a person in a subservient position could feel able to unreservedly speak their mind. A friendship where one must say 'your highness' or 'your lordship?' I cannot conceive of such a thing.

A letter from Colonel Fitzwilliam

The 7th day of September at Rosings Park

Dear Madam,

I write concerning the health of my esteemed cousin, for he is these two weeks indisposed. Not to risk the possibility of the transmission of any infection, he has asked me to send his regards to you, rather than to write them himself. This I have done.

He was at pains to add that you must feel no obligation to return said regards, for he is unable as yet to walk beyond the house and, therefore, may not travel to receive such.

Please be assured of my continued discretion.

Yours with great sincerity,

Col. Fitzwilliam

Letter 5

Monday 14th September, Rosings Park

Dear Madam,

Forgive my belated reply to your most*(ly)* welcome letter. It was not my intent to be so very tardy. Much to my surprise, a fortnight previous I was struck down by the Unmentionable and confined to my chamber, not solely for the sake of quarantine but also by my own design for I had no wish for witnesses. Where I contracted such is the subject of much enquiry, for I have been nowhere save the grounds and green, and seen no one save the current household. Certain, it was not as virulent as might have been expected, yet it was irksome enough, truth to tell. I sat up in a chair most days, reading as the mood took me and drinking a copious amount of tea and broth, readily brought to my door by Anne who had kindly taken it upon herself to see to it that I did not starve, while her mother, Miss Bingley and Mrs Norris removed themselves to a more distant wing. The Colonel and Bingley naturally could not be expected to wait upon me, yet still I was supplied with the occasional brandy and a fresh book from time to time.

Gratefully I report that, with the exception of a somewhat lingering cough, I am most full restored to health, and thus far have infected no one else — quite the miracle.

I am obliged to you for the lengthy descriptions of your immediate heritage. I am now most enlightened, particularly concerning your Mama. Yet I must ask, do you believe it natural, inevitable even, that your father's reluctant governance should secure, instead, the authority of your mother? Forgive the bluntness of my enquiry, I realise you will broach no censure of your family; consider it instead rather a general musing upon what would appear to be the inevitable redistribution of leadership.

I was also most interested to learn of your mother's concerns for her own security, yet surely such fears can have no distinct foundation? She must know that, should she find herself in the predicament she greatly fears, her brother would soon enough ensure her a comfortable position within his own home.

It is remarkable that you should mention the Fourth Earl of Chesterfield with some derision, for I must say that I know of one* in particular who in his university years devoured and followed that gentleman's letters to the...er...letter. Indeed, as far as ever I may tell, he fervently continues so to do. As this person is quite evidently highly regarded by you yet, I shall say no more. Except to ask – the 'others' to whom you refer concerning your 'grievous low opinion' of my 'standards of behaviour' and also, I perceive, 'exclusionary schemes' – are you quite sure that they *(or he)* are as reliable a source as you would wish to employ in forming so very unfavourable an opinion of myself? While I must humbly concede that you are naturally far more intimately acquainted with your sister's true character than I could ever hope to be, may you not also likewise grant that the person to whom I believe we both refer might be far more thoroughly known to myself than to you?

(You have become rather free of late, I note, with imaginings of what I may, or may not, say or think. Must we now become once more a fiction to each other?)

Your defence of your sister is nothing short of fearsome, and while I must sincere admire your loyalty, I nevertheless believe that it has somewhat blinded your powers of achieving an impartiality of judgement. But perhaps the very notion that any may be impartial when in defence of a close friend or relative is unreasonable.

Shame is a foolish and superfluous emotion; it is the inevitable symptom of an action previously ill thought through. As I always consider my ensuing actions most fully, I am fortunate to experience little consequential shame. Were I both impulsive and irrational, I imagine I would be oft beset by it. I would also remark that I did not boast, nor do I. Why would such be necessary? As I understand it, 'twas the Colonel who considered my achievement a 'triumph.' I simply considered it a necessity.

I am curious, how do you imagine that the counsel of my friend somehow facilitated my own happiness? I have searched and searched the resources of my mind, yet I may find no logical answer.

I do appreciate your reticence in pursuing an accusation and thus accordingly withdraw my own. Would there were more like you.

Out of the deference you truly deserve, and being saddened to find myself, for whatever reason, the object of your poor opinion, I will comply in brief with your apparent desire for further explanation: I observed closely Miss Bennet and my friend upon the evening of the dance at Netherfield, having received the unprecedented information from Sir William Lucas that their marriage was widely considered quite the certain event. From my examination, I noted that while Bingley himself seemed most seriously attached to Miss Bennet, indeed, beyond anything I had witnessed in him prior, your sister appeared instead unmoved, I would go so far as to say indifferent. As I recall *(at this distance! How superfluous it yet seems to attempt to recount this now)* her look and manners, though engaging as ever, revealed no clear symptom of particular regard and it was evident to the discerning eye that although she appeared to receive my friend's attentions with some pleasure, she simply humoured him through courtesy and nothing more. Had their roles been reversed and your sister evidently simply humoured, I doubt you would have resisted the impulse to warn and deflect as I then did. While you have my sincere sympathy for any distress inadvertently caused, I could not in all conscience allow my friend to embark upon a marriage where he is like to give far more than he might ever receive. He has a loving heart and deserves an equal mate. I say again, that knowing your frankness as I do, I can hardly imagine your having acted otherwise when given the opportunity to divert a dear friend, or sister, from a choice which would doubtless cause them future misery. Perhaps our experiences at the time had been very different; yet now, in your current position, can you honestly say you would not have taken such a step as I, given both the foresight and opportunity?

Therefore, to your accusation that I have somehow excluded your sister, I would answer that I quite absolutely refute such. I simply encouraged my friend to incline to think more generously towards himself with regard to his future. He has that right. Then, concerning Miss Bingley, I often have observed her to behave thus and have frequent wondered if it were unusual. That is all.

Yet I cannot but wonder, considering the confession you have made that you have 'studiously developed' the appearance of calm within society, if it is possible that your sister may have likewise misrepresented herself? Could you find objectivity enough to concede this? You speak of the pretence that all must undergo when among company. I would agree that this seems so, and add that having attempted on countless occasions to act with what I would consider to be integrity, I have found myself condemned by many, yourself included, for appearing both unsociable and taciturn, unpractised even. *(How oft have I relived your wry rebukes within my mind. How is it that such impudence seems to have expanded so my heart?)* I do not say that you were incorrect, but would argue that at least I deceived not, for I acted exactly in accordance with my feelings. Is it not this very *lack* of honesty that brings so much confusion?

As I am honouring you with absolute candour, I must in all conscience also add to my testimony that your nearest relations – with the exception only of yourself and your eldest sister – exposed themselves frequently and before all eyes to a total and quite alarming want of propriety which, in my estimation, would only contribute further to a most unhappy connection for my friend. You will pardon me, knowing that it pains me to offend you so. I have fully absorbed the explanation you so kindly took the time to give concerning your Mama, and although I would extend my compassion, I cannot say it in any way allows me to condone her general lack of civility and deportment. In short, while you have blamed me most extensively, you have quite deliberate turned away from a closer culpability. Yet this bickering serves neither of us. I sincerely hope we may now say no more upon the matter.

(How I am led yet again to defend and justify what I would rather speak not of. Must I allow myself to be thus goaded? I would offer comfort, for much of your last letter did concern me greatly. Very well, I

will attempt now to fulfil my original intent as best I may. If I may.)

As far as music is concerned, you have my sympathy. For many months, indeed, we had only the Colonel's intermittent whistling to regale us upon occasion. In very recent days, Georgiana has broken her recurrent solitude and is frequently to be found within the drawing room upon the piano forte. It is a true delight to listen to her for she genuinely loves to play, and although her choices have been, thus far, somewhat dismal, it has been a relief to all of us, I believe, that the house be of a sudden filled with music. This has had an additional consequence, for my Aunt – out of an irrepressible gratitude, I imagine, at least in part – has, of a sudden, taken Georgiana under her wing, and is persuasively planning future excursions and treats. 'The poor little soul,' she declares whenever she might be heard, 'has suffered through such trials in that abominable London. Is it any wonder that she should look so pale and wan? You, Fitzwilliam both, do not your duty by her! Oh, she is the very image of my dear sister, so beautiful, so refined, so demure, so obedient.' This has created only further confusion within the breast of Anne, who whilst still fully rebellious is also clearly experiencing quite strong sentiments of what may only be described as envy towards her cousin. Naturally, this is my Aunt's intention and I believe she will see it through to its fullest conclusion.

By the by, affirmatively I have indeed heard your sister play and sing. *(Clearly our ears have been at odds. Yet now I understand that she inherits many of her faculties from her Mama.)*

May I ask, what occurred *after* you clanged the gong? I only wonder that as you find yourself unable to counter your cousin's pre-eminence verbally, you feel you may yet do so in the manner of gong.

Ah yes, Miss Bingley – whose popularity has been upon the wane since her arrival – has this very day lost all possible favour with Anne by accidentally shooting her beloved Rufus. You will remember the small scrap of dog aforementioned? Bingley, the Colonel and I had been out upon the lawns to combine both exercise and sport by reducing the red grouse population that has grown exponentially during the summer months, as it is wont to do. Anne had been throwing a cricket ball to Rufus to fetch – with moderate success, for while he will chase and capture it cheerfully enough, he is not keen to give return – while Miss Bingley loitered near to us, offering 'assistance' to her brother should he need such (he did not). I still cannot think what possessed Miss Bingley to pick up a gun in the first place for, as far as may be discerned, she had prior no experience whatsoever. Indeed, we had all three been preoccupied with a suitably distanced conversation when the gun went off, violently hurling Miss Bingley some way backwards into a hedge. Once we had pulled her from the foliage and Anne had given her a handkerchief — for she wept quite profusely (and rather angrily, I think) with shock — Bingley noticed that young Rufus had stopped his usual capering and lay quite still upon a tuft of distant grass. Naturally most ran towards him, Anne calling his name and then scooping him up into her arms. It was evident that he was only slightly hurt and his stillness simple fright, for he soon wriggled upright to lick her nose and face. Anne at once resolved to immediate and in secret summon a woman from the village who is well known for having a way with both animals and curative preparations. This proved a good instinct indeed, for his ear was stitched and he back upon his paws within the hour. He now misses a small portion of his left ear which gives him, somehow, a piratical demeanour. Of course, he has been a great deal petted and cosseted since and thoroughly relishes the attention. Yet I fear that Anne will ne'er forgive Miss Bingley; not for the shooting itself, but for indicating neither remorse nor concern for Rufus in its wake. Being all affability, as you know, the Colonel has attempted to intercede, indicating to Anne that Miss Bingley must also have suffered greatly from shock at being so precipitated and could hardly have had time to find the proper way to act. 'Nonsense,' retorted Anne. 'She is heartless quite.' And that, as they say, is that.

Incidentally, Miss Bingley has gifted me with an intricately embroidered cushion of her own construction. In the centre my initials are represented writ in gold, and on one side what I believe may be a lion, or perhaps a vole, and on the other an elephant or piglet. I was duly confounded and then, I hope, appreciative. It was greatly admired by Georgiana as a work of some intricacy, yet I have no idea quite what I am supposed to do with it. I am also the recipient of a velvet-bowed bottle to 'help' my cough. Gratis, I might add. When I removed the stopper, it revealed an aroma something akin to Pease soup.

To continue upon a theme, it transpires that Georgiana's reluctance in leaving our house in Grosvenor Square was not, after all, a fear of travelling with too few gowns. Rather, she had formed an unfortunate attachment to the servant who so willingly offered to carry her necessities, an attachment which he naturally encouraged and professed to ardently return. She confessed as much to me last evening after I had made some rather fleeting remark as to falsehoods and how oft they do return to plague us. While I need not describe my disappointment at her use of pretence, not to mention her foolish vanity in believing such a man either capable or worthy of forming a sincere passion for a woman of her station and fortune, I privately comprehend this experience to be a natural expression of her youthful naivety. I know she would never have been so foolish as to contemplate an *(another)* elopement. Naturally he has been dismissed and we shall have to do without his assistance. Upon reflection, this may explain her choice of music.

My sister, as you know, is many years my junior and that in itself diffuses the 'absurdity' or my role as guardian. I know not to what you may refer regarding 'discipline.' We speak, I offer amendment to her notions and behaviour, and that will be an end to it. There is no imprisonment or suffering, I do assure you.

(Now to it) You are right to consider your anxiety closely linked to anger, in addition to the emotion of fear. I have found, in my experience, that they

are close relations. Yes, in answer to your question, I *have* felt fear of that scale, although I am conscious that it is foolhardy to confess such weakness to you, or indeed to any. Such is the nature of our correspondence. You have privileged me with your sincerity and trust; how could I give less in response? It was one morning at Pemberley, not long after we had lost our father. I awoke early. The night had been stormy and the windows rattled yet. My chamber was gloomy, the house mostly asleep. I remember keeping my eyes tight closed for as long as I could in an attempt to suppress the thoughts that would still come. My heart pounded so hard within my chest, I thought it might burst out. I could not breathe. I wanted to tear the bedclothes forth and run as far and fast as I could away, yet I could not force myself to move. I felt forsaken, I believe, angered at myself, at fate, at those who had departed, and quite utterly alone in this world; it threatened almost to engulf me. At last, I remembered to breathe, deeply and fully, holding on to each gulp of air for as long as I could. Then I remembered my sister, and that there was more to this life than we can see. I remembered God. After a while I sat up and began my day. No one would have known; no one ever did. It is so for all of us. Yet perhaps you are right to question whether it is good to believe we are quite so alone in our feelings, when the experiences of life are universal, and compassion so essential.

I have heard you. Let me offer my assistance. I perhaps once believed that a man and a woman were blessed with very differing natures, that women experienced little in the way of anger and no fear to mention, that might not easily be assuaged by heroics, although this seems ridiculous and childish to me now. Madam…I would ask you…my sister is now quite happy in the company of her Aunt, although I am still utterly perplexed as to why. They have formed a bond I cannot understand. Yet Anne is deeply unhappy and I have come to believe that she must be removed from Rosings. Would you consent to join us as my guest at Pemberley? I would emphasise, without need, that there would be no impropriety. You and Anne could be as companions to one another. I would stress also that it will not be an easy journey. We will travel at night and may not take the main road for fear of discovery. The house has been shut up these many months and we will have to shift for ourselves. I believe we are all capable of this. I will ask Mr Bingley to accompany us, although he may prefer to stand by his sister. If this is the case, I assure you without the slightest doubt of his discretion. The Colonel I have already consulted, and although he seemed mostly in favour, he is unsure as to whether he may yet relinquish his proximity to London.

I await your reply.

Yours etc.

P.S: With respect, just because one may not be able to conceive of something does not mean it cannot exist; merely that it does not exist for you.

P.P.S: My Aunt has agreed that Mrs Collins might have Mrs Jenkinson's piano forte on a long loan, on the terms that it must be returned once quarantine is at an end and a new companion established for her daughter. It is a perk, you see, for whomsoever takes up the role. Indeed, it was fortunate that Mrs Jenkinson could find no way to tow it with her when she left, for she removed almost every item that she might reasonably carry from her room upon departure. The piano forte will be despatched as soon as ever a cart may be procured. I imagine that with the harvest, this may be slightly longer than ideal, but perhaps you will inform Mrs Collins of this intention that she might look forward to the arrival?

P.P.P.S: The badger must be the most ancient of landowners in this sceptred isle. You are right to give him due deference.

P.P.P.P.S: One of my *'ilk'*?

(I need say no more. It is unnecessary. Churlish, even.)

Ilk? I do my utmost with the role I have inherited. I would not give up my land, it is true, knowing that my place should be instant filled should I decide to step away. It seems an unfortunate fact that those who take a stand for another's sake are oft rewarded with martyrdom and little else. It is another truth that those oppressed do oft o'er-balance and become oppressors in their turn if due care is not then early taken. I do not disagree regarding inherited opportunity; I consider myself well fitted for my role in life and I endeavour to continue to deserve it. Indeed, I would be ashamed to be otherwise. Like yourself, I am affronted not because I am specifically affected, but because I am a human being and what affects another is of great import to all.

(Curse my pedantry.)

A letter from Miss Caroline Bingley

Tuesday 15th September, Rosings Park, Residence of the de Bourgh's

My dear Miss Bennet,

*Although for the present only, we are near neighbours once more, and I thought to engage you in an epistolatory conversation for our mutual amusement. In this communication **par écrit**, I shall also ask you questions and you may then respond to these by return. You have my **garantie** of secrecy as I give you my sincere assurance never to breathe a single word of this exchange for as long as I live.*

*I am sure you may only imagine how tedious I find it here at Rosings, having passed so many months in town. My sister, as you may know, had chosen to remain rather than make the arduous journey here, and I discovered with vexing immediacy that she was quite correct in her judgement. Nevertheless, we must make the best of wherever we are **forced** to be, must we not? I am sure I could not bear myself if I succumbed to written gripes and miseries, not least in an endeavour to evoke **sympathies** and **affections** in another which would otherwise not have the slightest possibility of existence. It would be a most dreadful **exploitation*** of **another's** inherent **courtoisie**, through centuries of good-breeding, to force them to endure such egocentric ramblings.

Mais je m'égare. We may not all bear up with fortitude, may we? Some have not that spirit, no matter how blinded another may momentarily seem by their machinations.

I trust your mother is in good health. I am given to understand that she is often very poorly, which must account for the behaviour I have – alas – often witnessed. It must be trying indeed for your **cher père** to bear her evident decline into **sénilité précoce**.

I trust your eldest sister has settled once more at home. How desolate I have felt indeed to think of the **toll** these months of lockdown must have taken upon her. A woman in her position – indeed, a woman of her **delicate years** and want of connection – could surely not broach such a delay. I do hope she will not now be forced to remain at home indefinitely, yet confess that I do fear for her **most grievously** and recall her in my **daily prayers**. Surely, she has yet the hope to be both wife and mother? Please send her my most affectionate wishes whenever you are able, and my sincere desire that she may rally and ultimately succeed in the **gruelling** task that lies before her.

It is sad, is it not, that we all may not marry well? The world is quite dreadfully **injuste**. One must have means, must one not? I am grateful indeed that I dwell in such **immense certainty** of a most mutually advantageous match. How I wish the same were true for you.

Naturally I am most grateful for my time with Miss Georgiana Darcy, who is quite delighted by my company. We pass hours together every day and a bond is formed between us that may **never** be broken, I assure you. Miss Darcy, of course, is always in the best of health and spirits, yet even she has declared my presence quite the tonic that she would not do without.

Whilst attempting to amuse myself on yester afternoon, I fired a gun and shot some sort of rodent. What a kerfuffle! The hue and cry raised by Miss Anne de Bourgh was quite akin to a fishwife upon a market day, or so I would imagine. I never was so **mortified** for another in my life. 'What have you done?' She all but screamed at me, 'oh what have you done?' It was quite mystifying I assure you. The Colonel took her side of course 'that is Miss de Bourgh's pet dog,' he said. 'Why that is no excuse,' I declared, and I was quite right too. 'Such an unforgivable lack of composure to unleash!' With that I left them to each other, yet I could hear Miss de Bourgh howling like a banshee until I reached the house. Naturally Mr Darcy was of the same opinion as myself, although he voiced it not; we are of such common sensibilities that we know each other's thoughts. Yet what a fuss. 'Twas just a dog.

With **felicitations,**

C. B.

I enclose for your edification a portrait of myself in lockdown ensemble from early June. Of course, this is out of date by now. How **sequestered** one feels in the country. I know not how you could have stood it for this **many** a year.

Letter 6

Wednesday 16th September, Hunsford Parsonage

Dear Sir,

I was indeed saddened to learn that you had been unwell, and most glad to hear that you are now full near restored to health. Last week, I did receive a short missive from your cousin to indicate as much, for which I was grateful *(for I imagined our correspondence brought sudden to an end and this disturbed me more than I could say)*. Had I sooner known, I would at once have dispatched to you one of Mr Collins' latest experiments.

Concerning an escape to Pemberley, I am grateful for your consideration *(truly)*. Yet for all our society seems turned upon its head I cannot possibly consent. I must return to Hertfordshire and to my family. Nowhere else will do. *(I wish with all my heart that I might prevail upon your party to leave instead for Hertfordshire and Netherfield, yet I cannot make so great a presumption. I know not how I might bear the solitude when you go.)*

It is an immense kindness to offer Charlotte a piano forte on loan. I am sure she will be delighted.

I am disturbed to learn of Miss de Bourgh's increased distress. Would that I could offer assistance.

(I will attempt now to tread with care, for much as your keen insensitivity does displease and offend me, I have no wish to receive a further extended silence.)

Regarding Charlotte, for let us call a spade a shovel, I must assure you that I did make attempt to intervene as you suggest, if only in the form of astonished outburst when told of her engagement. My opinion was given in the briefest of exclamations and, being unsought and discernibly unwelcome, I did all I then could to remedy my mistake. Now, I have the most unpleasant satisfaction of an instinct proved correct. It is no satisfaction, indeed.

You speak of integrity, yet have you not *(often, I imagine)* attended gatherings where you had no earthly wish to be? True, you then do show your feelings plain, yet the very act of your attendance is a breach of truth, surely? It must be. But this tributary is simply a diversion. You and I both full well know that we may not say or do whatever we might wish, whenever we might wish it. Such actions are impossible; for there are those we love and would not offend, abodes and assemblies we must desire to revisit.

You speak of impropriety: might we agree that misdemeanour is a matter of opinion *(although, in truth, I blush to recall Mama's behaviour on occasion)*? To you, my mother is gauche, is she not? To others, she may appear carefree and amusing. To you, your inability to converse with impunity is excusable. To some, you might seem inconsiderate and *(dare I?)* ungentlemanlike, indicating what might be perceived, by those who know you not, as a certain discourtesy exempted by status, *(I cannot help myself!)* appearing then to sport a rather voluminous cloak of pride. Yes, I can concede that Mama's behaviour may seem improper to some, yet I would most firmly argue that the only person of whom I can possibly conceive who might be 'proper' enough to condemn another for impropriety is Jane, and she would be neither so unkind, nor so uncivil *(there!).*

That aside, you cannot possibly yet believe that there is any comparison between the marriage of my friend, and the feelings which subsist between my sister and Mr Bingley. It is palpable intransigence on your part. Clearly, we will never agree, but for my own peace of mind I will attempt once more to explain with clarity how mistakenly you have perceived Jane's feelings and, thus, how much you have wronged your friend *(although regretfully I must in private make concession that Jane may not have shown her regard quite as plain as she might, for did not Charlotte make the self-same observation once? Mind you, her own professions regarding happiness in marriage and a comfortable home, seem woefully misguided now).* With all due deference, I would ask you this – have you once considered that my sister, in her reticence, attempted fully to understand the character of Mr Bingley for herself? You imagine that we women must simply be o'erwhelmed with gratitude when a man, any man, shows an inclination towards us. So much so, that we must directly simper and flatter to swift secure his constancy, before we may be quite so certain of our own. I may assure you that Jane has no wish whatever to marry where she does not love, and her sincerity and integrity is such that nothing on earth could compel her to show continual encouragement towards a man for whom she did not care. You have woefully mistaken her character, her modesty, and her inclination, and I fear that no explanation you could give will change that.

Regarding the 'other,'* I will grant the possibility that I may not know all. Yet I cannot imagine that the information to which I have been made party could ever be false. It is impossible.

Concerning Mama and Uncle Gardiner, of course I am sure she has considered this. But I would ask you, even allowing for the vastness of Rosings, could you ever desire to remain as a permanent guest? I know well the answer. It is one thing to visit, and quite another to depend upon the benevolence of a family member or friend, to prevail constantly upon their filiality and thus make personal adaptation to their schedule and mode of living. Indeed, I can think of little else to set more strain upon an ardent friendship, than a lengthy stay.

Considering your musing with regard to dominance within a marriage, I would offer that my father is of an easy, gentle nature and Mama will broach no argument; that is their specific union. I would not believe it to be ever and always the case. A true marriage, in my conception, would be one of equals, where dominance and subjugation plays no part.

In the strange, circuitous way that prayers are often answered, I have received two missives in as many weeks, in addition to your own, though not by post. I am grateful for your cousin's communication, as aforesaid. As far as a letter received from Miss Bingley is concerned, however, I may only express my surprise and consternation, for I had not considered that she might know aught of our correspondence. Forgive me, this may not be so, but I had no thought of either I or my family persisting as the subject of any current public discourse. That I might not give impression of an accusation ill-founded, I must disclose that I acquired said letter from within the elm *(our elm)*. I have no idea whatever of composing a reply; indeed, I do not think it wise.

(I must order my thoughts. Yet what compelled her to write such a letter, I wonder? It is almost as though she had taken leave of her senses.)

Yesterday afternoon I was prevailed upon by my cousin to assist him in the filling of the holes and pits within the garden, dug by our striped friend. Having no reasonable excuse, I reluctantly consented, knowing well that they would be dug again within a night. Although he had most generously offered that we might 'share' the task, the reality transpired that I would dig and transport soil whilst he pontificated, gesticulated and perspired. Although we have seen neither hide nor hair of our neighbours for this many a day, he is still resolved to think the worst. I attempted to explain the nature of the actual perpetrator, yet he would not have it. I then described the badger, to which he merely laughed and offered knowingly: 'a badger, cousin Elizabeth, is a small and wriggling creature of reddish hue with a large bucktooth and a tuft of white hair upon his upper-lip.' Adding 'you should know this.' After discerning that he made no jest, I politely hinted in return that perhaps he described a squirrel or a weasel, although the portrait was something of a bafflement, yet he seemed riled enough to be so questioned and, for my own sake, I resolved to say no more. Thus, I dug in silence for some time, while he paced the perimeter hedge and performed a series of lunges and high knee raises for 'my humors' (here I would wickedly add that even the now meek Charlotte does not condone such exercise as it is inevitable that he will, once a week at least, stretch too far and tear asunder the forked seam of his pantaloons *(for he wears them rather snug)*). Then: 'I have a book within the parsonage that my dear wife gifted to me. In it you will see it writ that I am right.' I hesitated, being unsure as to what might follow, then discerning that he intended me to bring the book to him, I left him to his unfortunate exertions, returning to the house. Once inside with the door closed and my hand quite upon my forehead, I was startled to discern a muffled but yet quite audible sobbing from above. Treading carefully, that I might not disturb the emitter, yet determining to satisfy my own curiosity as priority, I tiptoed up the stairs and hesitated at their summit, realising fully – of course – the impropriety of my behaviour. I guessed full well that it was the mistress of the house, and that she wanted none to hear, having clearly waited until she was finally alone. At the summit, and chastising myself roundly, I turned to retrace my steps yet forgetting in my haste the pattern of creaks that must be avoided if subterfuge is to be achieved, trod upon one groaning step after another, alerting Charlotte to my presence. 'Eliza?' I heard my name. How on earth she knew it to be me I am yet unsure, although do we not come to know well the familiar tread of our intimates (or inmates)? I forced a cheerful, nonchalant tone and replied in the affirmative. The fall of her footsteps was followed by the appearance of a poor, sad and crumpled face. I gasped at the sight of her. Those who know Charlotte well might tell you that they have seldom, if ever, known her to shed a tear, for she is an indomitable master of herself and her emotions. I am yet surprised that she acknowledged me in so private a moment. Looking up at her, I nearly wept too. She came towards me as if to speak, but dissolved once more to tears and I threw my arms around her. We stayed some time like this, speaking not a word, then she pulled herself away and returned to her chamber and shut the door. After a moment of shock, I remembered that I had a mission to complete and that if I did not so do then the man himself might appear and find me out. Thus, I made my way back to my cousin, who had pranced repeated on an ants' nest in my absence and been bit substantial up and down each leg. I was grateful to the insects for their noble sacrifice, as it spared me any further explanation of either absent book, or present badger.

In the evening, after drawing her husband an oatmeal bath and encouraging him to go early to bed in order to restore the balance of his spirits, Charlotte and I sat alone together in the parlour for the first time in more weeks than I would care to recall. At first, we neither knew how we could begin and stayed half staring at one another in some discomfort. Then, Charlotte began to speak, hesitatingly at first, but soon at length. I will not reveal the detail of our conversation, for it would feel betrayal to my friend, yet much was discussed and much appeared explained and resolved. After an hour there came a loud bray and she was subpoenaed upstairs. I remained alone there until the chimes of ten, just because I could, revelling in the unprecedented restoration of my hopeful spirits.

If I had believed this the start of a new chapter, which I did, and our renewed intimacy to continue, I was sorely to be disappointed. In the morning, it was instantly apparent that all was to continue as though nothing out of the ordinary had previous occurred. Indeed, Charlotte went to great lengths to refer to 'we,' meaning she and Mr Collins, more times than I could have thought possible within so brief a time, and her resolute dedication to his bandaging and rebandaging was most unsettling. Worse still, Charlotte seems more greatly ill at ease within my presence than ever, as if in having revealed her most private thoughts to me I am now an enemy, not a confidant.

It does seem to me that if one is raised in a household where there are heightened levels of, shall we say, theatre, one will likely seek peace at all costs, but find spectacle without meaning to. It is what one is used to. I seek peace but find spectacle.

I did not fulfil my original plan concerning the gong. It seemed not worthy of the scene that would inevitably ensue. Yet I enjoyed the thought of it for a time. On the morrow, I attempted to appease my feelings of resentment by hinting to my cousin that my scratchings might well be a novel concerning the perils of existing within a realm of petty tyranny. Naturally he had no idea that I could or might refer to he, and no concern whatever that as a mere woman I might have the capacity to finish such an endeavour, even should I start it. But I weary myself with grievances. Why must I stay, I wonder? Why remain only to complain? Verily I would face a considerable fine were I caught. There might be roadside vagabonds a plenty. Yet in my current humour they would best beware of me, than I of they. Surely with home as my aim, a handful of uncomfortable and nervous hours would not be much to bear?

With respect, the bond of which you speak between your Aunt and Georgiana is rather more understandable than you might, at such close quarters, perceive. Your Aunt is the sister of your mother, is she not? That of itself makes perfect sense of it to me. I am sure your sister's intention was not originally deceit with regard to that which you confided. Our hearts may lead us to the most unsuitable places, especially when we find ourselves isolated and in confusion. It is not my place, I know this, yet I would urge you once again to speak of this with your sister, for secrecy may oft create only distance.

Mama dislikes the autumn, most particularly, I believe, because it leads to winter. Once the evenings begin to draw in and the leaves change to gold, she is to be seen in the garden weeping, wrapped within a shawl. 'It is such a sad time, Lizzy' she will say, 'do you not feel it, as another year fades away?' She has said this since I was six years old, possibly before. Hitherto, I confess, I have not felt so. I have always found the autumn a joyous season of beautiful colours, warmth and vivid skies. There is nothing to disappoint, only to revel in, and the more time I can spend out of doors the better. Yet, this year I have come to understand a little of what Mama has felt. I too have felt sorrow at the fading of the summer. I too have shuddered at the thought of darker nights. I have contemplated whether this is a sign of impending maturity, which frightened me, for Mr Collins is 'the very essence of maturity' (his words), but after giving myself quite the turn I laughed, realising instead that it is simply this particular year. I cannot express it quite, for I know it cannot be helped, yet I feel as though my life were being stolen. We hide within our homes or refuges, we may not hold or even speak to those we love, there have been great losses suffered that might once have been shouted from the bell-towers, yet instead have occurred as the briefest of sighs. I have never before experienced a time of so little choice, nor so much fear. For all History has shown us time and again that the bows will shake, at present it is as though our lives are caught within a thick syrup, and try as we may we cannot pull free.

(It is so long since I saw or heard from any of my family. If I close my eyes I can hear my father's voice, my mother's laugh, see Jane's gentle smile. I am at a loss to understand how this all occurs, and why it still continues. I feel defeated quite, and it is most unnatural and uncomfortable to me. I know it is a choice. I know better. Why do I not rally?)

Charlotte has been sent to speak with me. I am to move to the second guest room with immediate effect. I will no longer have the large window and wisteria, but a room with a window half the size and nothing beneath it but the ground. It is my own fault, for I was lulled to trade the confidence of my friend with that of my own. I will resume this communication tomorrow, but for now I am done.

Thursday 17th September, Hunsford Kitchen *(Dungeon)*

Last night I dreamt I punched Mr Collins on his big red bulbous snout. I recall it vividly and it restored me. Naturally I ran like one possessed after, but I can still recall the feeling of elation that I had to see him buckle. I do not condone my dream-actions completely *(or do I?)*, yet I believe the joy I have felt since as I have relived the moment in my mind over and over has given me intense relief. Had I actually hit him I would have offended Charlotte, ruined what slim familial ties we have, put my entire family at risk of his revenge and sorely hurt my hand. Yet in my heart I feel better. I feel released and able to think with more clarity now that I am not suppressing long-harboured anger. Our imaginations are our allies and we must allow their assistance as we negotiate our way through this muddle of existence.

My father once told me that in spite of what others may say, there are times in life when one must give one's self permission to run away. Perhaps it may be for an afternoon alone, or more than that, but if it is necessary, if one has become so cornered that it seems the only solution, then it must surely be allowed. 'Do not go down with your ship, my Lizzy,' he would say when in a philosophical frame of mind, 'it is not courage, indeed, but sheer stubbornness serving none but historians and novelists.' I would nod sagely, of course, yet I knew not what he meant till now. I could yet force myself to stay longer at Hunsford; another week or three, perhaps months, until time blends completely or is spent entire. I exaggerate, yet it frightens me to see how much one might just endure. I have become so fearfully uncomfortable, but would it not be worse to be so and then forget? I feel a definite and growing hope that I will find myself away from here soon, that I will find that courage within myself, and not through violence or attempts to change another who could not change, even if he wanted to.

(I will liberate myself, do you hear me world? It is only a matter of time.)

Yours etc.

P.S: It will not surprise you to learn, considering your disrespect for my rhapsodising upon the outdoors, that I have quite the low opinion of hunting for sport. Not least foxhunting. Out of interest, do you by any chance keep a pack of foxhounds and drink a bottle of wine a day?

P.P.S: Concerning your cushion of quite evidently extraordinary design, I wonder if I am alone in finding the process of gift giving completely alarming, unless it is for a person whom I truly love, whom I know well and who is likely to receive my gift with due affection and good humour. To tell truth, any other gift-giving feels a confusing flurry of attempts at pretending more intimacy than is actually present. Naturally, Jane is an expert giver of gifts and is neither confused nor insincere. Kitty embroiders beautifully, but is apt to decry her attempts in favour of Lydia's and unpick over and again, achieving a lesser result than she otherwise might. Lydia does well enough in the most spartan of ways, and her gifts are seldom boxed, for she 'has not the time.' Mary, who has time aplenty, is prone to embroidered morals. Mama gives in what could only be described as a rather chaotic abundance – indeed, I believe she carefully collects gifts for each of us throughout the year – being the absolute mistress of beautifully decorated little boxes for jewellery, of lavender bags and unexpected preserves and other dainties. Last, but not least, Papa is a generous distributer of 'top ups' to our pin money.

Also, while such is on my mind, I must query the End of Year Epistle from distant acquaintances, in which they inform you of their most recent triumphs or miseries, having had no desire to communicate with you for the entire preceding year. Why now, is all I ask?

P.P.P.S: *Ilk* does not sound flattering, I concede. I simply meant those who use their rank and fortune to separate themselves from others, superiority being a greater aim than mutual affinity, and deference the necessary due of entitlement.

P.P.P.P.S: Now I will tell you something rather shocking. I have been breaking crockery. Not the best Collins set, naturally, and only one piece a day. Perhaps it is a kind of madness, but I routinely take a plate or dish from the kitchen after breakfast and then keep it within my chamber all day. I look forward to the moment when I might go outside to the end of the parsonage grounds where there is a small brick cool house and may hurl it with all my might at the wall. I will then pick up every single shattered piece and hide them within a bush in the garden that covers a multitude of sins. I know, of course, that I must be discovered soon enough, for although they have been gifted with a quite extraordinary abundance of tableware, it is not without its limits. I have pin money saved at home and will send them a replacement when we are free. If we are free.

(I do not like what is become of me here. I am custodian of myself and I seem to fail at every turn. I have three younger sisters – what would they think of me?)

Letter 7

Friday 18th September, Rosings Park

Dear Madam,

I thank you for your good wishes concerning my health; they are appreciated indeed. Also, my sincere gratitude that you did *not* send a Collins Concoction, for it might have been unwitting administered by a well-meaning de Bourgh and then who knows how I might have fared.

With regard to Pemberley, I envisaged you might respond as such *(indeed, I would expect no less of you)*. I will speak further upon the subject with Bingley and should he believe an alternative removal to Hertfordshire and Netherfield a viable possibility then I shall immediately dedicate my energy thus, and through that means return you home. For the sake of deceiving you not, however, I must in all conscience add that discussions in that direction previous have led to the self-same conclusion: it would seem an impossibility for our presence at Netherfield to remain a secret. At Pemberley we would likely escape detection longer. Were it only an imminent fine as looming punishment, we would pay and gladly so. As indefinite imprisonment is rather more likely the order of the day, you will comprehend our hesitation.

Your words are appreciated concerning Anne. There are moments yet where her spirit returns clear and true once more, with Rufus proving an evident source of the most tremendous joy. Yet, as you say, for some the bonds become too tight to breathe, and escape appears essential.

As a priority, I would unequivocally confirm that Miss Bingley has been given no knowledge whatsoever of our correspondence, and neither you nor your family are the subject of any discourse within the walls or grounds of Rosings, beyond the briefest of speculation as to your current general well-being. The Colonel alone is aware of our communication, and I have no doubt of his silence upon this matter. As for your discovery of Miss Bingley's letter within the elm, I must venture only that she had perhaps followed me; yet I have no knowledge or evidence that the lady has once left Rosings since our arrival. I will think further upon how I may proceed in this regard, yet in the meantime must trust to your belief in my continued and dedicated discretion.

(Indeed, I hope perhaps you may ask no more concerning this subject. For how may I convey my

consternation at finding my desk disturbed and letters of yours clearly opened and read by another. Nor would I tell you of the countless occasions upon which Miss Bingley has attempted to raise a supposedly humorous discourse concerning members of your family, near and far. Thankfully, my Aunt takes little interest in that which does not directly concern herself, and no other person present would join to speak so unkindly.)

Unexpected occurrences aside, I must now refer once more to the earlier portion of your previous letter in the hope of finally creating a sincere comprehension between us. Thus: -

Regarding Bingley, I would assure you once again that my opinion was both sought and welcomed. Had my friend vigorously disagreed, I would have attempted further to persuade him, it is true, but would ultimately *(surely)* have conceded, had he then explicitly chosen to pursue his own course.

You are right, of course and I must forfeit with a good grace. I certainly did attend events where I had no earthly wish to be, and frequently so. Perhaps I would not feel so now *(indeed, not if you were there).*

Regretfully, I cannot agree regarding misdemeanour. We have codes of conduct, do we not? To be overly ribald is to wilfully, often quite significantly, decrease the pleasure of an evening for others in attendance, without consideration for the collective enjoyment, but solely for one's own. To be withdrawn is surely a far lesser crime, for it affects only those who, unwelcome, approach when they had clearly far better stay away. Perhaps I do indeed appear to wear 'a cloak of pride,' before those who know me not, yet as to 'ungentlemanlike' I will give no response. No doubt you are correct, however, concerning your sister's judgement of others and, also, concerning her nature. I must draw a line, however and for good, with regard to further discussion of my involvement in the attachment between Miss Bennet and my friend. It serves no earthly purpose, for it is done.

(Ungentlemanlike! How such a word does cut me to the quick. Not least that it should come from you.)

Concerning Mr Wickham, for let us call a trowel a trowel, I am afeard that your imagination, if only in this regard, is sorely restricted. You see, while my old acquaintance's manners may indeed appear easy and affable, his company most desirable, he is rather more truthfully and eagerly concerned with the management of his reputation, so much so that he will energetically endeavour to regale others with a deeply subjective version of past events, long before said others have even thought to enquire. It is impossible, you see, for Mr Wickham to describe his own true behaviour, for he will surely then find little approval among those he wishes to momentarily befriend. He must therefore make invention, controlling their opinions and ensuring not only their sympathy, but generously offered credit and willing loans.

(Too much! Too much!)

As you have asked, albeit it indirectly, I would tell you briefly why I so greatly distrust and must hitherto reject the man. Yet I find I cannot, will not, embark upon any further communication which may lead to acrimony between us. Recognising your disinclination to trust my word before that of Mr Wickham, I will ask the Colonel, instead, to write a true and consecutive account of the past *events* which have led to so irreparable a rift. As one of the executors of my father's will, the Colonel has been unavoidably acquainted with every particular. I will deliver this letter to the elm within a day and no later than by four in the afternoon. I trust you may find the liberty to retrieve it in due course.

(I emphasise 'events' and hope you will comprehend my meaning, for I would hardly be so unjust as to break with a friend or acquaintance upon one slight misstep alone.)

I must divert and ask now if you are fully recovered from your 'ordeal' yesterday? I employ the use of inverted commas advisedly, for I am unsure yet as to whether it was indeed an 'ordeal' or an impulsive bid for freedom effected by one who will not long be brought down.

The Honourable Mr Collins took quite the fright. He appeared before Rosings at a half past nine in the morning, fully masked, and calling out in half-hysterics 'my charge has escaped!' followed by 'oh the ingratitude, the immeasurable *ingratitude!*' over and again. After much confabulation within – during which he was seen continuously to shuffle, then spin upon the spot with arms outstretched – a window was opened by Mrs Norris that my Aunt might perch uncomfortably 'in the draft of it,' clutching her shawl around her throat for fear of 'irksome maladies.'

'Good heavens, Mr Collins,' cried my Aunt, having waited not a moment, 'must I speak for you?'

'Oh n-no, your supreme ladyship,' stuttered he, 'I simply hesitated, wishing not to offend...'

'You have awoken me from my requisite slumber at a most unjustifiable hour. The offence is taken! Now, tell me why.'

The Irksome Malady shifted uncomfortably, waving a rather unsightly handkerchief across his forehead and beginning to remove his jacket before remembering himself and pulling it hastily back on.

'Miss Bennet, Ma'am, has this early morning vanished (pronounced 'vanish-ed'). That is to say, she was present before and then, of a sudden, gone.'

'Yes, yes, I know well the meaning of 'vanish-ed,' withered my Aunt. 'Well, and what am I to do about it, pray?'

'Why no, your ladyship. For while I believe no prayers could be of more effect than yours...'

'That is not what I said!' Rapped back her ladyship. 'For heaven's sake man, come to the point. I advance in years as we speak.'

So did we all.

'I wished to ask your most Esteemed Ladyship for your indispensable advice, nay, assistance even, in the matter, if I may be so bold. That is, to be brief, having no wish to disturb you...'

'Collins!!!'

After a cough which might well have been a sob: 'what must I do?'

'Do? Are you simple, man? Heavens, how would you fare were I not here? Or any of you, for that matter? My advice! Why, you and Mrs Collins must set forth at once to discover the renegade.'

'Yes, yes and I thank you, indeed...'

My Aunt beckons within and Mrs Norris is at the ready to close the window.

'Yet...! I know not where Miss Bennet could be. Doubtless she could not have gone far for she is unused to being out of doors, as are we all, Ma'am, and for our own safety. I am afeard she will become diseased, distressed, or...sunburned. She is a female of delicate moods and will not fare well, I am sure of it, alone and in the wilds.'

My Aunt surveys him for some minutes, no doubt half as punishment for daring to make so long an oration. At last, she speaks: 'Mr Bingley will go and make a thorough search of the area, for I have no need of him this day. I will grant him that permission.' With that she leaves the sill and Mrs Norris slams the window closed behind her.

With the best will in the world, it was unlikely that dear Bingley could find the Hunsford Green, let alone a wandering apostate with no wish to be discovered, for he has no experience of the local terrain and would likely simply become lost himself. Thus, having no wish to form a later search party for our esteemed friend, the Colonel and I agreed to mutually assist your cousin who yet stood below wringing his hands in an agony of indecision. Bingley, who it transpired did indeed have nothing better to do that day, gallantly offered to escort Mr Collins back to the parsonage that he might perhaps recover his wits and await your return. They set off at a distance from one another of at least fifteen hands, the noble Bingley clearly offering a series of comforting remarks as they faded from view, while your cousin persistently shooed him further and further away.

I set off at once for the stables, the Colonel promising that he would follow but a moment behind, for he needs must inform Anne of his departure; why, I could not imagine. While he offered to ride the circumference of the village and then to the heights in hope of spotting you from afar, I thought instead to search the riverbank. Not, I hasten to add, because I imagined you might have attempted an act of desperation, but remembering a past and confident assurance of concealment there. Thus, it was not half an hour before I discovered you, seated upon the grass beneath a tall oak tree. You saw and heard me not, so lost in thought were you. *(I remained and watched a quarter of an hour. You looked so peaceful, so very beautiful. Bonnetless, the sunlight glinted through your hair, bestowing the dark curls with the slightest hue of auburn that I had not seen before, and never shall forget.)* Seeing you as safe and seeming quite content I thought to tide you well. I had no wish to untimely end your retreat, so resolving to leave you to yourself I returned to Hunsford and the parsonage, where I gave assurance to Mr and Mrs Collins that I doubted not your safe return in due course.

'She left not a word; not one word,' retorted Mr Collins without hesitation. 'Oh, the ingratitude. The unmollified ingratitude.' He then collapsed once more and was helped within by Mrs Collins.

Incidentally, Mrs Collins did seem most sincerely concerned for your well-being.

I understand that you returned at dusk, for her ladyship received a rather long epistle from Mr Collins (lightly singed, of course) giving thanks to the Colonel and I for our *attempted* assistance. Bingley, who had spent more than an hour on guard at the Parsonage was uncharacteristically out of humour for the remainder of the day and at supper even spoke a brief word of reproach to his sister for some slight, but typical, misdemeanour.

Unheard of. Miss Bingley is shocked and angered yet.

Considering your trials are likely far from over, I would most sincerely request that should you, understandably, desire to run away once more and further, that you do not flee into the night alone *(for I fear you might yet be pushed just wild enough to attempt such extremity)*. The roads are unsafe indeed, there are vagabonds aplenty and they discriminate not. I would rather break lockdown, call at the parsonage and hang Mr Collins from a pair of his own antlers than see you put yourself in any danger to escape his clutches. Fond walker that you are, it is many miles indeed to Hertfordshire and I know you possess neither horse nor the experience to ride well. I have no doubt that you will fulfil your mission to return home eventually, yet if it is within my power to ease your passage I must be allowed to oblige.

I have yet to speak to my sister concerning your advice. I have every intention so to do, it has simply been a matter of time *(and writhing postponement)*.

I have it on good authority from the Colonel that the post is soon to be reinstated. It seems that old Filo has been caught repeatedly a-roistering at a series of impromptu gatherings to celebrate his return to power. Naturally the newspapers were instantly informed and his popularity plummeted exponentially, thus he now attempts to divert attention by restoring a privilege. I doubt it will have the effect he wishes, but we shall see. It has always faintly surprised me, apropos of nothing, that the government has met at all during this unprecedented experience. True, the country must still be governed, yet I had not expected such courage from any member in the face of the Unmentionable. Perhaps they do indeed have an immunity hitherto unavailable to the rest of us, but clearly the bubonic plague this is not – for who with the luxury of choice would take such a risk, let alone host a festivity, if they believed the contraction of such was any real possibility?

Over said newspapers this early evening, the Colonel and I did laugh at the descriptions of quite outrageously high fines imposed this lockdown for even the slightest infringement of the latest restrictions. Indeed, it is astonishing to learn of the profiteering that has arisen during the Unmentionable. The week before last I read of tests devised that 'essential workers' might tell if they are infected and thus stem the spread with prior knowledge. To be accurate, one must pay a government official for permission to travel beyond one's original permit to work, then discover and pay a government-approved apothecary who will invite one to spittle in a bucket, whereupon a pinch of saffron, a head of clover and a spoonful of gin is added, the mixture stirred three times to the left and four to the right. After a wait of several moments, one will receive a result - if the mixture has turned blue, one is infected, if pink, then one is not. Naturally it is most expensive and reliably inaccurate. Last week it was additionally revealed that several government officials had found a way to alter their results from 'uninfected' to 'infected' by bribing the apothecary to add a squeeze of lemon, thus attempting to avoid their posts for a duration of self-imposed-isolation. This surprised me indeed, having had quite enough of quarantine myself; but each to their own. The consequence of this is that the government has now swiftly introduced a 'Congestion Charge,' whereby any essential worker discovered attempting to deceive thus will be prodigiously fined for 'falsifying mucus.' Charming. This is not to be confused with the ongoing 'Congestion Scheme' by which, as you may know, the already financially put-upon are charged a large daily toll to bring their horse, cart or hired carriage into the heart of London and must either pay such or circumnavigate on foot via Battersea. Naturally, it is impossible for most to journey so and meet their daily obligations. In addition, our profiteering friend will surely charge them considerably to traverse his patched-up bridge, as aforementioned. Most spurious of all, this toll is said to 'give cleaner air' to London, ridding the centre of 'working-class horses' who are 'ill-bred, foulsome and copiously damaging to our environs'. Why we must all be forced to pretend to believe this nonsense could be anything more than a further way to line coffers is beyond me. Were something deemed truly so dangerous to the health of all, it would simply be instantly and completely prohibited, surely? Daylight robbery, as the saying goes.

After supper, Bingley, the Colonel and I amused ourselves in the exchange of suggestions as to what they might find to tax us upon yet. Beard clippings perhaps, or a restriction upon how many handkerchiefs one might own? The latter was Bingley's suggestion, for he is very fond of a handkerchief.

Humour aside, we must be aware that those who seek power seek also to hold to it by whatever means they can. Taxation is seldom solely about the money, but rather a way of seizing control, often when it has come close to being lost. It is a parent punishing a child who dares to question, by asserting their authority. It is an ensuring that we remain afraid for our survival, that our means of living could be, of a sudden, restricted or removed, should we object.

Yours etc.

P.S: Concerning the Unmentionable tests, Miss Bingley is beside herself with excitement at the inevitable privatisation of such, for she sees in that an avenue for further business ventures. She is determined that *her* tests, accompanied then by *her* cures, will become the very pinnacle of high fashion. Indeed, she has it in mind once we are freed to encourage the widespread testing of any who wish to partake in elegant social gatherings, refusing one entry if one has not done so. I must admire her entrepreneurial spirit, I suppose.

P.P.S: Concerning a pack of foxhounds, I do not. Concerning a bottle of wine a day, currently my answer must be 'no comment.'

P.P.P.S: Regarding gift giving and alarm, you are not alone. Admittedly, I seldom partake in such for it is not expected of me. On occasions when I must, however, I will decide beforehand exactly what must be purchased, precisely where it may be purchased and then make no deviation, that it be over and done with as swiftly as ever it may.

P.P.P.P.S: Arrangements have now been made for the piano forte to be transported to Hunsford Parsonage this very Monday. Lady Catherine has requested that Mrs Collins should only play while gloved. No doubt there will be an extensive list of further instructions enclosed.

P.P.P.P.P.S I shall refrain from further comment upon 'ilk,' but must offer a sound 'bravo' concerning the crockery. It seems a most necessary, most laudable expression of feelings. To horribly misquote Hippocrates 'for extreme Collinses, extreme methods of cure are surely most suitable.'
(I attempt humour. Perhaps it is not my fortis...yet 'tis too late, I may not strike it through.)

(A most alarming number of postscripts.)

Letter 8

Tuesday 22nd September, Hunsford Parsonage

Dear Sir,

I must sincerely offer my thanks to you, then, for my day of full escape. You were quite correct, for I was happy indeed and, although reluctant to return, have existed ever since within the certain knowledge of such future possibilities. It is as though, having finally lived fully the feeling of an extended freedom once more, I have now assured faith in its potential.

I readily affirm that I have no intention indeed of walking to Hertfordshire; as fond as I am of walking, that would be many a step too far. You have my further assurance that should I decide to fully flee I will first make application to you for some assistance *(but not rescue, for I desire no such weighty obligation...I ought to emphasise this)*. Although I would need no rescue, indeed, I do thank you for your friendship and considerate intentions. I doubt ever to employ such a measure, yet once again it is of comfort to know that such opportunity might exist.

I would, however, amend a slight misunderstanding concerning my horsewomanship. I *do* ride reasonably enough, yet, like Miss de Bourgh, find it a decidedly foolish and rather irksome pastime. The side-saddle is a distinctly unnatural invention, a device to twist and destabilise where one ought surely to be situated in the greatest achievable comfort and steadiness. While I am certain it is an elegant enough vision from afar, lauded by both the prim and the preposterous, the immense likelihood of catapultian is hardly appealing to any rider of good sense. Besides, were one inevitably to be propelled over the head of one's horse and into an obliging ditch, elegance would swift become a matter of memory.

Much as I shall continue to enjoy the notion of Mr Collins suspended from a pair of antlers, I regret to inform you that there are no such trophies within the parsonage. Not everyone owns a pair, you know. You might call instead to slap him hard with a glove for pinning butterflies behind glass. Who could do such to a fellow creature? How would he feel if someone stuck a pin in his middle and placed him behind a frame? Naturally, his innate lack of remarkability would certainly keep him safe from such a prospect *(yet not from my pen, it is true. How I wish he would not dominate my thoughts so, for I seem half-obsessed. It is because my mind can make no sense of how God-like he appears to himself, and how not so he appears to me).*

Naturally, my cousin lectures long, and my 'renegade infamy' (his words) will surely live for as many weeks or months as it fails to be duly superseded. Thankfully, our Rochester neighbours are come out of hiding and I am hopeful of an imminent reprieve from his watchful eye and reproachful tongue. Charlotte, on the other hand, has treated me with great kindness since my escapade, not least by insisting to her husband that he allow me an hour out of doors each day for the good of my health. I know not how this was achieved entirely, for I was not present, though clearly it took many hours of rumbling from him, but I do know that she has managed to persuade him of my being less likely to run 'for good and all' if only I am allowed this special dispensation. However reluctantly this freedom was granted, I am wholly grateful for it. Especially as my cousin was at great pains to describe the fearful risk this privilege engenders, the hosting family being themselves faced with a fine should a 'dependent' break quarantine, something of which I was hitherto unaware. I truly believed that a fine was only mine to bear, should it arise. Although I could not, even then, bring myself to remain within, I am resolved to apply far greater caution. If caught, and with the crockery to reimburse, I know not how I might ever afford to pay them back.

(I hope you will read between the lines of this and tell me if Mr Collins speaks true. I wish not to accuse him directly of deception, but his words felt most unnaturally delivered and I am most uneasy to accept such without query, however circuitous.)

That being said, on Saturday I diverted and used my sanctioned walk to pay an outdoor call to Maria Lucas at last, having long felt deeply concerned at her neglect. It was an intense relief so to do. To my surprise, however, Maria appeared neither dejected nor despondent in the slightest. Doubtless she misses her sister, yet this is clear outweighed by a happy sense of independence. I had no inkling prior that Mrs Timmins, the woman with whom she had been placed, was the very same who attended Miss de Bourgh's little dog earlier this month. Indeed, in the interim weeks, where I have been besieged by misery, Maria has been employed in the industrious learning of herbs, poultices, their applications and a whole host of other usefulness. In short, she has blossomed quite. It seems Charlotte may have chosen rather wisely after all, more so than I imagined, for she knew well enough the woman's nature and skills, having frequently visited for a restorative after imbibing a home cure, or for advice regarding the goats, chickens or Mr Collins. I plan to visit often, for it is a fascination to me, and also to find Maria's company so much developed in so brief a time. Before I left, she bade me take her sister a small vial of lavender oil and some dried chamomile to make into a tea, which I did as soon as a private moment presented itself. My secrecy was futile, for Mr Collins found out soon enough. He was more furious than I have seen him yet. On previous occasions their marital disagreements have been but brief and whispered. On this, he cried out within my very presence that his wife had 'betrayed his trust.' Then, 'it is to me you owe your obedience, your allegiance and your life. That is till the end. You break your word with God; worse, you have cut me to the quick, to the core, to the very bone.' Then he wept. Upon the morrow he sulked, on the Monday he lectured, and this morning found Charlotte engaged in a form of redemptive action; on this occasion the writing of two-hundred lines. He is such an infant.

Incidentally, I have begun to imagine Mr Collins as a donkey in a bonnet. It happened soon after my return from the Darent. He was pacing the floor of his study declaiming loud that 'in your father's absence, the mantel of your personal management must fall to me,' when two large grey ears did sprout upon his head. Then, with 'I am deeply, *deeply,* wounded,' his nose became a long, furry muzzle. I am unsure from whence the bonnet came, for the donkey seems obvious enough, yet now I cannot separate the two. This has offered more assistance than I can say, for when forced to endure yet another remedial interview I simply picture the donkey and, while hearing nothing but braying, I devote my energies to decorating his bonnet with a fresh style each day.

I confess, I have been in a quandary of thought since Charlotte's recent benevolence. I found myself wondering if the very independence I had previously so admired in my friend had led ultimately to her current situation. However, after due contemplation, I concluded not. It is instead, I believe, her sense of being 'burdensome' that directed the sacrifice of her own rational well-being. I considered also whether Sir William and Lady Lucas truly thought her a burden, or if, indeed, such an idea was never discussed between the three, but simply fearfully surmised by Charlotte. Yet did they not encourage the match? A fear of scarcity, of destitution, leads nearly all to favour financial security far above that of emotional contentment. Yet are the two always to be mutually exclusive, or is such simply another outdated idea, undisputed for far too long?

Ah yes, you mentioned the shuffling and spinning before Rosings: this is an extension of my cousin's Humor Regime as previously described, these particular patterns being employed exclusively for moments of intense anxiety. I know not the intention of the shuffles exactly, but am given to understand that the spinning is incorporated for the dual purpose of both 'stirring' each Humor at once, and preventing any looming encroachment of the Unmentionable towards his person. Perhaps the shuffles are an attempt at dashing. Mr Collins is no athlete, as I believe I have implied. Indeed, the fastest I have ever seen him run was away from his wife.

Here are ten facts you may not, and need not, know concerning Mr Collins *(how I do procrastinate)*: -

1. His most favoured word is 'aggrieved.'
2. His phrase of choice, 'I have no words,' invariably demonstrates the exact opposite and for at least an hour.
3. He has come lately to believe that the Unmentionable may be contractable through the ears, and has encouraged Charlotte to knit him a series of different coloured mufflers, one for each day of the week.

4. He has thus adapted his government potion to be administered aurally.

5. The mufflers make his ears itch incessantly.

6. Each morning Charlotte takes dictation, transcribes and files his latest afflatus, with which he then regales us both at supper, during which Charlotte must 'ooh' and 'aah' at his brilliance, as if for the first time.

7. At present, his heart is set upon the invention of an extended wheelbarrow. From what I have reluctantly absorbed, it varies only from a usual kind of wheelbarrow by being greatly lengthened in both the tray and in the handles, with a larger than usual wheel.

8. It is to be called: 'The Collins Extended Wheelbarrow.'

9. He also wishes the C.E.W. to go faster than any other ordinary wheelbarrow. I know not how, but that he might somehow run faster with it than any other wheelbarrow owner. This is unlikely.

10. Mr Collins has heels upon his footwear that are neither insubstantial nor unremarkable. Perhaps the extension of a wheelbarrow is not the only extension with which he is preoccupied.

(Now to it.)

(There is much upon which I find I now would rather remain silent. There are no more enquiries regarding Miss Bingley that could possibly be made without other, more intimate and confounding enquiries, to be made within my own self.)

(Regarding further mention of Mr Wickham, I am now truly at a loss. Upon this matter, however, I feel I must make some acknowledgement. At times, one must confess culpability, no matter how painful it may be.)

I went to the elm after four as directed and found, to my surprise, no letter but, instead, the Colonel himself.

(Oh, I can almost find no words. To realise oneself so deeply deceived. To then reflect upon what has previous been said and acted on as a result... The repeated sensations of foolishness, of shame; why, it is almost more than I can bear. Yet how thoroughly I feel it is deserved, necessary even. How painfully I am reminded of the shelter of my formative existence, the confidence I once held in swiftly made, ill-considered judgements...)

We took a walk within the woodland of your Aunt's estate and I am now fully acquainted with the particulars of your experiences with Mr Wickham.

I must, therefore, see your concession regarding social dichotomy and raise you mine concerning that *gentleman* (poor attempts at levity aside, I trust you will discern the irony within the italics).* I would say no more, in the hopeful anticipation that you will appreciate how very distressing it is to suffer the responsibility of so great a misunderstanding when accompanied with the realisation that an apology could hardly signify. Yet, if it should do so, please be assured that you have mine, truly and unreservedly.

Knowing what I now know, I am all amazement at your tolerance and self-restraint. How could you bear to have him speak so and not long to issue a statement of your own to retaliate?

(Knowing my own blindness concerning said gentleman, allowing myself to be deceived not only by his words, but by the shrewd manipulation of my own vanity and pride against myself, I must surely now relent concerning our disagreement over my sister. I will never consider your actions to be right or just, but I concede that you, in all sincerity, do believe that they were so. I will hold to the thought that you will one day see otherwise, yet I believe further argument from me will only move that day further away. It is for you to discover, not for me to instruct. There are occasions, indeed there are,

where in spite of Mr Shakespeare's rather over-used decree, what's done may indeed be undone. Especially where natures are loving and affable. I will hold to this, and fight no more.)

(In addition, how may I speak truthfully and continue to disagree concerning the behaviour of Mama and my sisters? Have I not often felt so myself? I might perhaps protest further that you could expect me to receive criticism of so intimate a nature with any objectivity; but that is only embarking upon more misadventures in obstinacy, and I would have none of it.)

(Oh, how I miss my family! How I do grow increasingly sentimental... I must regain some composure.)

Here are the aspects I love most of home, in no particular order. The sense of my family, the feeling of having those most dear close by, Jane and Papa particularly, always within calling distance. The feeling of warmth; for our home is always warm, even in the depths of winter. I know not how, perhaps a happy accident of fireplaces – yet it is so. The parsonage at Hunsford is a dwelling of very thick walls, yet strangely warm in summer when one might expect cool, and cool in spring when one might expect warmth. But there, I expect no convenience of the place now that I cannot be free of it. Returning once more to Longbourn; I love the familiar sound of the leaves in the trees at night. Oh, it is a balm to my soul and ever has been since I was a small child. That gentle semi-circle of Scots pines that shed their needles so extravagantly and have Papa out with a broom upon occasion, when he would clearly much rather be beside the fire within his library with a favourite volume; yet he considers it his one most particular task. The kitchen, yes, the preparations that we all hear and sense with anticipation, the time spent within its cordiality, the place I speak most with Mama, seated upon a small footrest, as I have since I was very young. Our drawing room, so full of an array of muddle, to be all at once bundled within a large wooden chest when visitors of a sudden arrive. The gardens! Is there any felicity in this world exceeding that of a wide expanse of lawn? Are there any who do not thrill somehow to the idea of *land*? Even those who would rather admire than tend to it feel, surely, that age-old sentiment of earth speaking to spirit. My chamber windows look to the east. I wake to the rising of the sun, the light which glimmers through the trees and never fails us, even though she may hide her face at times. Of an evening the house is filled with golden light, touching everyone and every item with warmth and beauty (although Mary complains that she cannot see to play, so not all are quite as enraptured). At the perimeter of our estate is a large and unruly laurel hedge with an archway in its midst, wide enough for a person to pass through, but no greater than that. I can see it from my windows. I used to imagine it an archway to another realm, yet in truth it leads to a wilder-than-wild wilderness (not the fashionable kind – we have one of those at the front of the house where no one is ashamed of it). In the spring it is full of bluebells, in the summer a tangle of prickly brambles and nettles, there is a small slope which one may run down, and always fallen leaves upon fallen leaves bestrew the ground, for the woodland lies beyond. If I should decide to marry, I will have another home, and I have no doubt that I will find my way to an abiding fondness, yet Longbourn and my family is the home of my heart, and I do not see how it could ever be fully replaced.

(Well, congratulations indeed Elizabeth. There is nothing sentimental in that whatsoever.)

We are creatures of the present, a saving-grace, and where we are becomes all to us in time, supposing we have chosen wisely.

(Oh, change the subject!)

I do hope you are correctly informed concerning the post. I can hardly keep still at the thought of impending letters from home; I long so for news. Tempted as I am to write to every member of my family in anticipation, I am denying myself that pleasure until it is made official, for if Filo goes back upon his word, I do not think I could bear to look at so sad a heap of correspondence, even for a moment.

(Yet this is nonsense, for have I not an absolute intention to write to each one of them the very moment this letter is complete?)

(I am not surprised in the slightest to hear that in the fireside company of your friends you make merry at the thought of impending taxes. I suppose you would find that amusing, deprivation being a matter of choice for you all, rather than a rather questionable and convenient 'predetermination.' I should not criticise, however, nor condemn. What know I of deprivation, truly?)

I knew not of the clean air tax. Naturally I am inclined towards amazement that the government are able so to manage the quality of city air. Besides, do factories not surely contribute far more substantially to poor air quality than livestock?

Naturally the reasons for an increase in taxation are always evident; why, there are copious unofficial celebrations to be paid for, are there not?

Yet, all this aside, I must return to the same thought which will not leave my mind; that it all begins with us. We must be the change we long for. We wish for gardens, then we must plant them – wherever and however we may. We wish for peace, then we must first discover that coveted peace within. Likewise, love, friendship, compassion. Each moment of every day I may choose. That is surely freedom.

I do not, never have, disputed the presence of the Unmentionable. Clearly some have been most unwell and too many have been lost. Yet in the aftermath which must surely come, how may we in all integrity fail to make enquiry into those who have so greatly profiteered during these months? My father often says 'if you would needs understand why something persists when all good sense decrees it need not longer be so, then you must simply follow the gold.' Where a person may make money, injustice is oft encouraged to prevail. Thus, it is of great interest to me to ponder the industries and individuals who have gained exponentially during this time of crisis. I am given to understand from Mr Collins that the government speaks frequently of keeping the populace 'safe.' My cousin is greatly convinced by this and extolls such generous virtues at length. Yet I wonder indeed, what exactly do they mean? I suppose it matters not, yet to be 'safe' appears to be restricted, almost as if one's arms have been tied fast behind one's back. Yes, I believe our best hope is ever to learn to shift for ourselves. We must seek independence, avoiding any encouragement to become the fatted calf.

I wonder, is it ever too early to consider the world which we are creating to be passed on? What we allow to prevail is too often deemed the responsibility of a future generation, and not our own.

Yours etc.

P.S. I have no comment regarding Miss Bingley 'entrepreneurial spirit,' except to say that fashion ever does baffle me.

P.P.S: Ah, another rumour then, unfounded in part.
P.P.P.S: The piano forte did indeed arrive yesterday to Charlotte's unsuppressed delight. Thankfully Mr

Collins was out 'attending distantly to his flock,' so an hour of unalloyed pleasure was hers. I know that she has written to Lady Catherine herself, yet I would also say with the most earnest gratitude that it was an unlooked for, yet most necessary and appreciated kindness.

P.P.P.P.S: I confess to rather liking that Hippocratic misquote, and shall adopt it. It had me laugh aloud.

P.P.P.P.P.S: The badger has returned, if ever he left, and his vengeance has been both prompt and prolific. I have named him Patrick. Whether he knows it or not, we are friends.

P.P.P.P.P.P.S: Coincidental with my newly approved excursions, Felicity is now allowed an hour of liberty also, and chose this day to spend her time with me — or rather, near me, for she scampered here, there, everywhere and back again, chattering copiously as she went. I know not whether this privilege may continue, for naturally enough where I dutifully returned within the designated interval, she — seeing her master at the window — shot instantly beneath a nearby hedge (a Pyracantha, as it happens — very thorny) and refused to come within.
(Am I become competitive concerning postscripts?)

Letter 9

Saturday 26th September, Rosings Park

Dear Madam,

You are indeed most welcome and your qualification regarding rescue duly noted. *(Truly, I could not imagine how one might begin to rescue such independence of thought and spirit.)* Also, regarding the piano forte for Mrs Collins; the work of a moment, truly.

Very well then, Lady Hester — no side-saddle for you. I will also make it my mission to furnish your cousin with a pair of his own antlers, for they seem a most necessary addition to his residence. No doubt they will be in almost constant use. I would decline to challenge Mr Collins to a duel, however, for it would seem unfair — even in defence of butterflies.

At risk of increasing your frustration with your cousin, I do yet feel it only fair to mention that you were indeed quite correct in your initial feeling that all are still allowed time each day outdoors, within a garden or for a short walk beyond. Neither you nor your hosting family could be levied for such. It is your cousin, it seems, who has extended the restrictions so and, as much as I know, only within your household.

From the newspapers, I am tentatively heartened to report that with Filo's evident and increasing confidence following the immense popularity of the reinstatement of the post (yes, I was wrong and I gladly admit it), the gentleman has indicated a determination to at last lift the imposition of fines and lead us to a more general easing of restrictions over what he envisages to be a mere matter of days, weeks at most. Reportedly, he has spoken thus, 'we must now learn to exist with the Unmentionable, accepting it as much a rite of passage as a mild chill.' This was a less popular remark, I understand, yet the general and impending granting of freedom has overwhelmed all other reports and it matters far less than it might.

In other, yet related, news, our dear Prince Regent and his entourage have, of course, been exposed as having not abided by lockdown on occasions too frequent to count. In fact, so liberal has the Prince Regent been with himself and his own freedoms that he and several compadres were spotted running through the mostly shuttered city after nightfall in little more than their undergarments. Ever the roisterer, is he not? Naturally he will ignore the general anger at his insensitivity, citing as excuse 'exemption by divine appointment.' Indeed, a report has been issued, with which Filo must surely agree, affirming in detail that since time immemorial those placed upon the earth at the bottom of the pile have proved themselves more prone to ailments and infections than those graced by God with a greater social standing. Naturally, one might argue that those born to privilege are more easily able to afford food, warmth and medical attention, whenever such is required. Yet there are futile battles, are there not, and those one simply cannot tell.

There is no apology necessary concerning the Trowel*. I require none such. Under no circumstances would I wish for your distress; please understand, therefore, that I consider you entirely blameless. You could not know.

(I note and appreciate that you mention not your sister and my friend. While I shall raise the matter no further, I confess – if solely to myself – I am less certain of my actions than once I was.)

Concerning your query as to how I bore Mr Wickham's presence in Meryton, I would politely intimate that I did not always manage quite so well as you have kindly indicated. When surprised, as first I was, I found myself inclined to react poorly and without due restraint, something which was later a matter of some private regret. Generally, however, I have endeavoured, and with increasing success, to offer no thought at all in that direction. I have found this the best and only solution. He must speak as he will and I can do little to stop him. Thankfully, the man is also generally at great pains to remain a stranger.

(I need not speak of the immense frustration that the evident friendship between the two of you initiated within my breast. I know better, surely, than to attempt to wrestle such external demons, yet for many weeks my mind would drift that way, imagining righteous, public altercations and to no good end.)

To general astonishment, the first of the post arrived yesterday, Miss Bingley being the eager recipient of a lengthy letter from her sister which, before she could be stopped or any of us flee, she instantly read aloud. Aside from the paragraphs of general dissatisfaction which all were compelled to endure, it seems that Mrs Hurst and her husband have been much enthralled by the unfortunate information that many in certain particular areas of

London have been recently obliged to offer their homes for sale, owing to the cessation of various businesses and an alarming decline in income. This news resulted in a lengthy disagreement between Mr Bingley and his sister over whether or not they might then set out to purchase several of the properties at far less than they are surely worth, with the intention of either selling them on at vast profit, or becoming landlords and offering tenancies. Bingley thought it a gross advantage taking of current events and would adamantly have 'no part' in it. His sister thought quite the opposite and went so far as to call him 'a foolish, sentimental, squeeze wax!' before hastily leaving the dining room with a clatter and a slam. He would not relent, however, and thankfully it remains entirely within his jurisdiction to say aye or nay. This morning at breakfast, Miss Bingley bounced into the drawing room full of fresh ideas with which to persuade her brother. By far the most objectionable was the suggestion that having sold said homes, they might then establish a charitable venture to offer solace and shelter to those whom they had helped to dispossess. Bingley was so astonished that he spoke not a word and could eat no further breakfast. Naturally, Miss Bingley took this as ascension and chattered away happily until, of a sudden, he rose from the table, strode to the door, hesitated, turned and said softly 'Caroline, there are times when I do not believe we are related.' Then, turning quietly away once more, he left the room and has kept away ever since.

Before I tempt you to defend woman-kind, I would be clear that I do not object to the lady having an opinion regarding business. Not in the slightest. My objection in this particular case is that the opinion was wholly lacking compassion, the focus solely on profit, removed from the common humanity which, in such circumstances, is surely more than ever a required necessity. If support and solace were truly to be offered, then surely the seeking of a remedy to enable those near dispossessed to stay within their homes, to regain their stability, would be a far more philanthropic endeavour? I recall your once writing that 'all should have a place to live that cheers the heart, that one may call one's own.' I could not agree more. You will find that strange, perhaps, when all is considered; yet your notion of a home for all, completely and independently owned, is something to be universally striven for and achieved. I see no possible future good in a continuing world of landlords, unless we desire another revolution.

(Speaking of revolutions, I hesitate to impart the following information, for it will seem as though I were offering gossip concerning scandal; a most

uncomfortable idea. Nevertheless, determining that I would prefer you to receive an account directly from myself, rather than another, I will proceed.)

I have news of the most surprising nature to communicate. Well, indeed, *I* am surprised to be certain, yet I wonder if, upon reflection, I truly ought to be of if, rather, I have been quite exceptionally short-sighted. Nevertheless, I feel at liberty to convey this information with some freedom now, for it transpires to be a situation with which Miss Lucas is also closely connected and, if not already, you will very soon be equally a party to these particulars.

(Yet it is hardly surprising that two people thrown much together might form an attachment. But that they have acted upon it, that each have shown the daring...well, I am confounded by that at the very least.)

My cousin Anne – well, both my cousins, actually – have eloped. With Rufus. That is, Colonel Fitzwilliam and Anne are to be married, or will as soon as ever they may, for I doubt not their true and good intent. I confess, I *had* noticed the Colonel's increasing affection for Anne. Indeed, the more she – would the word be 'blossomed'? It does not seem to fit quite – the more she *astounded* us all with her initial rise in spirits, the more he appeared enchanted. Of course, you are aware that she has been much subdued of late, and I do suspect the continuing decline in her state of mind to have proved a vital factor in their determination to take such action.

This is not a match that was looked for or intended by my Aunt. Would I use the word 'furious?' No, it does not cover it, I think, not even a toe.

Yet I ramble. I will begin at the beginning. On Wednesday, Anne had been missing all afternoon. By the evening her absence was formally noted, the house searched and a letter at last discovered within that chest of earlier conflict (how long ago that seems, though it were only spring). Within said letter, Anne disclosed the recent confession between the two of a mutual and abiding passion, confirming then their subsequent determination to marry at the earliest convenience. Naturally they realised that the actuality of a ceremony would be somewhat dependent upon the forthcoming cessation of restrictions, yet they had earnestly decided it both desirable and best to now depart Rosings with every possible expedience, journeying to a distant relative of the Colonel's, whom they doubted not would give them shelter and protection for as long as might be necessary.

While it must seem the most tremendous, even reckless of risks to take, you will no doubt appreciate their determination, having yourself previously acknowledged the prospect of an instance where one's best and only option might just be to flee.

That morning after breakfast, Anne had indicated that she was decided upon taking Rufus to visit the woman of remedies within the village, that the removal of his stitches might be affected. It appears from her letter that since the shooting, she had often visited this Mrs Timmins to achieve regular checks upon Rufus's health and, during the first excursion, she and Miss Lucas, becoming more easily acquainted than ever they might at Rosings, had struck up quite the friendship. Becoming an almost instant confidant, Miss Lucas had readily agreed to assist the two, not least by the gradual stowing of both garments and provisions, with Anne bringing a little with her each time, in anticipation of their future departure.

Thus, leaving Rosings after midday, it appears that she was collected in a carriage procured by the Colonel himself, perhaps as much as eight hours before her absence was first remarked upon with any serious concern. Of course, the Colonel had neither needed nor supplied an excuse for any absence, for it is hardly out of character for him to vanish for hours at a time and without explanation.

When the letter was first located and read, Lady Catherine uttered forth one terrible scream. It was the sort of emission one might expect from the Gorgon just before she was decapitated, or the Cyclops as he was stabbed in the eye. So much for classical references. To my surprise, she uttered no decree to have them followed. Rather, for three nights and two days she stayed locked within her own chamber, refusing to speak to anyone, refusing sustenance. I doubt she slept at all, for I could often hear her restless footsteps. At the first opportunity, Bingley dispatched himself towards the village with the intention of speaking with Miss Lucas and her mentor, but found neither at home, though he waited more than an hour and returned again the next two days.

Then this morning, Lady Catherine appeared at breakfast still clutching the letter as if it had not left her grasp and reading aloud as she entered the drawing room, in a tone of both astonishment and derision: 'I did not wish to fight you, Mama. I never have. I trust you may come to realise this in time. I know you have always considered me your creature to mould, yet I do not feel this should be so. I believe we children come to remind you of what has been forgotten, not to be hued in your own image.' Here Lady Catherine snorted. 'Children! Forgotten! What is it she speaks of? Forgotten! I have an excellent memory. Is this not the most distasteful nonsense a person has ever been forced to endure? Children! As if she were yet a child! Creature to hue! *Feel!* How dare she fabricate so?'

There followed then a most unprecedented moment, for Bingley who, with his natural gallantry, would remain standing until my Aunt was seated, gently placed one hand upon her shoulder, looking kindly into her eyes. Although I am now less certain, I was momentarily quite convinced of seeing her chin quiver. Yet within an instant his hand was shrugged away and her place at table gained as though nothing unusual had occurred.

I attempted to offer comfort to my Aunt in my own way, assuring her that she 'need not fear for her daughter's safety, knowing that the Colonel would give his life...' It was only to be expected that I might not complete my sentence.

'Oh, Anne!' Lady Catherine declared without hesitation. 'I do not worry about her. She is, and ever has been, a simpering fool of a girl. She will return soon enough and of her own free will. I need not lift a finger.'

'But Aunt,' said I. 'She will be married. I doubt it not.'

'Ah yes, she will,' re-joined my Aunt. 'But not to him; that incompetent noddy! Anne will change her mind before the ceremony can take place. You doubt me, but I will be proven right as always. Understand nephew, the key to my daughter is her guilt. She will always return because she will always reflect upon what she has done, given due time and silence to think upon it, concluding irrevocably upon her own inadequacy and ingratitude.'

I inwardly translated this as 'over time I have instilled within my daughter such a profound sense of shame, that in the wake of my anger she will quaver, buckle and ultimately do as I wish, believing it her own will.'

'Do you ever wonder, nephew, what it is like to be me?' Continued Lady Catherine after a short silence.

I affirmed that I did not.

'My life is very hard. *Very hard indeed*. I am surrounded by the needy and ungrateful, and am obliged by rank oft to offer assistance. I am, as it were, the mother of hundreds of ne'er do wells with gluttonous beaks agape. 'Might they not perfectly well feed themselves?' I hear you cry (I did not). No. No indeed. Sadly, they are not capable, nor never will be so.'

We both were silent for a time, I scheming my escape in a variety of ways. There is no person on earth whose company is less easy to evade than my Aunt's, once one is in her clutches.

'I will tell you a story, nephew.' (I inwardly wished that she would not, darting my eyes to the doorway yet again) 'Don't roll your eyes! You look like a madman.'

'Sorry Aunt.'

'Yes. Well. When I was a young girl, oh far younger than Anne is now, I realised that I was like Queen Bess. That my life would also be one of duty and sacrifice. I would make few friends worthy of the name, for most would be sycophants offering small service in exchange for tremendous recompense. I would be isolated by both fortune *and* breeding. I would exist as a Sovereign within a Realm of Fools. I would have money enough, yes, but I must learn to manage this effectively and with stoicism, for most would happily relieve me of such, should I allow it. In short, I recognised that I must become formidable. Do you see, nephew?'

I did, with reservations.

'I am as a gleaming stallion in pig pen,' she continued sadly. 'I do not agree with my daughter's choice. It was not her right to do as she did. The role of a guardian is sacred and she has behaved with unforgiveable ingratitude and foolishness. Yet I will not condemn her, as I can see you imagine I shall.' Adding suddenly, 'she called this house a mausoleum!'

'I believe she said it had become so, not that it was,' I interjected politely.

'Tush! No difference.'

'Indeed, Aunt, there is a tremendous difference.'

'Good heavens, nephew, do you argue for your cousin?'

'I do.'

'You are fond of her, then?'

'Indeed I am.'

'How strange. I cannot imagine why.' Then, 'your mother and I believed you would be a match.'

'No Aunt.'

'Don't be ridiculous.'

A moment of bafflement on my part.

'I will not cut my daughter off; you may put your mind at rest on that score. You are a foolish, sentimental boy though, for you would benefit the most should I do so.'

'Believe me, Aunt, I have no desire to 'benefit' in so distasteful a way.'

'I will inform her of my decision in a month or so. We will let them both wriggle for a while, for our amusement. You will keep silent, nephew.'

'Yes Aunt,' I consented, privately agreeing with myself that if wriggling turned somehow to starving, I would break my word within a heartbeat.

'It is down to you now, Fitzwilliam. Thank heavens you have no parents living to hurt so! It is your duty to revoke the harm to our family that your cousins have committed with their selfishness.'

To this I made no reply, which naturally was taken as agreement, and no more will now be said upon the subject by my Aunt. Prior knowledge of her ladyship makes this an absolute certainty.

Concerning Lady Catherine's views upon the likelihood of my cousins' impending nuptials ever taking place, I must emphasise once more my resolute disagreement. This being a step neither nature would have undertaken lightly, I am thus absolutely certain they will do as they intend. I believe my Aunt simply does not, cannot, understand how little Anne could further tolerate what once she seemed to bear without a murmur. My cousin had come too far, experienced too much evolution, one might say, to return once more to her designated corner.

While I am distressed for my Aunt, whose disappointment is palpable, if poorly expressed, I am yet glad for my cousins. It was perhaps not ideally accomplished, but it is certainly for the best.

How much has changed within a very few months. I have at last spoken fully with my sister *(spurred to action, admittedly, by these recent events)* and would express my further gratitude to you for encouraging me so to do. You were indeed correct in your conjecture concerning Georgiana's feelings of intense isolation prior to the London riots. Although it was no easy matter for either one of us for, somehow, we have evaded almost completely such conversations in the past, we are now far better acquainted. Having had no prior idea of Georgiana's unwillingness to speak candidly with me, I trust this newly offered freedom will only improve her trust of me in time, and with due consideration on my part, for I have no wish to be to my sister what my Aunt has become to Anne.

Yours etc.

P.S: I very much enjoyed your account of Longbourn. There is an area of Pemberley of which I am similarly fond, although it is much less a wild-wilderness, and rather more of a folly. My father had it built for my mother, according to a dream she once had of a Saxon tower. It stands upon the highest point of our estate and one can see a vastly pleasing distance from the top.

P.P.S: 'Follow the gold'? Yes, I do like that, it is most apt. In this morning's newspaper, printed upon the very last page, a short column attested to the formal decree of protests being now officially banned. Like Mr Collins, I have no words.

(I would like to ask you to take a walk with me one afternoon. I hope you might accept. I understand not entirely why the thought of such a simple request has me so inexpressibly unsettled; but that it does is undeniable. Perhaps within my next communication, I may find the words.)

Letter 10

Monday 28th September, Hunsford Parsonage

Dear Sir,

Having no opportunity to observe the two, I had no idea of the prospect of such fondness between your cousins. Yet, I must offer my sincere congratulations and heartfelt gladness that they have come together in mutual affection so. It does not sound so very ill-conceived a scheme to me, astonished as I am to hear myself say so.

I was indeed appraised of information concerning your cousins' departure upon the evening of the day it took place, and, it seems, additional intelligence which I am amazed remains yet a secret. For indeed, it is certainly confirmed that Maria, her landlady Mrs Timmins, and one other, accompanied the escapees, rather than remain behind. Hence, Mr Bingley having found Mrs Timmins' establishment unoccupied upon his visits.

Akin to your Aunt, my cousin, upon discovery of this unprecedented turn of events, took at once to his chamber and is even yet to re-emerge, although I am without doubt of his taking regular refreshment. Of course, he is affronted beyond all reason at the prospect of a match unsanctioned by himself, Lady Catherine, and God, in that order, and one would not think for a moment that it was he who insisted Maria be removed from his house. Under more ordinary circumstances, no doubt he would have appeared by now at Rosings requiring advice and seeking solace. Under such as these, however, he is clearly struck with quite another feeling. I would not hazard to imagine him contrite at all, yet, rather more likely, entirely fearful for his own safety with regard to Sir William Lucas.

I draw out this relation for my own amusement. The sixth occupant of the carriage was a young man by the name of Mr Edward Greene, the second son of a local farmer, who had apparently formed a strong attachment to Maria, and she to he, while seeking more gentle alternate remedies for his recently ailing family than the designated cure. Spurred on by your cousins' determination, it appears from Maria's own letter to Charlotte that they too decided upon elopement and, informing Mrs Timmins of their intentions, received her agreement on the condition that she should accompany the pair as chaperone.

Naturally upon receipt, Charlotte wrote almost immediately to her family to acquaint them with the news, and within a day received a very definitive response in which Mr Collins was quite universally considered to be culpable. From Charlotte, I am given to understand that while they are displeased with their daughter and consider her rather too young and impulsive, they are grateful for the presence of both the daughter of Lady Catherine de Bourgh and a chaperone. Above all else, they were confounded to find their child these months both ostracised and without the protection of her nearest family, requesting a detailed and immediate response from their eldest daughter as to how this had occurred. I had thought to bring tea to the parlour, where Charlotte had been busily ensconced to attend to this task, but upon entering found her not at her writing desk, but seated instead by the window in what seemed almost a trance. Resolving at once to set the tea down and retreat quietly, I was at the door when I felt my friend's hand tug at my own, then drawing me with her to the settle I watched as she shook her head again and again, then of a sudden stood and almost laughed, then returned to the settle, nearly spoke, and pouring the tea I had prepared for her, impulsively handed it instead to me.

'Charlotte,' I began at last, replacing the cup and saucer upon the tray and reaching for her hand. She sprang back.

'Oh Eliza,' she said, with a look of such sadness that I almost wept too. 'I am very much to blame, am I not?'

I knew not what to say. Thankfully she seemed not to expect an answer, continuing instead:

'I may offer no excuse; she is my sister and deserved far greater kindness. Oh Eliza, I found my own position so utterly insurmountable. I was at great pains to convince myself of having done the very best I could by Maria, under the circumstances, but I deceived myself and I knew I did.'

There seemed little more to say, yet wishing not to part company immediately we sat together, taking turns to sip from different sides of the same teacup, and I, at least, fully experiencing the most comfortable relief of a gentle silence between old friends.

On Saturday, another letter was received from Lady Lucas offering both concern and forgiveness to Charlotte, and carrying with it an unprecedented piece of information, for Maria is now most unexpectedly returned to Lucas Lodge with Mr Greene considered a not entirely welcome guest while his transportation back to Hunsford is arranged. It would seem that once the carriage drew close to Hertfordshire, Maria grew most restless to return home and begged to go no further. Naturally the Colonel and Miss de Bourgh — who were, incidentally, reported in both excellent health and spirits — were willing to divert through Meryton for Maria's sake, even delaying while Mrs Timmins accompanied the pair to confirm and explain their actions to Sir William and Lady Lucas. Thankfully the relief at having their daughter home safe, with little harm done, outweighed any excessive reproach (or, indeed, the fear of being fined, now unlikely yet not impossible). Mrs Timmins then resolved to continue the journey with your cousins, that they might also have the protection of her company. She seems a good woman.

I am exceedingly alarmed to learn of the ban upon protests. In our modern age, how could this be allowed? I realise that matters in June gathered an unprecedented momentum, yet is our government in no way obliged to take responsibility for their reaction to that initial most peaceful protest? Must they always fail to listen, driving desperate people almost inevitably towards violence in their fear for survival? I am ever confounded by those chosen to serve.

Yet, consider, need we truly be afraid? No matter what laws are passed, freedom is first and foremost within our own hearts and homes; for if among our families and connections we may speak freely, if forgiveness is swift and readily offered, if there is love and kindness aplenty, then it matters not what dwells within the wider world, for our nearer and inner world shall be strong and resilient.

I am so very glad to learn of your conversation with your sister. There is an understanding of both affinity and nurture, wholly desirable, that I am fortunate to experience with both my father and with Jane. It is beyond words to me, and utterly irreplaceable.

I have news of the most extraordinary, the most unlooked for, and yet the most, the very most, welcome blessing I could possibly imagine to convey. My father is here to fetch me home! I can hardly believe it. Indeed, I have paused twice in the writing of this brief paragraph to look through the window at the carriage below, believing myself mistaken. But yes, indeed he is here. My father has left Longbourn and *he is here*! My heart is very full indeed and I must gather my belongings swiftly and to a purpose, for I leave almost immediately and we will travel through the night. I will take what I have written thus far to place within the old elm as we pass by, and continue this letter once I have reached home. Home! I can scarce believe it. Please be assured that I will write as soon as ever I may and will send to you at Pemberley, knowing that you will likely find your way again there soon enough. I appreciate that a correspondence may no longer continue between us, now that lockdown appears fully and finally at its end, yet I feel there is nothing improper in completing a letter already begun.

Yours, for the present, etc.

P.S: Oh, I knew it! I knew that my liberty had been unfairly removed by my cousin; I suspected as much, yet could not believe he would be so very untruthful. It matters not, it matters not, yet how it does gall, I confess. Perhaps I will see the humour of it in time...

P.P.S: How wonderful it is that our fortunes may alter for good in a matter of moments!

Monday 12th October, Longbourn *(Oh, it does my heart good to write this now!)*

Dear Sir,

I trust this letter finds you in good health and returned home in both safety and contentment, with Miss Darcy, at last. For my own part, I am full happier than I have been for this many a month.

I had not time to fully explain how my father came to arrive so unexpectedly upon the last Monday of September, for I had received no letter at all from home advising me of his departure.

Having the leisure now to elucidate, I can tell you that he travelled not alone, but in the company of Sir William Lucas, and young Mr Edward Greene. Having written to his daughter, as aforementioned, Sir William decided then that the very best remedy for the whole misadventure was to return Mr Greene to Hunsford at the earliest opportunity, where he might be reunited with his own family and further discussion could, in time, be entered into regarding the arrangement of a long engagement between the ardent pair. Sir William is not an unreasonable man, seldom given to extreme bouts of anger, yet so incensed was he at his son-in-law's treatment of his younger daughter, that he was irrevocably resolved to make the journey there and back without pausing to spend even a night at the parsonage. Naturally, Mama was a party to this information before Sir William had breakfasted upon the day of departure, thus my father was equally the wiser in only a little more time. Being most anxious for my own safe return, Papa then resolved to accompany Sir William, not least, I expect, in the happy knowledge that he would soon be re-ensconced within his library without the unwelcome endurance of an unnecessarily extended sojourn.

(I will spare you the details of our reunion, although, in truth, I doubt not your indulgence for its tearfulness. 'How I have missed you, my Lizzy,' cried my father as he jumped (yes, jumped!) from the carriage, holding out his arms to me. I was so surprised, so utterly taken aback, that I stood for a moment quite stock still, then half-stumbled towards him, flinging myself against his chest and remaining there for many minutes. For as long as I live, I shall never forget the joyfulness of those moments, nor the feeling of that place upon my father's chest and shoulder where I do love to rest my head, grown woman though I be. I wonder, do we ever move beyond that love of our Papas? I hope not. I could not believe it possible.)

We left Hunsford with all due haste, for the daylight was already fading. Besides, Sir William had refused in all adamance to step inside the parsonage for fear that he might 'throttle' Mr Collins, so any lingering farewells were not encouraged. Having safely seen my luggage stowed, embraced my dear Charlotte and then nodded with all the courtesy I could muster towards my cousin, we departed and I sat in silence for many moments, half o'er-whelmed at the sudden attainment of the instance I had so often hoped for. During our goodbye, Charlotte had whispered to me 'please, remember to look back, and soon, Eliza,' then nodding intently added 'be not too quick to turn the corner.' Knowing not her meaning, I yet did look back and almost by my own instinct, only to see a small, rapidly approaching scrap of black fur scampering as swiftly as possible towards the carriage. Felicity had been released! I cried out to stop the carriage, then, flinging open the door and before I could even clamber down, that dear little being had sprung at once within and, much to Sir William's consternation and Papa's amused acceptance, chose to settle upon my lap and stoically make that long journey with us.

It is curious indeed to be home at last, after so many months. I had got to longing for it so. I would lie awake in my Hunsford chamber for hours, trying to imagine it were my very own at Longbourn. I am so powerfully relieved to be here. Perhaps I had got to thinking that I never would again. It is strange how we become, over periods of isolation, how very distant home can seem.

The first week of my return was full of happy reunions; so many dear folks to embrace over and again, then a gradual settling in to what had been before. Well, no, I may not say so. For what we thought we knew is different and we cannot forget it. There is a nervousness in the world now, I sense it. Where once a prevailing feeling of anxiousness seemed solely the domain of Mama, this has now pervaded our town. No income seems secure, no shop affixed. Yet we must find our feet again. We must move forward. We must take the experiences of lockdown and, having lived without them for a time, treasure with full hearts our freedoms, our loved ones, our dreams for a happy future. It is up to us, and ever shall be.

I am not, however, peevish enough to feel myself so changed by recent experiences that I cannot bask in the feeling of home and comfort. Already, and on several occasions, I have sat out with Papa to watch the golden light. I spend most of my days thanking the heavens for my safe return at last, even as Mama sees fit to regale me with every single speck of news that I have missed. My goodness, the miseries to which she and Aunt Phillips have been privy, and all observed and retold with a certain glee akin to those tricoteuse we heard of, knitting by the guillotine. Ordinarily, I would give no ear to it, but so happy am I to see my Mama once more that I care not. Indeed, I often hardly hear her. I have been watching the light, instead, bounce from different objects in our drawing room, savouring the scents of home, the great delight that my Jane is at last easily within calling distance and appears both instantly and happily, however many times I do exploit her good nature. My relief that she is both well and happy is inexpressible.

Mama speaks proudly yet of an entertainment got up by Lydia, Kitty and various gentlemen-acquaintances, with direction and musical accompaniment by Mary, in celebration of Midsummer. This was swiftly, and somewhat prematurely, performed during those two days of freedom when all ran riot. Yet it seemed that Lydia particularly was already well prepared. She had written a short play to present, which seemed mostly to involve 'a-capering, 'a-flouncing, and 'a-simpering' (Papa's words) under the 'guise of creative artistry.' It seems Mary had quite the task to keep them all in order, while she and Lydia fought almost constantly, and have even yet to fully reconcile. Still, the players enjoyed themselves, I hear, the audience survived and Mama served such a table after, that whatever regrettableness had been witnessed was quite soon and thankfully forgot among the merriment. Apart from that betwixt Mary and Lydia, of course.

In July, Mary introduced the idea of ringing a large bell once a week to convey thanks to our Sovereign and our government. For what, no one could exactly say, yet for weeks it went ahead with much solidarity and good humour on the part of local residents. Gradually, as spirits declined, so did the bell-ringing, until there was only Mary left, ringing a sombre and lonely bell through that rather misty August, until Mama very firmly asked her to stop, her motherly pride at her daughter's inventive inception giving way to the general nervousness that the sound of a solitary bell was provoking amongst our nearer neighbours. She was also frequently mistaken for a letter carrier, causing ever more disappointment and consternation.

Last week, my youngest sister sought permission from our parents to betake herself to Brighton with a married friend. That is to say, Lydia has informed Mama of her intentions, firmly expecting no opposition from either parent. In this she is quite correct. I attempted to intervene, but found no sympathetic audience for my concerns. My father's liberality has been a tremendous blessing in many ways, and I would not have him otherwise. Yet Lydia is our youngest and although she may appear rather worldly in the freedom with which she expresses, well, everything, I may assure you that she is not so. The truth is, Mama has clung to Lydia as if she remains an infant, seeing no more harm in her behaviour than if she were still a child of five years old. They are also somewhat similar. Hey ho. I can change nothing. Kitty is wailing yet, having received no invitation herself, Mary attempts to soothe her with a favourite aria which seems only to exacerbate her sister's tears. Thus, Jane and I take frequent, delightful walks.

Papa has often noted that Mama should keep a favour tally. That is, Mama is well known within the town for her generous assistance of others *(especially those who occupy noteworthy positions within the community)*. Naturally this is 'for the sake of my daughters.' Having no sense that her motives could be other than altruistic, she is yet strongly aware at all times of which favours have and have not been returned. One might say Mama herself is deeply involved in trade, a 'merchant of favours' if you will. That makes her sound bad. I should explain precisely what I mean by favours. Very well, here is the example I was leading to as it was. Prior to lockdown, one of the finer houses in town was taken by a woman and her daughter. Naturally the town was deeply suspicious of these interlopers and resolved to keep them at arm's length for at least twenty year or so, until a rumour began to circulate that the mother was likely the daughter of a French aristocrat and an English lady, and that they were living incognito within the town while their estate was renovated, or some such. The point is, they were wealthy, very wealthy, and well-connected in London.

Well, everyone in Meryton realised in the same instant that they had been most inhospitable, nay, unjust, and set about doing all they could to remedy their initial frostiness. Mama herself went every day to demonstrate 'friendship and forgiveness' (her words) and could not do enough for these two ladies, who were themselves so eager in allowing the town to remedy their initial mistake, that they despatched each willing penitent with piles of mending, darning, and readily accepted an abundant flow of local dishes and tonics. Never have two ladies been made so welcome within a town. Before lockdown, Mama became most certainly their firmest and most helpful friend. Then, during the months that followed, she would ensure their receipt of a share of whatever was made or baked each day, dispatching Mary or Kitty to leave such offerings upon their doorstep. I had a letter from Mama in the early stages of this friendship, rhapsodising over the beauty of this woman, her flaxen hair and slender figure, and how it was evident that she must descend from royalty. Mama does nothing by halves and her affections will know no bounds; at first.

In June, with the friendship yet unmarred by the return of a single favour, a crisis occurred. Mama received a note penned by the fair hand of the mother declaring that her daughter was gravely ill. It appeared that while out walking for solitary exercise, said daughter had been approached by a maskless young gentleman from the village, who had tipped his hat to her and coughed extravagantly. She was instantly afflicted with the Unmentionable. Mama was naturally vociferously outraged on their behalf, immediately replying to demand a description of the unmasked fiend, and offer any conceivable solace she might muster. A response was received within the hour. Mrs Grisalee required nothing for her daughter but the remedy of such a wrong. A detailed description of the young man was given and the militia called upon to track him down and bring him to justice. Dark hair and eyes, ruddy complexion, tall, slim build, around twenty years of age. Heavens! There were three possible candidates. None would confess, each protested their innocence. The village was in a frenzy to know who had so recklessly endangered the life of one of their most prized inhabitants. It took all the charm of the militia to keep everyone indoors. The three young men accused were escorted to the Grisalee abode and made to stand one at a time near the window of the drawing room to be identified. The curtains were closed, but for a small gap. One twitch of the curtain indicated 'no,' two twitches 'yes.' At last Mr Jonathan Goldby was identified as 'the cougher' and taken away for questioning. The town fell into an uproar of embarrassed indignation, dispatching medicines and parcels of food to the Grisalees. Mama even started a collection, putting a great deal of her pin money towards aid for the family that they might daily summon the doctor. Each gift was met with silence. Mama was beside herself. What could she do to atone for the evils of her town? She thought for an afternoon, and then sat up all night writing petitions to each household of note, asking them to give whatever money they might spare for the family. Papa attempted to intervene, but she would have none of it. 'She is a good woman,' she declared, over and over again. The mortified town gave generously, and Mama was able to dispatch Mary to the house with a considerable parcel of money.

A week later there was still no report from the Grisalees and Mama was beside herself. Late one night, finding she could stand it no more, she resolved to break the curfew herself and venture to the house to offer what assistance she might to the ailing daughter. Covering herself in shawls and clutching a jar of thyme in syrup, she made her way there. When she reached the house, however, she was most perturbed to discover the front door flung wide open and a large black carriage waiting at the front. She hid behind a hedge, clutching her jar. She could hear voices within, laughter. Peering through the foliage, she was able to see a tall, bearded man with a rounded silhouette standing in the doorway, holding a candle whilst urging quiet in a fierce whisper. His hair was long and Ill-kempt and, when he turned, the candle illuminated his face and he looked to her as though he were very angry.

'We must away,' he growled.

Mrs Grisalee appeared in the doorway, dressed for travel in immense finery and holding that very parcel of money which Mama had so staunchly collected.

'Ridiculous man. I assure you there is no need to hurry. No one suspects. Yet if you must submit to such cowardice, by all means carry your daughter from the house and then we may say to the owl who sees us that we are taking her south for restorative sea-air.'

Now, the next part Mama is unsure of as it was partially whispered, but she believes he said, 'you are a foul creature.'

To which she replied, 'thankfully I care not for your approbation, nor ever have. Perhaps if you were more of a man, we would not have to stoop so to feed our child.'

'This is not for our daughter!' the man re-joined in less of a whisper. 'You would do this had you no offspring and all the money in the world.' With this he snatched the money parcel from her hand and vigorously shook it, as if to emphasise his point.

At this moment, Mama says it was as if she were 'taken over,' for 'there was always something about that woman I did not trust or like, yet suppressed out of civic duty. She wore grey, Lizzy, so much grey and a sort of violent mustard and...and brown in stripes! Oh, I should have known! No woman of any virtue would wear such shades.'

She dropped the jar of syrup-thyme and it smashed to pieces upon the ground. Then, shrieking one loud, angry cry, hurled herself though the gate and up the path towards her nemesis, elbowing the scruffy man out of the way, and seizing Mrs Grisalee by the hair. 'You evil, lying, fraudster!' She exclaimed. 'How dare you! How *dare* you!'

By now, the town was awakening, candles appearing in windows and the swift to dress assembled soon nearby, at a reasonable distance from one another.

'I trusted you. You lied!' Cried Mama.

Here she believes the woman attempted to defend herself, but to no avail, for Mama bellowed at her once more 'you lied!!!'

The daughter appeared in the doorway, clearly not at all unwell, and those of the town present gasped in unison at the apparition. The father, who had been all of a stupor, attempted to cry out 'it's a miracle!' But had not the charisma to see it through.

To make short of rather a long tale, the three of them are now with the militia, Mr Goldby immediately returned to his family, the town in a further uproar of indignation unlikely to abate, the money redistributed and Mama 'deeply scarred' and 'unlike to trust another human being ever, ever again.' 'It was her eyes, Lizzy,' she says now. 'I knew something was not right. Those pale blue eyes, set far too wide apart. Unblinking. Remorseless! Oh, I cannot rest to think of them. The evil in those eyes. How could I be so foolish? I knew. I knew yet I allowed it.'

Whereupon I say, 'how could you know?' Which is what she really thinks.

'And her hair was dyed!'

The most unbearable revelation of all.

'And half of it was false!'

An examination by the militia discovered that this woman was indeed wanted for questioning over embezzlement and the selling of penny shares in many different parts of the south of England, the man and daughter her rather enfeebled accomplices.

My father, upon whose nerves lockdown has taken quite the toll, was extravagantly unsympathetic towards his wife, pointing out that her motives were entirely selfish and she deserved to be duped. 'In both her happiness and her sadness your Mama is somewhat shrill, Lizzy,' he said recently and rather dolefully. 'Therefore, I cannot win.'

'Perhaps, Papa. Yet we are fortunate, indeed we are.'

My father shook his head, 'You know well how beautiful I found your Mama when first we met, for I have often told you so. Indeed, I find her still a beauty, in many ways I do. Our courtship was brief enough, and I naive as she. Neither of us considered that there might be little in common between us to see us through a marriage. So it is with many. We get by.'

To my surprise, I found myself answering, 'Papa, with the deepest love and respect in the world to you, whatever your regrets regarding Mama, they are nothing to what Charlotte's are in marriage and surely will yet be. You have a household full of love, and yes, it is noisy and frustrating at times, for there is a more than an ample amount of foolishness, yet for all that, there is much to admire and appreciate.'

He stopped short, looked aghast, turned almost pale, then retreated into his library and closed the door. I stood in shock. I do not recall a time when I have ever tried to censor my conversation with Papa. Something I do cherish, whilst taking it for granted of course. I stayed for many moments, hesitating, not knowing whether to follow or to leave him be. As I ruminated, the library door opened once more and Papa's face peered out, followed by a hand that beckoned me inwards. I followed, unsure quite what to expect. He gestured for me to be seated in my usual spot, betaking himself to the fireplace and prodding unnecessarily at the fire.

'I am very sorry, Lizzy, and ashamed,' he said to the flames. 'To have placed you in so awkward a position. I have been hitherto foolishly unaware of the freedom with which I shared certain ideas with you.'

'Papa, I do not mind...' I returned, but he held up his hand to stop me.

'Your rebuke was just and well-spoken, child. Do not apologise. It is my fault, indeed, that you should feel it necessary. Let us say no more about it.'

I nodded in ready agreement and he at once began an alternative discourse which I was most happy to be part of.

I left the library at last in a frame of wonderment. Yet again I am confronted by my own good fortune. Should Mr Collins have a daughter, I cannot imagine he ever broaching so much as a moment of opposition from her, however well-intended. He will be King, and should his subjects question his authority he will make home such a place of sombre misery that they must either leave or capitulate. I recall your use once of 'familia' as 'household slaves'. It amused me, yet it should not be so. A family should surely be a place where *all* may thrive. When one alone insists on utter dominance this cannot be possible, for the atmosphere will, in time, be one of disloyalty, of bitterness, and a sense of relentless discomfort not to be endured.

I see and know now that I have been raised in such freedom. I confess that although I often felt and appreciated it, I never truly knew the contrasting possibilities until this time. I have never been without. I have a father who encouraged my reading and a mother who stood not in his way. I have been free to wander the countryside, unencumbered by thoughts or fears that hold so many in restraint. Perhaps my sisters and I have not always had the finest clothes, yet we have the privilege of something far greater than material goods. We have had a better beginning, I am certain, than many for whom my younger sisters might yet, and often, feel a touch of envy.

I thank you in all sincerity for your friendship over this time. It has meant more to me than I might reasonably express.

Yours, with all good wishes, etc.

P.S: I have this day received a letter from Charlotte in which she indicates that she will soon start for Meryton. She is to undertake a long visit with her family, and has resolved to come alone.

P.P.S: In her renewed freedom Felicity is become more affectionate than ever and sits a full hour at least upon my lap every day of fine autumn weather, of which there are blessed many at present.

P.P.P.S Feeling it not yet the best time to return to Gracechurch Street, my Aunt and Uncle Gardiner have decided upon a month's excursion, leaving their children in the care of our family – well, chiefly Jane and Mama. Although I am most loathe to leave my home again so soon, I am strongly persuaded that such will be a wholly desirable remedy to so many months of lockdown in Hunsford, and I shall accompany them. It will be most unusual to summer in the autumn yet, certain, I shall delight fully in both scenery and companionship.

(I know I shall think of you often, as we travel close to Derbyshire.)

Dear Reader, you know well what happens next...

Glossary

Bathurst, Lord	Henry Bathurst, 3rd Earl Bathurst, (22 May 1762 – 27 July 1834). Reportedly, rather dull, though loyal and competent. Referring to old Battersea Bridge, a wooden toll bridge designed by Henry Holland and built by John Phillips. The bridge was frequently in need of costly repair, being easily damaged by both ice and passing ships.
Bellingham, Mr Johan	Found guilty of the assassination of Prime Minister Spencer Perceval on 11th May 1812. Although executed, he did engender a considerable amount of support for his actions, on the basis that he had 'taught ministers that they should do justice, and grant audience when it is asked of them.'
Bennet, Miss Elizabeth	Spirited protagonist of Jane Austen's 'Pride & Prejudice.'

	Frequently known as 'Lizzy' or 'Eliza' by her friends and family. She is the second-eldest of the five Bennet sisters.
Bennet, Miss Jane	The eldest Bennet sister. Beautiful and kind, she tends only to see the best in others. She falls in love with Charles Bingley, a rich young gentleman recently moved to Hertfordshire, but he is persuaded that she does not care for him and so, reluctantly, jilts her.
Bennet, Miss Catherine 'Kitty'	The fourth Bennet sister, very much under the influence of her younger sister Lydia.
Bennet, Miss Lydia	The youngest Miss Bennet; a tremendous flirt, careless of others, wilful and imprudent.
Bennet, Miss Mary	The middle Bennet sister; earnest and studious.
Bennet, Mr	Lizzy's Papa, who feels tremendous affinity with his second-eldest daughter. Well-read, with a very dry wit, rather tired of his wife and younger daughters. His

	estate, Longbourn, is entailed to the male line.
Bennet, Mrs	Lizzy's Mama. Prone to nervous fits and tremors. Her focus is almost entirely upon marrying off each of her daughters to wealthy men. Often heavy-handed and socially unskilled.
Bingley, Miss Caroline	Mr Bingley's rather vain and snobbish sister who has set her sights on becoming the wife of Mr Darcy.
Bingley, Mr Charles	Darcy's close friend and suitor to Jane Bennet. Handsome, kind and wealthy, but easily persuaded away from his own true inclinations. Darcy has mis-observed Jane's modesty when around Bingley, assuming that it denotes a lack of feeling. He has used this to persuade his friend not to pursue his courtship.
Chesterfield, Earl of	Philip Dormer Stanhope, 4th Earl of Chesterfield, (22 September 1694 – 24 March 1773). Infamous for his 'Letters Written to His Natural

Son on Manners and Morals' (1774), which comprise a thirty-year correspondence in more than four-hundred letters, never intended for publication.

Collins, Charlotte	Mrs	Recent wife to Mr Collins, daughter to Sir William Lucas and Lady Lucas, and Lizzy's closest friend. At twenty-seven, believing her marital prospects to be hopeless, she agrees to marry Mr Collins, thus gaining financial security and relieving herself of the fear that she is a burden to her parents.
Collins, William	Mr	Mr Bennet's distant second cousin, a clergyman, and the current heir to the estate of Longbourn House. He is a pompous, wearisome man, fawningly devoted to his patroness, Lady Catherine de Bourgh. On visiting Longbourn, he set his sights on marrying Jane Bennet, but finding she was soon to be engaged to Mr Bingley,

		proposed to Lizzy instead. When she rejected him, he proposed to Charlotte Lucas and was accepted.
Darent, the		A river in Kent
Darcy, Fitzwilliam	Mr	The romantic hero of Pride and Prejudice. A wealthy man who owns a large estate in Derbyshire called Pemberley. Initially, he appears to be unpleasant and haughty, but – as the novel progresses – he is revealed to have a noble heart, capable of tremendous love and loyalty.
Darcy, Georgiana	Miss	Darcy's sister, younger by a decade. She is gentle and accomplished, with a dowry of £30,000. Mr Wickham persuaded her to elope with him when she was fifteen, but she was saved by the intervention of her brother.
De Bourgh, Anne	Miss	The only child of the late Sir Lewis and Lady Catherine de Bourgh. She is heir to the de Bourgh estate, Rosings Park.

De Bourgh, Lady Catherine	Aunt to Mr Darcy and Colonel Fitzwilliam. Used to having her own way.
Filo	Darcy's nickname for the Prime Minister
First Lord	Referring to the Prime Minister (First Lord of the Treasury)
Fitzwilliam, Colonel	Nephew of Lady Catherine de Bourgh and Lady Anne Darcy (Darcy's mother); cousin to Anne de Bourgh and the Darcy siblings.
For extreme Collinses, extreme methods...	Darcy is paraphrasing Hippocrates' 'extreme remedies are very appropriate for extreme diseases.'
Gardiner, Aunt & Uncle	Mrs Bennet's brother and sister-in-law. He is a successful tradesman, which earns the scorn of Caroline Bingley, even though – or perhaps because – her own fortune comes from trade. Both he and his wife are kind, level-headed and close to their nieces Jane and Elizabeth.

Gracechurch Street	A main road in the historic and financial centre of the City of London. Home to the Gardiner Family.
Hester, Lady	Lady Hester Lucy Stanhope (12 March 1776 – 23 June 1839) was a British aristocrat, adventurer, antiquarian, and one of the most famous travellers of her age. She shaved her head, wore a turban and rode astride, rather than side-saddle.
Humors	The four humors of Hippocratic medicine being black bile, yellow bile, phlegm, and blood, each corresponding to one of the four temperaments.
Hunsford	A Parsonage near Westerham and the home of Mr and Mrs Collins
Jenkinson, Mrs	The paid companion of Anne de Bourgh in Pride & Prejudice.
Lazarettos	A quarantine station for maritime travellers. Can refer to ships permanently at

	anchor, isolated islands, or mainland buildings. The first lazaretto was established In Venice (1423) on the island of Santa Maria di Nazareth.
Longbourn	Hertfordshire residence of The Bennet Family.
Lucas Lodge	Hertfordshire residence of the Lucas Family.
Lucas, Miss Maria	Younger sister to Charlotte Collins, sister-in-law to Mr Collins and daughter to Sir William and Lady Lucas.
Lucas, Sir William & Lady	Neighbours and friends to The Bennet family.
Meryton	A fictional town in 'Pride & Prejudice', located near Longbourn and Netherfield in Hertfordshire.
Miasma	Bad air, or night air. A now obsolete theory that diseases were caused by a miasma, imparted from decaying organic matter.
Militia	A military force of civilians, raised to supplement the regular army in case of emergency.

Norris, Mrs	Lady Catherine's Housekeeper in 'Lizzy & Darcy in Lockdown.'
Pemberley	Derbyshire estate owned by Fitzwilliam Darcy.
Perceval, Spencer	Spencer Perceval, 1 November 1762 – 11 May 1812. A British statesman and barrister, serving as Prime Minister from October 1809. He is the only UK Prime Minister to be assassinated. He was opposed to hunting, gambling and adultery; did not drink as much as most MPs at the time, gave generously to charity, and enjoyed spending time with his thirteen children.
Phillips, Aunt	The sister of Mrs Bennet and Edward Gardiner, Aunt to the Bennet and Gardiner children. She is widely thought to be rather vulgar.
Piano Forte	A fortepiano is an early piano dating from around 1700 to the early 19th century. During Pride & Prejudice, Lady Catherine states to Lizzy of

music that 'there are few people in England, I suppose, who have more true enjoyment of music than myself, or a better natural taste. If I had ever learnt, I should have been a great proficient. And so would Anne, if her health had allowed her to apply.' She encourages Mrs Collins to play the piano forte in Mrs Jenkinson's room, where she will be in 'nobody's way.'

Pomanders (Apple of amber) A ball of perfumes, worn or carried in a vase and thought to protect against infections. For these specific purposes, an orange decorated with cloves.

Primus Inter Pares Latin for 'first among equals.' The Prime Minister.

Prince Regent, the Later George IV (1762 – 1830). The eldest son of King George III and Queen Charlotte. From 1811 until his accession, he served as Regent during his father's final illness. He was known among the people as a

	profligate, thanks to a careless and extravagant lifestyle.
Rochester Neighbours	The Collins's neighbours who arrived in Hunsford during 'Lizzy & Darcy in Lockdown' and were not thought well of, nor welcomed by Mr Collins.
Rotten Row	After a rather wild and dubious early history, Rotten Row, a thoroughfare in Hyde Park, became a fashionable meeting place for London Society from the early Eighteenth Century onwards. The upper classes would parade their finery there, often for a watching general public who would line the railings.
Rosings Park	The palatial dwelling of Lady Catherine de Bourgh, located in Kent. Hunsford Parsonage – home of the Collins – shares one of its boundaries.
Serjeant (at Arms)	The Serjeant at Arms is responsible for keeping order within the House of Commons.

Slubberdegullion	A filthy, slobbering person.
Soldiers of Fortune	Men pursuing a military career for profit, adventure, or pleasure.
Squeeze wax	A good-natured, foolish fellow, naively willing to stand as security for another.
St Paul's	Cathedral Church of St Paul the Apostle. A London icon on Ludgate Hill, the highest part of the city. Designed by Sir Christopher Wren.
St Stephen's Chapel	St Stephen's Chapel (or the Royal Chapel of St Stephen) located in the old Palace of Westminster, serving as the chamber of the House of Commons from 1547 – 1834.
Stultus	Latin for 'stupid, fool, jester.'
Tricoteuse	French for 'knitting woman.' A commonly used nickname for the women who attended executions during the French Revolution, knitting throughout.
Wesleyness	Lizzy is referring to Cleric John Wesley (1703 – 1791). The saying 'cleanliness is next to

	Godliness,' is commonly attributed to him.
Wickham, Mr	Infamous rake of Pride & Prejudice; charming and untruthful. He befriends Lizzy, relaying a false history of his acquaintance with Mr Darcy, and encouraging her prejudice towards him to further develop. Later in the novel, he seduces Lydia Bennet, exposing the Bennet family to potential ruin.
'Where Wav'ring Man, betray'd by vent'rous Pride...'	Lady Catherine is quoting from Samuel Johnson's 'The Vanity of Human Wishes.'

With sincere gratitude to: -

Miss Jane Austen
Austen Authors
The Jane Austen Centre
Jane Austen's World
Pemberley.com
Randombitsoffascination.com
The Jane Austen Wiki
Vic Sanborn
Wikipedia

So much love and gratitude to my wonderful James, my Mr Darcy, always so loving, supportive and full of enthusiasm for everything I write, and to my gorgeous gang of friends, near and far, who accept that I will disappear into another world for weeks at a time and are happy to see me again once I re-emerge.

'Lizzy & Darcy in Lockdown' is also available to watch on YouTube via Summer Light Theatre's Channel
https://www.youtube.com/c/SummerLightTheatre

Printed in Great Britain
by Amazon

20080143R00231